Collected here are the rich and poig*~~ ~~*
Camden Joy's reputation as "~~ ~~
music writers" (Ira Glass). *~~ ~~*
which disappeared songs or b~~ ~~
Some speak of fleeting passion~~ ~~
identities gone missing. Some or~~ ~~ ...n *the form of*
polemical tracts, or as ephemera~~ ~~ ~~.~~*ne streets of New*
York City. Others existed only as ~~r~~ ~~umors,~~ *beyond the reach of*
any reader. Each, until now, has been lost.

"I know of no one who writes with more passion
and more soul."
—DAVE EGGERS

"Pop culture obsessives will hear echoes of all sorts in
Joy's voice—ecstatic art seraphs Patti Smith and Allen
Ginsberg, Greil Marcus and Lester Bangs—not to mention
the wild cadences of crank religious missives . . . It makes
you lust for a world of heightened feelings and values
beyond the one we live in—just like art is supposed to do."
—WILL HERMES, CITY PAGES

"Camden Joy is one of the great rock writers of our age."
—ROLLING STONE

"[Joy writes with] a hyperventilating, loose-
gasket appreciation of popular culture, from
the autobiographical POV of an addict, a jilted
lover, or a music fan who loves too much."
—RICHARD GEHR, SPIN

"Guerrilla writer Camden Joy is a unique voice . . .
His moral seriousness—which rarely deflects his sense
of humor—ignites his lyric imagery and linguistic
virtuosity. Hero worship, celebrity, the dialectic
between art and commerce all inform his work."
—JON GARELICK, BOSTON PHOENIX

OTHER BOOKS BY CAMDEN JOY

The Last Rock Star Book, or: Liz Phair, a Rant
Boy Island
3 Novellas

LOST JOY

Camden Joy

Verse Chorus Press

"Dum Dum Boys" first appeared in *Little Engines*; "The Launch of
the MJ-97" in *Mommy and I Are One*; "Total Systems Failure" and
"Call Off the Fatwa" in the *Village Voice*; "Rattled by the Rush" in the
Chicago Reader; "Surviving Sinatra" on *This American Life*; "Observing
Murder" in *McSweeney's*; "My Life in Eighteen Songs" in *Greatest Hits*;
and "The Greatest Record Album Band That Ever Was" in *Puncture*.
  "The Greatest Record Album Ever Told" first appeared as
Lost Pamphlet #1; "The Greatest Record Album Singer Ever" as
Lost Pamphlet #2; "Them Lost Manifestoes" as *The Lost Manifestoes
of Camden Joy*; "This Poster Will Change Your Life" as *This Poster
Will Change Your Life*; "Dear cmj..." as *Dear CMJ: We Left the Coliseum
Discouraged: Posters of Protest from the CMJOY Gang*; and "Thirty-Seven
Posters About Souled American" (including excerpts of an interview
conducted with Steve Connell) as *Make Me Laugh, Make Me Cry*.

Cover by Mark Lerner / Rag & Bone Shop

Country of manufacture as stated on the last page of this book

ISBN 978-1-891241-06-2 (paperback)
ISBN 978-1-891241-76-5 (e-book)
Library of Congress Control Number: 2015935686

Verse Chorus Press
PO Box 14806, Portland OR 97293
www.versechorus.com

CONTENTS

SEVEN POSTERS ABOUT LOST JOY
JONATHAN LETHEM

1.

In the last century in Brooklyn there were a few of us who'd meet regularly in a bar on the corner of Bergen and Hoyt - this was for me personally at a sort of hinge moment, large only at that instant, while we were living inside it, in fact hurtling into the past with an awesome unforgivingness - when the Brooklyn where as a child I'd been beaten and robbed - stripped of cheap wristwatches given me by uncles - on the same street corner was still legible, not only to me, but to others; it was still tangible on the ground. So the fact that we convened there in jubilant defiant self-invention, at that particular axis, held a rich strange intensity; we were, now I see, a few of us, claiming that world even as we helped wreck it through mythology and romance at the same time that others wrecked it through real estate dollars. Nobody could be blamed now for seeing us as part of the problem. We were drunk on enthusiasm, at least, as well as pints.

It was there that I came to know Camden Joy. I had that luck. Before *The Last Rock Star Book, or: Liz Phair, a Rant*, well before *Boy Island*, let alone the nice solid baseball books as Tom Adelman (I'll never understand why he assumed that obviously false civilian name, but *whatever*). He was the author of pamphlets bound so beautifully they evoked boutique chocolate bars, and of some pieces in the *Village Voice*, and, yes, posters. The writing in here is the first writing of Joy's I knew, and I was around for some of its making. In fact, I was enlisted into the Posters for Souled American project, and wrote one (not one collected here, these here are Joy's alone) which I suppose was wheat-pasted onto some New York street-corner as part of the project. I don't know for sure, I never saw it on a wall. But I wrote it. We read them aloud at the KGB Bar, I think, too. It was a time, what a time it was. And then it was gone. I haven't known Joy since. I understand that under the "Tom Adelman" name he's gone and made a family, in some remote state. Under my own name I've gone and done the same. But we don't know one another. It strikes me now that we met, Joy and I, on a boy island, or anyway an island where we could still do more than glimpse boyhood; we could be fed by it – by our own, I mean – as I for one no longer can be, and that's likely for the better. We were in the same band, for about five minutes.

2.

The critic Manny Farber made a famous distinction, between "White Elephant Art" and "Termite Art". The implicit suggestion, to pursue the path of the termite, has meant a tremendous amount to so many of us who feel the burden of capital-A Art on our shoulders, and try to work from under that prospect, who dodge sideways into vernacular and genre gestures, who come at the problem of putting the 8-ball in the corner pocket only by means, as Howard Hawks was prone to say, of the *three-corner shot*. Of course it is only vanity to declare oneself a termite, and in fact to care at all may be to have failed the test. It isn't clear that Farber, who was trying to praise underrated Hollywood movies, meant it as a prescription anyhow, or as something you could achieve intentionally. But: Camden Joy, in the work in this book, and needless to say above all in the postering projects, exemplified termite-artist behavior. He worked the floorboards, he bored holes in the house of standing assumptions around how the intelligent writer was meant to position him or herself in regard to the objects of their pop culture desires, using his delight to shine the light and his aversions as teeth. And like the best termites, he got lost in his own holes. They began to interconnect and form a design capable of fascination. Camden Joy's negotiation with his own self-fascination, even as he prostrates himself in self-mockery before the objects of his veneration - the "record albums" which have seemed to give him his life, his key to himself - is the generator of his amazed reader's Joy. Throughout this book Joy is hiding, and failing to hide at the same time, and in so doing he flushes our own yearning and sadness and joy out into the open.

3.

But the Joy termite wasn't only boring holes in the monolith of how pop culture regards itself. He was a student, like many of us, at the college of which Robert Christgau is the Dean - the body of pop culture criticism which had, in fanzines like *Crawdaddy* and then increasingly professionally, in *Rolling Stone* and elsewhere, constructed a discourse out of whole cloth, or perhaps even out of scraps of cloth. A termite discourse itself, when it began - for who could consider that pop music deserved a criticism, at the outset? It seemed ludicrous. Nonetheless, by the time Joy came along, such connoisseurship had become institutional, even to some degree self-assessing and self-enshrining, pointing the way towards institutions yet to come: the Experience Music Project, the voting body of "experts" for the Rock and Roll Hall of Fame, and so forth. Even the quick and slippery commodification of "college rock", and subcategories of taste like "Americana", which produced an enfolding conformity that could neutralize the weirdness of an outsider artifact like Joy's beloved Souled American - these encroached on the private and eccentric fan-to-music connection that had galvanized this form of writing in the first place. So, by inventing himself as a dissident, as a semi-autistic protest voice, kicking against even many things that he himself was capable of liking (cf. Freedy Johnston), Joy-as-termite bored holes in the consensus that music criticism had "grown up" or "come into its own".

4.

What this reminds me of is how a Spanish-language writer like Roberto Bolaño, and others in his age cohort, had to work themselves out from under the canonical "Magic Realists" of the Latin American "boom" generation: Marquez & Co. And that's the writer Camden Joy actually calls to mind for me the most: Roberto Bolaño. The slippery method by which he inserts himself everywhere and nowhere in his writing, his obsessed-fan awe but also the devouring contempt he feels for the artworks he loves, the cataclysms he feels preying inside his devotion. Actually, I'd say Camden Joy reminds me of a character in a Bolaño novel even more than he does Bolaño himself: if *The Savage Detectives* had included a young American pop critic, it would have been Camden Joy. Of course, such a character would have had to be fated to vanish or die, and in fact that is what Camden Joy (I mean the character now, and not the writer; this is confusing, yes) eventually was fated to do. And then to come back and haunt us.

5.

Another, much simpler claim: Camden Joy is the Dean of something himself, now, much as he might be chagrined to admit it. He is the Dean of a crucial (albeit still distaff) style of music writing now found, sporadically, in the 33 1/3 series, whenever the authors go off the research track, into fiction or memoir or some other kind of unholy meditation: John Darnielle's on *Master of Reality*, Kate Schatz's on *Rid of Me*, Joe Pernice's on *Meat Is Murder*, and John Niven's on *Music from Big Pink*. Another example is Nicholas Rombes' *A Cultural Dictionary of Punk*, which resorts to sideways fictions and left-field comparisons to surround its subject.

6.

Three brief personal asides (here's the part to skip if you've had enough of me): First: the poster I wrote for the Souled American project was partly incorporated into the first personal essay I ever wrote, "Defending *The Searchers*", which inaugurated the sequence that became *The Disappointment Artist*. So, Camden Joy's DNA is in that book, and in my surprise fate to be any kind of essayist at all – I'd never intended it. Second: within "Dear CMJ..." is a poster calling for the discovery of a "lost" band called Memorial Garage. At the time I read this poster Camden Joy had still never succeeded in hearing that band – but it happened that not only was Memorial Garage the brainchild of my old friend Philip Price (later of the Maggies, now of Winterpills), but I'd even written a few lyrics for the band. So I was able to give Joy a couple of their self-released tapes. Third: I based Perkus Tooth, in *Chronic City*, in part on Joy. I gave him the posters, for one thing.

7.

I've got a book on my shelves the title of which I've always found peculiar to contemplate: *The Uncollected Stories of William Faulkner*. The title is self-disproving, since the stories were collected the moment it was published. *Lost Joy* is the same sort of thing, isn't it? How can Joy be lost? Joy is right here.

FOREWORD TO THE FIRST EDITION
DENNIS COOPER

RECENTLY A FRENCH JOURNALIST with a thing for American rock criticism asked me why the new generation of critics in the United States weren't artists. He couldn't understand why there weren't young *auteurs* in the mode of Lester Bangs and Richard Meltzer—or, if they did in fact exist, why he didn't know about them. When I couldn't name a current writer who satisfied his criteria, I argued that there must be young artist-critics on a par with the maestros. Readers would have a hard time finding them, however, since no prominent American music magazine gives much of a shit about prose. I explained how the old writer-friendly publications like *Rolling Stone* and *Spin* had grown tone-deaf, filling their pages with variations on a kind of young, hip, middlebrow voice whose only edge lay in the area of opinion. Even the smaller magazines devoted to intelligent, artful rock seemed too concerned with getting the word out to nurture the word itself. So, my argument went, it's not that there aren't terrific rock critics per se, they just aren't necessarily into writing literature anymore.

I hope that French guy reads this book, because Camden Joy turns out to be the perfect answer to his question. I've been an awestruck reader of Joy's fiction for years. I knew he also wrote what might be called 'rock criticism', but, seeing as how he's a very sporadic contributor to the print media, and famously likes to express his opinions in hard-to-find chapbooks and posters that he plasters around New York City, where I don't happen to live, this amazing collection comes as a surprise to me, and probably to most of you. If you've read Joy's novels and novellas, you already know that he's one of the best writers on the subject of rock music and its attendant culture. He's sort of the Irvine Welsh of American rock, setting music to narrative with a knowingness and grace that elucidates what it means to be a rock star and/or fan more persuasively than any other contemporary novelist. His almost religious belief in music and his brilliance as a wordsmith combine to create works of fiction that are so fresh that they qualify as innovative.

If that weren't impressive enough, it turns out Camden Joy might just be our finest younger rock critic as well. I can't think of another writer who writes so resonantly about the emotional and intellectual consequences of being a discriminating devotee of popular music *du jour*. Just as the hyper, hallucinatory rants of Bangs and Meltzer seemed to have an almost psychic connection to the aggressively heady rock artists of earlier decades, Joy's discursive, romantic, volatile, and super-intuitive essays translate the complex, introverted sensibilities of contemporaries like Frank Black, Pavement, and Yo La Tengo, and reignite the works of elder figures like Al Green and the Kinks. He's the kind of writer you pray will love and ruminate on your own favorites, not just because his passionate, exquisitely written tomes could convert the masses. Camden Joy isn't just a seductive critic with admirably good taste. He's as great an artist as the musicians he addresses, and you'd have go back to a time when rock criticism was the medium of geniuses to find another American writer whose output so clearly and thrillingly justifies that claim.

ACKNOWLEDGMENTS

With gratitude to all who gave me floors on which to sleep and drove me places (1995-1997), including but not limited to: the Adelmans, SE Barnet, Dani Bedau, Nancy Braver, Megan Cash, Iumari Castillo, Bill Carmean, Mark Donato, Ben Donenberg, Dorland Mountain Arts Colony, the Fryers, Piper Gray, George and Beverly Grider, Phillip Hollahan, Nancy Lynn Howell, Steve Itano, Laura Kaminker, Mike King, Lyuba Konopasek, Jim and Ernie Lafky, Mark Lerner, Jennifer India Scott and Kerin Lifland, Jane Littman, Kent Matricardi, Jamie Mayer, Kelly Meech, Jim and Sally Oldham, Karen Parrott, Meg Richman, the Rosses, Mady Schutzman, Stewart Schwartz, Benjamin Shykind, Janet Steen, Heidi Swedberg, Jim Taylor, Cathy Vibert, Hope Windle, Cintra Wilson, Allan Wood; also Amanda, Ella, Smuj, Zachary, and Zinky.

Thanks to my editors and friends: Richard Abate, Tobin Anderson and Vincent Standley of 3rd Bed, Matt Ashare, Caeri Bertrand, Matthew Berube, Paul Coleman and Jef Czekaj of Sinkcharmer, Steve Connell and Katherine Spielmann of Verse Chorus Press, Andee Connors, Tom Devlin of Highwater Books, Chuck Eddy, Jon Garelick, Richard Gehr, Ira Glass, Carter Hasegawa, Stephen Heuser, Erik Huber, Andrew Hulktrans, Jessica Hundley, Jonathan Lethem, Michaelangelo Matos, Sia Michel, Natalie Nichols, Heidi-Anne Noel, Matt Poitras of Buch Spieler, Pamela Polston, Jay Ruttenberg of the

Lowbrow Reader, Steve Salardino and Garret Scullin of Skylight Books, Ben Schafer, Geoff Shandler, Jill Stauffer of H_2SO_4, Alison True, Adam and Joy Voith, Eric Weisbard.

I love you, Hannah.

LOST JOY

If you start thinking in a moment like that, you're lost.

— Marcus Allen, after scoring on
a 74-yard run, Super Bowl XVIII

DUM DUM BOYS

THE THING I REMEMBER about Cameron—he would start smiling as soon as you'd start talking to him. Can't remember a single conversation we ever had, just remember him smiling. Don't think he knew he was smiling, it just happened, he couldn't help it, couldn't help but trust you, couldn't help but smile at you just for talking to him, watching you with his perfectly round blue-grey eyes, eyes the color of the Civil War, and when you got mid-sentence those eyes would open wider, momentarily surprised, then go back to watching, patiently waiting out your sarcasm with a disarming smile, slim good looks, a little stoned, leaning back, waiting on you to make him laugh, to earn that smile of his, to send his mouth open with laughter, his mouth with those perfect teeth.

Cameron and I first met when we were thirteen, and he alone remained as my comrade from junior high into high school, whereas my other pals of that time were lost along the way to the marching band or the swim team or the yearbook committee or the drama club. Together Cameron and I avoided the lure of school-sponsored activities. "You're running," we'd smirk at some former friend whom we'd catch training for a track and field event. They'd glance up dazed, their expression flushed, looking near death, sweat-covered, short of breath, their bodies ruddy, almost naked in those trim jerseys and gym shorts. Cameron and I would be warmly dressed as usual, long pants, trench coats preserving a pasty pallor. "What are you running *from?*" He and I distrusted the sudden crop of boring new pals one found following such pursuits. We were the only guys who by ninth grade had advanced to spray painting punk rock graffiti, gouging "Flipper" or "Nervous Gender" into the lacquered tops of school desks while our former buddies were still carving nonsense like "REO Speedwagon" or "Boston" or "The Wall." Eventually we met others who sympathized with our graffiti, who also lacked affiliations with any extra-curricular projects, and these became our new friends.

Cameron wrote a song on the guitar I lent him, the beat-up tomato-red Fender Duo-Sonic I bought off the dentist's son for $25. You can hear that model of guitar a lot nowadays, a toy-sized treble-rich guitar with no sustain. I let that guitar of mine go for almost nothing; starved for cash and desperate to get out of my hometown I, against my better judgment, hauled the Duo-Sonic into the music store, where they pointed at this and that defect and—positive that I was fencing stolen goods—said they could only offer me $60 for it. I took their money, then later heard that the Duo-Sonic was in their window—"a classic antique"—wearing a $490 price tag.

I attempted to teach Cameron to play that guitar in my parent's garage after school, weekdays, tried to turn him into a band member, but frankly he wasn't very adept. His interest in guitar technique was quashed after meeting Greg of the Circle Jerks. Greg told him about the "Magic Chord," told him that you need just two fingers, that you finger the roots of the bar chord, pluck those strings together very fast, turn the amplifier to full distortion, and everyone will feel you're plenty talented. Greg had Cameron convinced that the rest of the guitar—the other four strings, the pick-up switches and bass/treble knobs—were made for wussy jazz and that no one who played rock and roll should touch them.

So Cameron wrote a song, sorta like you'd imagine, a fast distorted 4/4 hard-core basher which was played on only two strings, with Cameron just shifting the Magic Chord up and down the frets every half-measure. The song had no melody, no words, no title; we covered it, my band, long after Cameron stopped showing up for our garage rehearsals, and we dubbed it "Cameron's Song" in his honor but I doubt he ever came and saw us and I'm not certain, even if he had, whether he would have recognized the piece.

The thing I remember about giving him guitar lessons is Cameron smiling at me the whole time, nodding enthusiastically with a short "Okay, okay" each time I'd show him something.

"You want to hold your pick—"

"Okay, okay."

"Like this."

"Okay, okay."

We'd take our fake identification cards and together go to shows at the Starwood or the Whisky or the Cuckoo's Nest where the headliners dressed as we dressed, plain jeans, normal tee shirts, short hair, where the singers couldn't be heard above the instruments though they screamed themselves hoarse trying, their bent-up mouths appearing like dark wounds gashed into their pallid faces, features in terrific pain, the musicians brazenly using made-up names like "Jello" and "Smear," "Zoom" and "Crash." Our favorite singer was named Dinah Cancer, our favorite bassist Derf Scratch, our favorite drummer D.J. Bonebrake. Occasionally, Cameron and I would come out having favored different folks on the bill—he'd generally enjoy no-nonsense barrage, I'd prefer stronger melodies, better words. But still, we went to the gigs together, endured them all the way through, and to my mind that was the important part, the part that truly made us friends.

My mother calls and I'm immediately suspicious. I haven't been home in some time, and I know she's anxious to see me, to draw me back any way she can, to position me there, a permanent cushion between her and my little sister. But this time she doesn't sound that way at all; she just isn't sure I've seen the news. It has been drizzling in my hometown for weeks and now the storms are intensifying. Flash flood warnings have closed down most of the local campgrounds, including one located just a quarter-mile from my parent's house, the house I grew up in. In recent years, maybe due to the campground's proximity to freight tracks and the main highway, this particular site has housed a steady flow of unpaying inhabitants—drifters and runaways, migrant workers and homeless, their belongings in milk-crates, their tents improvised out of painter's tarps, their laundry draped like Christmas ornaments over the oleander. This campground straddles a dry creekbed, a broad sand ditch lined with pepper trees where my friends and I would hunt for fossils on summer afternoons.

A few weeks each winter the creekbed fills to capacity with roiling waters, the overflow from mountain dams located high over us in the Condor Sanctuary, rushing thousands of feet down, racing and scurrying and taking along gnarled husks of fallen oak and trunks of pine, turning the logs over and over in haste, momentum growing, a crashing river hiding within its foam so many half-visible scraps of weighty things that standing on the bank you might glimpse the top of a stove or a closet full of clothes or a sheared-off car door drifting by, strewn with uprooted tumbleweeds and greasewood.

Mom explains that the sheriff scoured the campground after the flash flood warning and removed all the transients, hauling them to higher ground, to safety. But the sheriff had inadvertently missed an occupant, some deranged man, a homeless guy, who drowned soon after in the middle of the night when the river burst its banks, water inundating the site with such force that trash cans and picnic tables were picked up and carried nearly ten miles downstream, washed almost to the beach.

In the obituary my mother was surprised to read that the dead man had actually been quite young, was a recent graduate from our local high school. She thought I might have known him because we were the same age, graduated the same year. His name sounds familiar to her. Didn't you know some boy, she asks, named Cam-something, whose last name was Joyce?

Cameron was the kind of kid who reassured parents, easygoing, amiable, even ingenuous, and mean to no one but himself. It used to offend me when I read of people being warned against punk's amorality and anti-ethics because though I often considered myself passionately bankrupt of values, devoutly bored with manners, wonderfully unimpressed with most any grown-up, still this did not seem true of Cameron, who was another kind of punk altogether, irregular, inconsistent, unreliable, yes, but shy too, always kind, civilized.

I would laugh at those anguished predictions about kids my age when I thought of Cameron, riding his quietly pleasant

Vespa scooter around the sun-drenched valley, overdressed in his fishtail Union Jack parka with the fur-lined hood.

Tell Cameron not to do something and he wouldn't, whereas most of the rest of us would out of spite. They'd tell us not to skateboard over the pads in front of the automatic doors at the grocery store, they'd tell us time and again, not realizing the more they told us the more fun it was; but Cameron wouldn't do it, they asked him not to and he abruptly lost interest in it.

And yet Cameron was more complicated than that too, for he came along with us when we sourly stalked the school halls, my few friends and me, and any people we passed whom we didn't like we would nod at, declare "After the revolution . . .", and then draw a finger across our throat. And we liked almost none of them, not teachers, not students, and gradually we amassed detailed plans to kill most every one of them.

Leaning on our favorite wall of combination lockers, close to the edge of campus, some of us crouched, positioned so that the wall supported only our heads, others standing, one knee bent, we would proudly pass around well-worn copies of berserk books whose scenarios fit us more comfortably than high school, although I must point out that in this Cameron was not one of us, he never ascribed to these bibles of ours. Cameron's rebel status — the reason he sought the company of petty thieves, liars, and braggarts like us — was more intuitive, less thought-out; he did not internalize, the way some of us did, the distant romance of anomie-struck youth in holy literature; Cameron in a sense wrote his own story, which he kept to himself and told none of us, and he shrugged away the books and essays we'd offer while smiling patiently, tall and lean, seldom speaking, eventually pushing off from our favorite wall, waving a small 'so long' at us without pulling his hands from the deep pockets of his parka, and then putt-putt-putting away on his polite white Vespa.

We would drive long distances together, all of us, in order to see any showings of *A Clockwork Orange* or *Quadrophenia*, films we knew every line of dialogue from. One of us would usually have stolen a half-gallon of alcohol from the back of some parent's liquor cabinet, that untouched chardonnay from Christmas long ago, that cognac which a grown-up was reserving for a special occasion, that fancy malt-something which adults keep for later, and we'd pass it back and forth during the film, sloppy and more alive there than anywhere, each of us Alex and each of us Jimmy, cocky, defiant, sexy, intoxicated, dismissive of authority. It seemed to us these films alone appreciated us. *Never Grow Old*, they insisted, for once mature you would be Jimmy, heartbroken over his return to Brighton, or Alex, helpless in the hands of well-meaning, bungling adults.

Stretched out in the theater darkness, warm in the bath of flickering light, I grew bold enough to reflect on how we boys turned out this way, our hearts like onions, like stones, and why so lost, why so lonely, got far enough in contemplating these concerns to recognize that such musings should proceed no further if I wanted us still to retain our camaraderie. So I would simply stop, suddenly and completely, and seek to forget that I had ever raised such imponderables, and maybe ask for the bottle to be passed down my way once more, and work to be drawn back again into the movie.

I tell my Mom that it's too bad about Cameron but that I'm doing fine and no, I won't be coming back for the memorial service. After that, weeks follow when I cannot quell my thoughts of Cameron. I am summoned home every few minutes by one memory or another. Every time I step into a hot bath I anticipate drowning. I begin to recognize Cameron's mannerisms in most everyone around me, every coat I see is a parka, every motorcycle a Vespa. At the video store, I linger over A Clockwork Orange, *finally decide to rent it, find I can't watch it anymore. The front window of my neighborhood record store advertises expensive digital remasterings from many of the bands we used to see, reissues of Twisted Roots and the B-People and Middle Class. And one night, digging through my drawers looking for a set of thumbtacks, I uncover instead the receipt for the Duo-Sonic, the guitar I sold after Cameron gave up on it, and the receipt is just a piece of paper with a date and "$60.00" written on it but it holds my attention for an hour until I sigh, pack my bags. Finally, I drive home.*

I remember being with Cameron the first time he did black beauties. He swallowed three, then insisted I haul him over to the Arastradero, this all-ages disco at a nearby strip mall. There was no liquor allowed inside so Cameron and I first sat out on the concrete block at the head of our parking space, me drinking a shoplifted forty-ounce bumper of beer, Cameron jiggling a foot, sharing very little of what he was experiencing. We were sixteen. Once inside, I danced with this college student to one lame new wave hit after another—"One Step Beyond" then "Planet Claire" then "Pump it Up." I felt like a goddamn martyr, faking my pleasure at these songs solely to have this girl come out to the car with me. I looked across at Cameron, who sat beside the dance floor, nervously tapping on a tabletop, utterly enraptured by the sight of the Arastradero's rotating mirrored ball. "I got a bottle in the car," I told the girl, and impulsively I grabbed her hand. "Let's go outside!"

Just then the start of "Heart of Glass" blasted onto the sound system.

"No way!" she shook me off. "And miss *this* song?"

She started her wiggling again so I just walked off, dragged Cameron out with me. He revealed that he was seeing spiderweb bridges and stalactites, asked me whether he was hallucinating, softly requested that we listen to some soothing Muzak on the car radio. We drove to get chili at Bob's Big Boy. Cameron had his teeth gritted, no appetite. He set about methodically crunching the crackers with the tips of his thumbs. He did this for some time, silent, suddenly stopped, looked up, squinted, tried to focus on me.

"I got our band name," he whispered. He couldn't stop blinking. "It's real good."

We were forever working to name our band, spent more time on that than rehearsing. I wasn't even sure that there was any band to name, but still I was interested.

He had this clammy look about him, very pale, sort of stuck. "Memorial Garage," he spoke thickly, wiped his nose, gazed off.

"You alright?"

He shuddered, didn't respond.

"You gonna be sick?"

He shook his head, leaned two slender fingers into his pale neck to check his own pulse.

"Okay," I sighed. "Memorial Garage. Do you think maybe

you can explain it?"

He clamped shut his eyes, opened them, once more shook his head. "Just Memorial Garage. That's all." I saw that he had started to cry. "Really you fucking gotta trust me on this, man."

My sister wears a Walkman to the dinner table, my dad asks for the pepper to please be passed, my mom says she fluffed my pillows and my old room is ready. My dad tells me my sister quit eighth grade flag football, my mom says my sister should be able to do whatever she wants, the Walkman plays Alice in Chains. I can make out the high-end rattle of the percussion leaking out the headphones across the table, can't distinguish the band's voices from its instruments. My dad says of course of course and that's not what he meant, my mom asks who wants another helping of squash, my sister loudly announces she has to go use the phone right now. My dad frowns at my mom, my mom shrugs, they look at me. Alice in Chains ends, Primus starts. I ask if there's some reason they're both looking at me, and they go back to their plates.

Once I'm gone I can speak up, I can notice how everything they say misfires, bounces off, I can pinpoint unhealthy patterns, sour dynamics, but when I'm in it, when I'm at their dinner table, everything is a haze, familiar, aching, confused, I can be no one but their disappointing son, I can do nothing else but choke out the few lines I have recited my entire life and shake my head at how little I feel, how little I comprehend this act called dinner with my family.

I wonder what the hell they are doing wrong because I personally can't think of a thing and yet the fact is that Cameron went mad for drugs the same way I went mad for girls, the fact is that whether or not it was his and my parents—he and I both went mad. I have to question what else they could have done, what could have been lacking, for when we were small boys our folks were the sort who always endeavored to comfort us, to encourage us, they raised us to appreciate sunsets and exercise, they gave us a chance at churchliness, moved us to suburbs close to the beach (they proudly told us this was once an "alluvial flood plain"), they made us camp out in the backyard to show us meteor showers and point out the North Star, bought us paint sets and bicycles and magazine subscriptions, they taught us to recognize good kite-flying weather and to say thanks and stop at stop signs and read newspapers and enjoy public television, and they worked hard at their jobs—perhaps a little too absent, a little too preoccupied, this is true, but still they worked hard nonetheless.

But maybe there was something murderous about this work ethic of theirs, maybe that was the source of the problem, for I think of how they would read our adolescent Christmas lists like aggrieved parents reading a ransom note, too proud to admit that they could not afford our teenage demands, confident that they could completely buy us back if they only drove themselves harder, removed themselves a little more, stayed late at work for enough nights. And then something happened where they began to work so hard at times we hardly saw them, and it felt as if we were being purposely kept out of their sight, as if we had already in fact been kidnapped, and our parents confirmed this for they began to behave as if they, in turn, were already set on being blackmailed. All I know is, despite the attention lavished on our early upbringings, by the time we were as old as my little sister we wanted none of it, all any of us hoped for was an early death, a violent early death. Out of all of us happily only one got what he'd hoped for; sadly, that was Cameron.

Cameron barely graduated, he was forever skipping school to cruise around on his Vespa or hitch-hike down to L.A. I think it can be accurately claimed that as his friends we had more to do with his graduating than he ever did, for I believe that he got out of high school mainly due to the gullibility of teachers who believed the stories we fed them, the endless excuses we gave as to why Cameron didn't show up today or yesterday or the day before or last week either for this or that class. The example I remember is Mrs. Constantine, our literature teacher.

Ever the punk rebel, Cameron had taken to wearing exceedingly normal polo shirts and cardigan sweaters to high school and so we, in turn, took to telling Mrs. Constantine that Cameron's frequent absences were the fault of the school golf team.

"I had never before heard that Cameron golfed with our golf team," she informed us skeptically.

"Of course. Why do you think he wears those dorky polo shirts and stupid cardigans all the time?"

Mrs. Constantine considered this. "I suppose," she said. "I might have heard of it if he were the type of boy who talks. Still, I should have seen his name on these lists that are circulated around, that have the names of all the golfers on them."

"Well naturally. But remember it's Cameron, after all. He doesn't want anyone to find out. You know how he is. He does everything he can to keep it a secret. 'L'Angelo Mysterioso,' all that."

Mrs. Constantine nodded, made a gesture to indicate the secret was safe with her because her lips were locked and she had tossed away the key, and then excused many of Cameron Joyce's absences in her ledger as "Necessary for School Business."

Cameron often took far too many uppers and then requested a lift to the disco. One time he was near to overdosing at the Arastradero on a handful of cross-tops. Two beautiful college girls kept checking us out. Eventually they came over and, with no other prelude, just liking the looks of us I guess, asked for Cameron and I to take them home. We drove them to their condo, followed them inside, watched the girls unceremoniously shrug out of their clothes.

"Oh," said Cameron. "Christ." He was suddenly moving away. He had that clammy look and he was staggering back and back, one hand darting behind him, unsuccessfully groping about for a chair, and then he quietly sank to the carpet, a pile of slouched limbs.

One of the girls giggled.

"Should we be worried?" they asked.

"Nope," I said, untangling Cameron's spindly arms and legs, smoothing him out so that he looked a bit more presentable laying there passed out cold on the condo's floor. "He's like this all the time."

"We should maybe call an ambulance though?"

"Amphetamines," I explained. "He'll wake up, he'll be fine." I made sure his breath was visible in a compact mirror and then I shed my own clothes.

The ice cream parlor closes at eight-thirty so we have to hurry. The dishwasher is quickly filled, my sister is dragged from the telephone, my dad from the computer. My mom, dad sit in the front of the car like always, my sister, me in back. The town goes by the window and nothing appears any different. My sister and I ignore each other. It's been four hours since I got home. We have yet to speak. Her Walkman and headphones rest in her lap, a threat.

At the ice cream counter my parents pretend to be newlyweds. My dad croons along with the music on the loudspeaker, my mom giggles, takes his hand, rests a cheek on his shoulder. My sister and I take our cones, move outside. She leans on the car, notices me watching a homeless guy approach. He is having a tough time of it, stumbling, dropping things.

Fuck, she laughs, indicating the homeless guy. It's the first word she's directed towards me. Who's this loser? I laugh with her, nod. Her eyes connect with mine, share something. Too weird, wheezes an unfamiliar voice. It's you, hey man. The homeless guy is speaking. He croaks my name a few times. My sister rolls her eyes, stamps her feet, recrosses her arms, licks her cone. Figures, she snorts.

The homeless guy wants me to shake his hand. How have you been, he asks, you heard what happened to our friend? Yeah, I reply. I can't recall this guy's name, but I briefly give him my hand. He looks like someone I might have hated in high school, probably someone we'd planned on killing after the revolution. Yeah, I say again, too bad. Could be it's better off, the guy shrugs, he wasn't well, you knew that. Yeah, I say, guess I did.

I think of the party I heard about where, after a few drinks, Cameron made everyone whisper because he insisted the government was listening. Everyone assumed he was joking but they indulged him anyway. A few days later, he attacked a group of Asians on the street, claiming that they had placed electrodes in his brain, that they were monitoring his thoughts for the CIA. No one told me what happened to him subsequently; I caught rumors he'd disappeared somewhere across the country, in Boston or New York, I heard that he was calling himself "Camden Joy," writing on some city's walls or some crazy thing, and I kept setting his smile against East Coast backdrops, I'd imagine him smiling as the New Yorkers spoke, smiling like he couldn't help it, couldn't help but trust them, leaning back, just watching, hands deep in his parka, smiling. I always figured I'd find him eventually, I'd imagine these elaborate schemes in which I'd smoke him out, make him reveal himself, like maybe I'd write under that name "Camden Joy" and he'd track me down as a result, schemes like that, which were far-fetched and spooky in a way I knew he'd like, and then after finding me we'd shake our heads over our impossible past, disputing it like an amnesiac might if awakening to a hoax, we'd mock memories of "the good old days," and he'd smile and smile.

Hey man, you really gotta come out and see us, the homeless guy is saying to me. I would, I say, but I'm just visiting, I'm leaving soon. Come out to the campground first, the guy encourages me, it's where him and me are staying. You and who, I ask. Him and me, the guy says. I got Camden out there. What, I ask. I got Camden with me out there, he says, man, they cremated his ass, don't you know. I got what's left of him out there with me. You should really see him before you go. I'll try, I say. I'm pressed for time, you understand. The guy fidgets for a long time, studying me. You haven't changed, man, he informs me at last, not at all, and he staggers off.

Cameron and my other friends and I remained close for a long while, for no other reason than that we simply dreaded explaining ourselves to anyone who didn't already get us, who didn't admire the complex hail of references which comprised our daily chit-chat.

Inevitably, Sex and Drugs got in the way of this friendship, for the intensity and immediacy of their sensate gratification so dwarfed the ordinary pleasure of our camaraderie as to make us entirely question the depth and commitment of our feelings towards one another, made us ask whether we truly knew each other, if we were ever even friends at all or just neighbor boys who had a few tastes in common, similar jokes and mannerisms, liked a couple of the same LPs and movies, nothing more.

What were such similarities in the face of Girls, who quickly meant everything to me, or Speed, which began to mean everything to Cameron? It grew crucial that we dismiss the friendship to pursue these bigger joys, and Cameron accepted—just as I was made to grasp and grudgingly admit—that he would have to make himself better understood in order to obtain access to these higher pleasures, and he began to hang out with agitated speed-freaks who endlessly described things they witnessed which were utterly invisible to the rest of us, and I began devoting myself to girls whom I respected solely for the tautness of their trim calves and the willingness in their open smiles. These were, in some ways, our uneasy attempts to apply for membership to new circles, signaling our willingness to be cheaply belittled and lamely categorized by these new so-called pals so that we might be allowed to drop a hungry hand into their grab-bag and come away having scored some of their goodies.

I stride down our block of tract homes and across the kiddie park, skirting the shopping center the whole while, then continue over the highway, down and up a tall cement embankment, wading through a field of knee-high green brush, across the railroad tracks, down a row of ditches which irrigate a field of baby's breath. Wild anise sprouts everywhere underfoot like weeds, encouraged by the winter's rains, the gentle morning breezes rippling its feathery leaves, the reek of licorice pouring from its sticky, cane-like stalk.

So you came, the homeless guy calls out, I knew you would. Well hey there, I say, I was just taking a walk. This is incredibly close to where my parents live, actually. The guy ignores me. I knew you would come, he repeats. We always figured if anyone got to be a household word, it'd be you. But then, you're not a household word, he mumbles dismally, not even you.

Not even me, I agree.

What's the point anyways, he says. Right? You heard Susan Lucci on the radio the other night. No, I reply. Well, he discloses, I got a radio, I got me Camden's radio set-up . . . Wanna see Camden? Not really, I tell him. You came all this way, he mutters. Wanna see where he lived?

Yeah, I concede, okay.

The guy motions for me to follow, starts across the campsite. Watch the poison oak, he declares. Leaves don't turn red till summer. The guy leads me around barbecue pits, sacks of trash. So, he says, Susan Lucci has had no easy time of it. And you think, if not Susan Lucci, you know, then who. Because what she deserves . . . that's some incredible talent. And that Emmys thing is so screwed. Too weird. Breaks your heart. Oh, I drily put in, absolutely. You don't care for Susan Lucci, he notices. Okay well, you will. I didn't once upon a time either.

He points to the top of a eucalyptus tree. That's it, he says simply. About nine feet up, three branches diverge off the frame of the main trunk. A piece of plywood rests between the limbs.

Cameron lived there, I ask.

Camden, he corrects me, yeah. He hasn't been Cameron since high school. But you know, the guy goes on, Camden always kept talking about you. What did he say, I ask, do you remember? No, he says, you couldn't always hear him real good. What's funny, I say, is I can't even remember anything we talked about, just him smiling all the time, you know? Right, the guy says, I know. I hadn't seen him, I say, in a long time. You kinda—the guy gesticulates frustratedly—we couldn't find you, right after Camden got picked up for going off on those Jap dudes.

I got real busy, I acknowledge. My career just . . . It took off.

Fine, he says.

I always heard Cameron went to New York City, I say. Sometimes I'd go there, I'd look all over for handwriting on the walls. The guy shakes his head, points up again at the plywood. He came home, he says. He was at the emergency room, they were calling him psychotic and all this, got him down on this cot, KO'd him with Thorazine. I met him up there at the crisis center, they were doing him up with four and a half milligrams of Haldol three times a day. We just took off together, man, it was getting wicked.

The crisis center was in town here?

Near here, he nods, yeah. So we've been here now, this is our third springtime. The state pays us general relief. Were you here that night, I ask, the night the cops came to get everyone out of the way of the water. Sure, he says. Well, I ask, where was . . . why didn't you take Cameron with you?

Well, he says, the difference there was, Camden didn't like the cops and so he went and hid in the river bottom, soon as they showed up. And the stupid fucks, they never even saw him down there.

We smile at each other, proud of our friend's ability to confound the law.

You know how he was, the guy murmurs, and we smile again.

Yeah, I admit, I know how he was. I begin to climb the eucalyptus.

Be careful, the guy warns me. Camden used to fall from there all the time. Yes, I think to myself, I can see why, because only two sides of the plywood have any sort of branch support, the other two open into thin air. None of his belongings are up here, just this bare plywood placed in the trees. Is this all there was, I ask. No, the guy replies, I took everything else, his books and shit I got down here with me. You wanna see them? You still gotta come down and see Camden, man. Can't believe you haven't even seen Camden.

I'm not really interested, I say. I am laying flat, my belly against the plywood, gazing off through the acrid haze of fried burgers and fast-food neon, and suddenly I jerk at the sight of something. Did you know, I start to ask, then stop. It's just a coincidence, it's gotta be. What, the guy asks. Well you can see, from this perch here, you look right at my parent's garage. Yeah, concurs the guy, where you guys used to rehearse. Exactly, I say. Yeah, he continues, I was aware of that, Camden did that on purpose. He did, I say. The guy shrugs. I couldn't tell you why.

I have my fingers interlaced, palms down, my head on my hands. So, I think to myself, Cameron was home all this time, delusional in the arms of his eucalyptus, conversing with his memories and watching that stupid garage. I shut my eyes against the sunshine and remember the winter weather, the way it hits here and holds on. I picture this board wobbling in a thundershower, Cameron unable to make out the sounds of the highway or the freight trains when above them both is the storm whistling through the treetops, breaking branches in the blackness, shaking loose water and leaves with a high, relentless whoosh. As a child, I remember falling asleep to the rain pelting our roof, and in my mind the source of the storm was a face as big as the sky, a face with its mouth stuck open, howling, and the face was gruesomely contorted, and it never ran out of breath.

I feel those childhood storms howling in the pit of my stomach right now, week-long storms which seemed never to go away. And every fear ever imagined sings in my bones, there is the fear of being locked up in my room too long alone, the fear of being devoured by the storm, the dwarfed feeling of being left behind, insignificant, a trifling speck of humanity. I know that as a boy, laying in bed, eyes closed, I regularly fell asleep to this feeling, this absolute certainty that I had been forgotten.

I feel the abrupt shudder of plywood beneath me. Hey, the homeless guy says, shaking the tree. Hey. You been up there long enough. Come down now and see him. You gotta see Camden, man. You haven't seen him yet.

In a minute, I say sleepily. Just give me half a minute. I'll be down.

THE ALMOST REVOLUTION

BACK BEFORE LIFE WAS OKAY, imbeciles with feathered hair parted down the middle and no acne organized suburban dances, where everyone bumped and gloriously french-kissed while vomiting hard liquor down one another's champion throats. Stuck-up morons mocked me openly, said things like, "Scram, Shrimp!" so they could practice their routines in the boy's room. They told everyone I was *cognoscenti* (because I outpointed them in dodgeball), *isolato* (because I lacked adequate fashion accessories), and *pozzolana* (because of my big bones). They walked unscathed from totaled hot rods while I sat up late with Marie, my girlfriend, and together we cursed Jesus H. Christ for allowing them to live, with their muscle cars and glass packs, beauty rings, righteous Sat. Nite Fever bud, and primo levi weed, their blithe insistence that nothing mattered except the continued tingling of tanned flesh beneath their polyester wraps. We were two fifteen-year-olds. Long-faced, slack-jawed and, of course, down-hearted, unable to bear the lack of *soixante-huitards* and *nouveaux philosophes* in our resort-style neighborhood, Marie and I rode bikes down to the shopping center one balmy afternoon, hauling a boombox, angrily intent on accomplishing some protest. But our brains were very young, just fifteen years old, and putting the predicate to a subject like "transgression" incapacitated us. Soon we settled on candy. We would eat candy. More candy than had ever been eaten. The world would wonder where all its candy went and we alone would possess the answer, having eaten it all. That kind of thing. Ingesting the goods of our crass *société de consommation* to call Western culture on its fascination with simulacra and facsimile, blah de blah blah. Lemonheads, Mike and Ikes, Atomic Fireballs, Branch's Peanut Butter Rickeys, Hot Tamales, Licorice Stumps, M&M's, Mounds, Mars, Marathon Bars, &c. You sense the magnitude of what we were planning. We bought, as I recall, thirteen dollars worth of candy; candy was cheaper then, this was a whole lot. We also bought a $3.99 cassette of *Donovan's Greatest Hits* which, displayed for sale near the cash register, seemed as indicative as anything else of what Johnny Baudrillard would've disdained about the dead-end way in which we were being raised.

The candy tasted good at first, especially since it was for a good cause. The first ten Hershey products went down fine. We consumed them while fidgeting around outside the store, heckling shoppers who rolled by with full carts, yelling (as kids will) about how we were going to teach you bastards a thing or two about fake serenity, about soft utopias, and so on.

We had the Donovan tape going on our boombox. A perfect soundtrack! As the digesting got tough, as we gagged on root beer barrels and choked back the stomach acids which rose, bewildered, in our over-sugared throats, Donovan too began to sound sick—but truthfully, didn't he always sound sick? The pain hardened in our guts, bellies pregnant with some devil offspring, civilization's *fin de siècle* hyperrealism made (ouch—!) concrete, but steadfast we continued to dine on candy, on candy, on candy (revolutions require strong stomachs). In fact, when (soon after) we began to vomit, decorating the shopping center walkway with festive rivers of speckled post-structuralist barf, we didn't even consider that the candy might've been responsible nor did we bother doubting our philosophical persuasions. We instinctively blamed Donovan. He sang in his fey queasy tone, he sang his inane ditties and we puked. Cause and effect. Perhaps our incipient revolution did founder on the shores of a sudden dextrose intolerance—but America, you can thank Donovan that you still have your candy, for without him I do believe our protest would've succeeded.

THE GREATEST
RECORD ALBUM
EVER TOLD

. . . Like the inflamed sea creature one suddenly discovers attached to one's body when previously some quiet wound resided thereat — on that day some open sore awakens into its fullest agitated condition of garish redness — this was the day I glanced down to find my TEENAGER OF THE YEAR.

I am not writing this for money's sake. Please understand that if you understand nothing else. I am writing this because I have just this one free night to deposit noise in your general direction — tonight! (I am off work all night.) I am not due again at the liquor store until tomorrow at 9 AM so now till then I plan to tell you this while I have time I have a strong pot of coffee and twelve sacks of M&M's and an itchy red rash on my right calf and no blossom-faced missus Marie and will not sleep for I cannot knowing what I just read in *People* that those in charge of giving us music have given up on our Teenager Of The Year Frank Black, that he is adrift and label-free — whoa! like hearing your dearest buddy is side-down on the cold cement sleeping behind 4th City Savings and Loan off Cahuenga Blvd. in the smoked glass recessed doorway in back beside the grey alarm security box — actually I have slept there three times before in my life and never once slept poorly but this is not about me, but about — Frank Black — and I am writing this because Frank Black is great (I want to be as great as Frank Black is!) — I am writing this not for money I am writing this from love. Love — I have seen eventually — does however cost one quite a lot (—!) so I expect this ultimately will bankrupt me utterly for such is the depth of my love for our disowned pudgy genius, such could I not have gotten through what I got through without *Teenager of the Year*, all the associative slipperinesses of meaning he is comfortably employing, the deranged tirades, no prosaic summing up "here's my point," instead of embraceable anthems only syntactical errors with sweeping implications, a splayed-out array of obscure pop ephemera meeting one another for the first time, a description, an overwrought response, a confident feeling, then some people, some places, some things. "Some gibberish it is so serious," says Black in advance of his theory during Track Ten, put plain his gibberish ends up as poetry, random thoughts meticulously arranged, not subject predicate but modifier modifier modifier noun. Many other "B" artists have guzzled this thirstily at the font of ill-lucidity and lyrical obscurity — Barrett, Beefheart, Bolan — but none go POP! as unabashedly as this enthusiastic Black man which is why I write this now to instruct you concerning the "Greatest Record Album Ever Told" —

An in-town glamour rag here in our valley of tar tagged and feathered Frank Black as one of the hundred coolest Angeleno peoples — even though he is a recent immigrant — their high priests and scribes writing thusly of him — "phenomenal" and "eccentric"! And then these self-same journalists — to all their compliments off-set so they are not to be read as slobbering sycophants — they bring up his gigantic waistline, they off-handedly call him "stout" "corpulent" "lard-filled" he is to them "pear-shaped" "bloated" and "sickly-swollen" a "tub of goo." But why, you ask, and how dare they and from whence doth such vitriol erupt, precisely? Is it from that undeniable truth that fat people are more jolly — does bitter envy spring forth from underfed, stick-like writers? Is each of us of such optimum weight that as readers we can abide perusing such ridicule? Who among us can truthfully say he has never stepped from a steaming bath with skin aggravated red as a big old beet and smelling as some fatty boiled dumpling? There is No Justice for Our Black Man—NO JUSTICE! To celebrate his music they insult his looks. To praise the greatest record album ever told they drop him from the label.

A friend I used to talk to talked to Black on the phone once—by accident really—but said he was odd. This, the world thinks. That Frank Black is odd—but I speak this loud he is not Odd but Normal and ours is the responsibility to catch up to him for like some H.G. Wells fictionalized individual Black has advanced in our time-space continuum advanced ahead of us so far in every direction—in all but the most unlucky manner—that only his physical corporeal self is being forced to inhabit our dim dimension to remind us from whence he originally came, thusly permitting him to be castigated, sent off, ridiculed, made to bear Job-like burdens—

If in fact—as some suggest—Richard Nixon invented Rock and Roll—which indeed reads preposterously but only means how the stifling political occurrences of the '60s and '70s—from the savage Nixon campaign against JFK which led to JFK's death to Vietnam to Kent State et al.—repeatedly foisted new significances and purposes upon rock and roll and thusly in a sense our suppressive American dictator inadvertently was attributable for the granting to rock and roll of its merry eternal life, if this Nixon-Invented-Rock-and-Roll Maxim holds true well then how appropriate is my home-taped version of *Teenager of the Year*—I have it also on CD but I prefer this cassette better because of how it begins after a radio interlude somebody taped for me of Talking Spooks—McCord, Hunt, those types—ferreting out riddles of that Watergate scandal which dethroned our rock-and-roll-inventing Great Dictator—muttering of the Florida thing, the O'Brien thing, Haldeman's diaries, Dem Nat'l Chair Lawrence O'Brien the consultant for "The Western Exterminator Co." founded by one Howard Hughes whose agent Bob Mayhew "defused difficulties" arising from $100,000 Bebe Reboso Campaign Contribution—the Florida thing—and F. Donald Nixon's receipt of suspicious loan from self-same Western Exterminators in the late '50s—well-documented though later

expurgated in pages of Haldeman diaries — all this mutters
on then *Teenager of the Year* arrives and sets up and begins to
play —

And oh dear reader have you never drunked chocolate milk
that like candied paint went down, gooey and fine, for this
best connotes that blissful day I first made the acquaintance
of this *Teenager of the Year*. I cannot really put words to how life
seemed before then: unpulled together, dreamy, disconnected,
I believe it was fine but who can say, who can guarantee this
vague past I recall is even my own and what is a true memory
anyways anymore amongst the high-paid programmers
and mind-controlling media agents of these 1990s I might
say I remember how people would come up offering their
assistance, children on swings, a blackbird takes flight, untold
grief, one city with signs in Cyrillic, another full of carts and
grumpy livestock, an embrace, a lazy cloud or two drifting
over the sun, the nasturtium glance of Marie over and over,
palm trees and fountains, the sun sharply yellow at some
certain hour and envy, such envy, these pines, angry words
and stamping off, pedestrian signals blinking don't walk eight
times, a glimpse of fishing boats in the bay, chatting weather
with someone at a service station, an orangey landscape pity-
flooded, trash-fish and pond-scum, Marie honey-necked and
gleeful, rollerbladers cradling Slurpees, licorice wrappers,
Disneyland tee shirts (— for everyone!), cars leaking pop
songs, military planes low overhead — any of this could be
accurate but it zips into focus "only" upon meeting *Teenager of
the Year* to which thereupon ensued a close study of this here
Frank Black factoid chart: Born same year as *Beatles '66*, as
a boy Charles Michael Kitridge Thompson IV is continually
teased for having same name as one of the Monkees. In
late '80s Thompson meets Kim Deal and — envying her
monosyllables — surreptitiously tricks her out of her name.
She retaliates by writing band's first hit "Gigantic," found
on a record album called *Rosa*-something (late '80s), labeled
by *Sounds* and *Melody Maker* "the best thing to come from
Boston since 'More Than a Feeling.'" This follows an EP which
came out around then or before. Next comes another record
album, called *Doo*-something, enters UK charts at Number so-

and-so, labeled by *Village Voice* and *Puncture* "the best Boston record album period." In bold parry, Deal seizes back name for all-girl record album celebrating girls and their cool names and record albums. No one buys this record album. In an unrelated event, to honor those killed in Dec. 3 massacre during Feast of St. Francis, Thompson now adopts mournful new name of Black Francis. This lasts until 1992 when once more he loses name, this time in tragic motorcycle accident. In the meantime, two more record albums that have names are released, each called "the best music ever made" by *Rolling Stone*. Disappointed by such comments and wanting to do still better (and encouraged by Lowery leaving Camper, Perry F. leaving Jane's Ad, Roy Orbison leaving Tr. Wilburys), in early '90s Black Francis tells bandmates to hide and promises he will find them by end of decade. He counts to ten and dutifully band disappears. Then tires skid on ice and motorcycle accident. At subsequent 'recovery' shows, he adopts moniker "Mr. Pixie" only next to find himself embroiled in federal lawsuit when candy manufacturer Topps Inc. (as maker of Pixie Sticks) files in U.S. District Court for "infringement of a trademarked character." In resulting settlement arising from binding arbitration, Thompson drops the "Mr. Pixie" name in exchange for promise of receiving lifetime supply of Topps' annual trading card series FAMOUS SAUCER ABDUCTIONS/ ARCHITECTS THROUGH HISTORY. Thompson attempts comeback cabaret show as "The Artist Formerly Known as Kim Deal" but attendance wanes and tour is canceled in midpoint. Next Thompson, hearing Eno's *Here Come the Warm Jets*, reads where "Blank Frank" is a song that was written in reverse and so reverses it back to make new name "Frank Blank." Unfortunately, his passport application is redrawn by clerk at Ellis Island to read "Frank Black," because clerk prefers that name and possesses darker ink. Proof of family lineage (for possible later conversion to Church of Latter Day Saints) potentially problematic when Cilla Black (1943–) disavows all cognizance of any offspring "Frank" and each of Anne Frank's surviving relatives deny having black descendants. Despite these setbacks, Elektra/Asylum (via smaller 4AD label) signs this "Frank Black" to solo career in late 1992 and expects great things.

Elektra/Asylum—*Asylum?!*—ha! there was none for Frank
Black.—[I must now admit this how during the entire
length of our relationship the whole time we were together
myself—your beloved pamphleteer—and angel-haired, candy-
mouthed Marie were watched over by this vast bunkered
home of the Western Exterminator Co. which loomed high
above us from its mighty mantel (Silver Lake at Temple) fenced
in with electrical wire aloof and giving no clue to its mission
but for its wall painted with a tall gent in top hat, cravat, and
gloves waggling a finger at a subdued rodent while behind his
back he hid a big tool and tiny neon mice blinked along the
facade racing to get away but automatically they circled back
to get squashed by that imperialist caricature, that cartoon
capitalist with the oversized hammer—ah, how like living in
the trail of Auschwitz ash this was and "how long," I ask,
could any love survive beneath this ugly billboard prose of
doomed mice when to come home each day meant to look out
each evening upon the overwhelming vulture of the Western
Exterminator Co. perched at our bedroom window—to see
all night that rendition of killer cartoon capitalists, this was
the plainest of signs that we had lost our everything and . . .
ah well! Some few of us have since come quite accidentally
to uncover impressive evidence of the Western Exterminator
Co. as a sinister enterprise, its monies spread everywhere
abundant—operating in effect as a present-day Dutch East
India Co.—they who in the 1600s/1700s ran the spice trade,
ran the high seas, ran everything—but Alas! said "Revelation"
must await a more focused delineation in some later tract but
I will eventually transmit that knowledge to you the reading
public I promise!]

"BUT JUST WHAT ARE SIGNIFICANT SALES?"

Who out there is paying attention and why should this
matter? 16 million viewers did not enough Nielsens provide
to save the Last Good TV Show from cancellation; 16 million
viewers! Sculptors, to get a showing, to draw a hundred, that
is a success in the today world of sculpturing; great men of
letters read by none but a handful of college kids; our best
poets drinking themselves to sleep beneath freeway bridges,

me behind the counter of your liquor store every damn hour, every damn day (I am not a hard boy to bear but when I am tired). And meanwhile "THEY"—these the same sorts as the Romanovs who merrily profited by restraining in serf-style backwardness Russia for upwards of four centuries—They dare play pong with our hearts and yank the inspirational Frank Black from our record album bins for his moving of only 75,000 units which they term insignificant sales and to tell us that the fat lady has sung on this fat boy's singing career, that the difficult Frank Black is not a merchandisable commodity in fiscally conservative times, in the daunting arrhythmia of our cultural pulse. . . . Let them lose no money, these chicken Romanov bastards, for their faith in Art rises and falls on its investment return, they have no patience with integrity, cannot live—as the restless Black advocates during track three—on an Abstract Plain. They call you a genius in television simply if forty million peoples look at you continually, in music if you sell half a million, in literature if anyone reads you, in poetry, well, everyone's a genius there once they're dead. Right now in the darkest damp night I look out upon spooky silence scratching my itchy calf, all others are asleep in this shivering mid-morning premonition for there is no sound but that of the Money Counters running downtown and I stand here in this big swirl singing this lullaby alone but for you here alongside me, dear Reader, and how confidence might well dip if I had not begun listening in my Walkman just now FULL-BLAST to Frank Black who restores me completely to myself by saying he wants to sing for me ("I want to sing for you/And make your head go POP!POP!POP!POP!POP!"). And POP it has! It has and what must the Board have made of this at their shareholder's meeting in the executive bunny room when they received these tapes ("There it is—Take it!") twenty-two tracks of the best pop marvels ever recorded, the whole endeavor transpiring over just sixty-two minutes and fifty-three seconds (for an average song length of two minutes forty-nine seconds—optimal AM radio length!), each song a compact feast dense as a collapsed star with melodies smushed into more melodies, offering as many varied colors and textures as a Moroccan carpeteria, each track with a thousand choruses, a bunch of bridges, untold verses, impossible guitar catchiness, everything spry and lovely and irresistible — "YET" — and here comes the boo-hoo-hoo face — there is "Challenging Content" here too — even "REVOLUTIONARY" — and one thing these wicked shareholding Romanov despots hate more than a release which does not sell is an artist chatting "Geographically" as in Laurasia, Calistan, Españo Nuevo, singing "Nobody owns/The pleasure of tones," singing "How many stars girl/Can you both count/And then classify?" singing "How can you free me/How can you free me/How can you free me/How can you free me/When I am free?" The pliant meek musicmakers, the tasteless producers and imitators, they are adored by the Romanovs yes, but just like Western Exterminators these Romanovs love the dead ones best, the Croces, Cobains, and Big Boppers, the Janis Joplins, Sid Viciouses, Gram Parsonses — how uncomplicated to market those tribute* albums, how little those stiffs resist, how completely they take on the amenable behavior of cash-dispensing corpses, the record album companies might just as well install vast ATMs into the celebrity sarcophaguses so brazenly do they profit from deceased talent — And so before their cash registers and adding machines — before all those gathered Western Exterminators — this Black man planted a stance ("There it is — Take it!") and bellowed NO! in a voice that tore flesh from bone (he requires no megaphone) and for this — because Frank Black shunned any publicity for his last CD, would permit NO pictures, grant NO interviews, make NO response to the insistent questions of the media horde, the inane rockarazzi ('How do you write songs? Why didn't you let Kim Deal sing more? What's a guitar? Have you always been so round? How come your lyrics are hard? Your thoughts on TicketMaster? How do you explain losing your hair? Am I being clever yet flirty yet cynical yet kiss-ass enough for you, Monsieur Le Noir?'), because he wanted his greatest life's work examined free of childish prejudice and artist's commentary — he was dispatched to a far-off kingdom to rot

---

* And when they were come to Capernaum, they that received tribute money came to Peter, and said, Doth not your master pay tribute? MATTHEW 17:24

and the Romanovs built a wall sixty hands high, nine cubits in breadth, and barbed they the top with Breeders discs to guard this immaculate space and prevent his reentry—

You all must mail letters of protest for you are as much to blame as anyone, even more so, for look inside your soul and answer honestly these hard-put questions: Did You Tout This CD to all you came in contact with (&c.), did you organize sign-up drives, incentives for Frank Black listeners, did you call radio stations to demand 'Less Breeders, More Black Man,' did you send the world your message proudly? Did you to catered gatherings go decked-out in festive garb and holding out but one CD which you persistently pressed upon the DJ and insisted she play in its entirety, did you into the yielding flesh of ficus and succulents carve and upon bus kiosks and overpasses and blank alley spaces daub Frank Black compliments so thusly those headed to work might consider these advertisings all day while at their labors? Did you figure out where the impressionable ones congregate and did you then approach them there, confront the wary, debate the cagey? Glib people might in a fast-moving car in which you were a passenger idly put down Frank Black as "too Clever, too Complicated, too Weird, too Slick"—and did you then announce loudly to them your disagreement and encourage them yet still to seek that enlightenment which was eluding them and grandly upon your body paint the news and upon every specimen of American currency you handled did you write how there is none finer than this record album *Teenager of the Year*—if to any single one of these you answered less than "yes" you are then obligated to undo this damage, you as a fan are as mighty as a president just swimming in the slop of this sauce of chaos and must grab responsibility now. They will of course respond that they can do nothing—it would be easy for those of us advocating change to take the Romanovs' word for it but it would be a Mistake—this can be remedied!

Let me hammer this into your idiot mouse-brains: you must "Write" "Write" and "Write"—"Write" the Western Exterminators, the Elektra/Asylum/4AD Romanov Despots, look them up each in the Million Dollar Directory at your local library and "write"—for this is an urgent action, "involve thyself"—you must "act" to stop these abuses and exchange this world for some better thing—remember that although you oppose human rights violations wherever they occur, you cannot defeat the greed-driven conglomerates or even a few deaf record album executives SO LETTERS SHOULD NOT BE ACCUSATORY, it is better to assume that the cruel profiteers at 4AD and Elektra are, in fact, willing to seek a remedy for stripping our greatest national asset of his livelihood "IF" they are properly informed. Please be courteous and send your letter promptly. You may wish—to reassure the badged men in front, given the recent difficulties—to upon your envelope write "NO EXPLOSIVES ENCLOSED HEREIN but merely things of EXPLOSIVE IMPACT." You must remember as you talk with them that sometimes when you have talked to someone you mistakenly believe yourselves in complete agreement like with blossom-faced, bough-armed Marie and me when she says, 'This is so cool' and you see her big lips draw back to smile, happy happy, and you're happy too, you say, 'Definitely, so cool' and you two kiss to the sound of "Velouria" in the great laser-riddled dancehall while thousands upon thousands gyrate in merriment and much later I come to find we were two totally wrong for each other—candy-mouthed Marie, you were watching bassist Mrs. John Murphy onstage as said wasted-looking bassist panted tobacco clouds and not like me focused on the microphoned prodigy of our times—his head a peeled grape, his voice a pained dog—who is so rare and special and magnificent I cry, I can cry over it—far more than I ever cried over us splitting(—!), although I have cried, I will, I will, I do I promise.

"TELL THEM!!"

Say unto them I am writing you this because no one has yet rammed Frank Black into your damn public head and his sponsors in fact as I have said threw high their frustrated arms and quit the set* and Frank Black's perspicacity is contractually bound now to no one, for like the wandering King of the Jews this despised Teenager of the Year has been chastised and

---

* And Pilate gave sentence it would be as they required. LUKE 23:24

let go and our Black man has already lost his name so many times how much more must he be faced with—this morning I baltered into the bollard at the bottom bank of the pedestrian overpass, my thigh is bruised and bothered I feel a wreck but truly I'm fine, just fine, and I am writing this because you never liked him and instead always told me to put on something else w/ more music, less words (aaaaaaaarrrrrrrrrrggghhh!) and thusly *Teenager of the Year* languished—from lazy listeners like lemon-eared Marie—clung low on the pop charts until it fell with a clatter (with no windows thrown wide/to see what was the matter).

For I say unto you near-sighted ones who can see this but have troubles reading all else (she too was blind this way, my last, holding papers at arm's length and scrunching her eyes up most delightsomely her name as I've explained was Honey-Necked Marie and now we are no more but I'm not sad so there—!) this I possess "The Knowledge" that soon you shall see—Myopia Cured!—and the wicked set straight and those otherwise impaired fixed for *Teenager of the Year* is the GREATEST RECORD ALBUM EVER TOLD and performs Magic. But you will want proof of my knowledge I have seen this. Proof that I know of what I say, proof that I am whom I say or vice versa, &c. For I have read things which treat *Teenager of the Year* as just another great record album, comparing it to *Imperial Bedroom* and *Pet Sounds* (how akin to equating fresh Coke to a flat soda!) and I do recognize that there are many here among you who know that life is but a joke and who—in learning of albums which contain fine lyrics like "The microscope/ On that secret place/Where we all wanna go/Is rock and roll" and "It frightens me/The awful truth/Of how sweet life can be" and "If it's not love then it's the bomb/The bomb the bomb the bomb/That will bring us together"—will desire that said record albums be written up instead as THE GREATEST EVER TOLD. Or "Other" record albums with which you would imaginarily be contentedly shipwrecked—the first Stooges or the first NY Dolls or the CCR one with "Midnight Special" on it or the Kinks one they did to accompany that television show or the Beach Boys one they chickened out and never released or the Patti Smith one with cover photographed by that Mapplethorpe guy and insides produced by that Cale guy or the one with The Boss and His Telstar* leaning against the shoulder of some kindly black gentleman or the one in which the Beatles announced Paul's death through clever use of bare feet, a dark suit, and a license plate on a Volkswagen. All of these fine, fine record albums which in simpler times have been perfectly okay to listen to, I accord you this. But contrast these with any scholarly study of songs from *Teenager of the Year* (abbreviated sample study to follow) and clearly evident is that Overwhelming Faith this Black man possesses in us, for beneath the humble attire of pop! music he has slyly gifted us with detailed renderings of broadly disparate historical occurrences—trusting us to muddle our mistily shrouded manner through to Enlightenment (You all must write letters! I say again). This abbreviated sample scholarly study of four songs is presented to you herewith—note how various are those events which inspire melodies in the head of our Black man—

Track One—"Whatever Happened To Pong?"

With the 1969 drop in the cost of integrated circuits, electrical engineer Nolan Bushnell at last saw the possibility of stirring computers into the mix of electro-mechanical midway carnival amusements. He hired Berkeley student Al Alcorn to "create the simplest game" he could think of ("Paddle the paddle to the side to the side/To the side to the side to the paddle the paddle/Paddle the paddle the side to the side"). "Nolan defined a ping-pong game that could be played on a TV screen," Alcorn explains. "He defined it and I built it, though there were little things like the sound that I did add." Alcorn recalls many arguments he had with Bushnell over whether the ball in Pong should be round or square. "What's the difference?" Alcorn—as the one favoring the square—had objected. "Who needs all the window dressing?" Alcorn still maintains that "the best instruction on any game was the one we had on Pong: 'Avoid missing ball for high score.'" Bushnell

---

* Telstar: Commonly accepted abbreviation for Fender Telecaster; also title of instrumental written by Joe Meek (winner of Ivor Novello Award, 1962). Unclear which is being referenced during Track Nineteen in line, "It's been so long since my Telstar."

named his company Atari. Pong was shipped to arcades in fall of 1972. Ultimately Pong's lack of sophistication and challenge contributed to its demise. Bushnell sold Atari in 1976 for $32 million.

Track Two — "Thalassocracy"

Despite Herodotus' remarks (Histories, III 122) on Polykrates of Samos and Minos of Crete and decayed relics of the list of thalassocracies quoted from Diodorus in Armenian translation of the Eusebian *Chronographia*, the concept of thalassocracies has neither archeological nor source validation. Consequently, the hotly debated notion of thalassocratic maritime supremacy (i.e., small, independent sea-power in more or less local waters) has few supporters amongst today's historiographers as it runs apparently contrary to any ancient histories which presuppose broad imperial Roman domination from without.

Track Ten — "Two Reeler"

As with Frank Black, the Three Stooges too lost their names. This was because they were asked to please not be Jewish and so Samuel Horwitz, he turned into Shemp Howard, Moses Horwitz into Moe Howard, Jerome Lester Horwitz into Curly Howard, and comic violinist Louis Feinberg into Larry Fine ("Louis was so very fine"). Black's history of the troupe is rendered accurately in every manner and bespeaks tremendous hours of dedicated microfiche research. Jerome/Curly was in truth a terribly unhappy individual, a drinker of liquor, a squanderer of money, a divorcer of women, "all his life was in pain." His depressed state was said to be exacerbated by the element of their act which required his pate to remain shaved. Though he became world-famous for said baldness, he was always terribly embarrassed ("Did you know he missed his comb?") and at a too young age — after numerous breakdowns and strokes — he was committed to a fancy pants sanitarium where he curled up and died ("Made us laugh never did complain"). After Curly's departure, Moe reintroduced his original partner back into the act, his brother Shemp ("returned once more to save the day"). Soon thereafter Shemp keeled over into a heap-heap-heap-heap from those lethal sorts of chest-pains so Moe, having at last undisputed primogeniture, next brought in Joe Besser, who was later replaced by 'Curly Joe' De Rita ("He got a Joe and another Joe/ He would not quit he would not quit"). The Stooges had the longest-running series of two reel comedies in the history of sound film (197 shorts). Columbia Pictures producer/director Jules White with studio Romanov head Harry Cohn at last exterminated the short film division in 1958, long after all other studios had done so ("And so it ends the two reeler short").

Track Twelve—"Olé Mulholland"

Unattributed on the lyric sheet are direct quotes from Los Angeles Chief Engineer William Mulholland. By turn of the century—exemplified by certain architectural feats, most notably downtown's Bradbury Building—the pending international status of L.A. was hampered only by its limited supply of drinking water. Mulholland transformed uninhabitable Southland desertscape into urban sprawl (a good thing?) by designing longest aqueduct in Western Hemisphere that ran from Sierra Nevada's snow pack to coastline, an engineering challenge some lately compare in difficulty to sending man to the moon. In late 1911 Socialist candidate for mayor Job Harriman called the L.A. Aqueduct a conspiratorial trick to benefit the city's ruling oligarchy; City Council subsequently ordered an investigation. After four straight days of draining testimony, Mulholland stormed out, erupting: "The concrete of the Aqueduct will last as long as the pyramids of Egypt or the Parthenon of Athens, long after Job Harriman is elected mayor of Los Angeles." The following morning, this quote appeared on every Californian newspaper's front page. Soon after, Harriman lost mayoral race (in the wake of bad publicity following dynamiting of the *Los Angeles Times*). The Aqueduct opened November 5, 1913 at massive public event. As first torrent of water came rushing through culvert, Mulholland commanded the forty-three thousand in attendance: "There it is—Take it!" And the thirsty public waded into the water as happily they drank.

Does this not move you, can you honestly say you have emerged from this abbreviated sample scholarly study unimpressed with Our Black Man? Then consider that the genius of our *Teenager of the Year* attracted together such fine collaborators—though actually as may need pointing out this Frank Black truly be in fact "No Teenager" but a grown man of twenty-eight—that twenty-eight the same age at which Einstein invents his special theory of relativity, Stravinsky first works with Diaghilev, Trotsky escapes Siberian banishment, McCartney splits up the Beatles, Mme. Curie begins to investigate uranium, Gropius builds his first factories, Thoreau constructs himself a small cabin at Walden Pond, Poe moves to New York City, Nijinsky goes mad—this same-style genius, as I say, lured in the aid of exceptional fellows (Prepare to be Impressed!) like Jeff Morris Tepper (the renowned illusionist who in 1978 got a job in Captain Beefheart's Magic Act) and Eric Drew Feldman (sleight-of-hand pianist for same Magic Act) and Joey Santiago (the guitar player who in 1985 shared a college dorm room with Charles Thompson in Massachusetts)—and that genius to which I refer of course is how exceptionally well Frank Black does NOT the dictum follow: "Write What You Know" but rather educates himself and proceeds to catalogue All That He Did Not Know—not particularly caring if anyone else did not know it either, not caring to have an academic explain it any further.

Oh you think you can live for some time without working especially now with expenses down with flower-headed Marie gone and everything—but then things start breaking—at first little things which seem inconceivable like your toothbrush snaps apart in your mouth (—?) and your favorite coffee mug slips from a shelf and then Triple A wants a check and if you're going to get anywhere in this town you need Triple A! And then—and this has only been four days of not working—the feral cat that lives on the stoop out front starts spasming and the vet (I explained to the vet that I had no job but like any ex-military dude he just laughed and laughed) wants his money before he'll fix anything and then you droop out of there a lot poorer and your hood's up and your stupid battery's been taken by some pathetic vandals and then out of nowhere some powerful somebody insists the pests and vermin in your building have to be taken care of so all the people at your place contribute $50 each to hire the Western

Exterminator Co. (MY GOD NO) and your tires get slashed by
perfume-eyed Marie's new friend and there's food to buy then
the power bill then before you know it the money's gone and
you're applying as a register dolt at "9 OK Liquor-Deli & Wine
Mkt" but if you "Want" the job you must commit "Heart and
Soul" and give them sixty seventy eighty hours a week (C'mon!
You're Not Up To It, My Man!) and it's like, you thought you
could NOT WORK but they can't abide that, the Western
Exterminator Co. will find you out and maybe now I should
be napping—the sky is yellow rose at ten minutes to sunrise
and I feel sorta light-headed and dizzy like maybe having had
too much coffee or hungry, weak or needing more coffee or
needing a little sleep, maybe that's it, calf still itchy, that
bruised thigh—while instead I'm going off on 'Frank Black
this and *Teenager of the Year* that' for now I have declared that
I would justify its status as The Greatest Record Album Ever
Told and—has this been done? How might this be done? It
might perhaps best be done thusly: if in fact—as some
suggest—EVERY RECORD ALBUM IS A POP OPERA—which means
consequently we listen to everything as a way of hearing
about the life of this singer, the towns whereat he's lived, the
folks to him that count—in other words most record albums
make dull stories as they only star the singer and his
feelings—than this *Teenager of the Year* documents minds being
lost, the shock of primitive peoples as sure things scatter—and
how all the more astounding is this *Teenager of the Year* for how
little we learn of Him, how completely this Black man
disguises his face and limbs behind every lyric, telling us
nothing. From hearing his record albums we learn no details
of Frank Blank's life, whether he is married or divorced, has
some children or some parents or the blues, looks forward to
the weekend, likes sports, all that autobiographical crap,
because he seems so busy visiting other Abstract Plains and
bringing us back stories of There that some listeners ask, for
example, if he Truly believes in UFOS (on the other hand there
are those—not easily dismissed—who insist this entire record
album is to be heard as the travel diary of someone kidnapped
by extraterrestrials recalling snatches of earth life while
gazing out at galaxies zipping past; for details of said

phenomenon, see case history of architect David Vincent) (and then there are others who will work to convince you that Black is addicted to some rare and expensive designer drug which crunches dimensions and sends the addict uncontrollably hurtling up and down through this planet's long history). For 'tis true that down onto every landscape which congeals from the head of this Black man there descends an aviational aberration (select random shuffle on the CD player and on nearly every track you will find objects traveling six trillion miles a year, invisible planes cracking the concrete, hopes that they crash in the sea, wishes that the singer can see a radar blip then he'll totally flip for if you say it's nothing but sky he will be one lonely guy, details of how one requires just photon power and eight minutes of an hour to make it to our sun, &c.), onto his radar screen there eternally gleams saucery light, a space alien having lost his way—on Track Twenty Frank Black works desperately to downplay his poetry and freakiness in order to convince the truckers and CB folks he is one of them "I've driven every place that they call land/I talk plain talk" when—as if he couldn't tell this would blow his entire case—he continues still more earnestly, "I've seen the moon sitting on the road." As for the seriousness of his affection for UFOs, okay, it's like when you follow someone out to their car to help load in something—they might be someone you're starting to dig, potential friend-stuff—until they pop the trunk and you see something *astonishing*, a side of them you never expected, your every preconception about them shifts, like when rose-nosed, candy-mouthed Marie blurted out that thing at that party about how "There should be a law against governments," like maybe they are closet astrology buffs and they carry a whole horoscopic kit in their trunk or they turn out to be hostile to Darwin or Marx or into B&D (or D&D!), they believe Reagan Was Right or they play in badminton championships, maybe they are practicing pagans with a trunkful of books about white witchery and the mystical properties of nettles and burnt cumin, they are revealed to be secretly "Different" in other words. Seeing such things one at first always naturally recoils in horror but we are next obliged to "INVESTIGATE" (as in: "A law against governments, bough-armed, peach-fuzzed Marie, what a cool idea but who'd enforce it?") for many people are first completely one thing and then completely another and they might have been dedicated Scientologists just a few years before—WHO ARE WE THAT WE "DARE" TO JUDGE—and this says what I mean to say about the affection Frank Black bears for items of a saucery flying nature: how we must tolerate it with sympathy for they are to him the only hope worth hoping, clearly all else pales next to life on other planets. So yes, perhaps Roswell *did* turn out to be No More than a crashed high-altitude aluminum balloon and other Unexplained Phenomena of The Sky often resolve themselves into less controversial searchlights, meteors, marsh gas, ball lightning, weed seeds, temperature inversions, even experimental runs of the Navy's XF5U and Yet Still even the skepticalest critics amongst us HOW CAN "THEY" EXPLAIN the nine bright cigar-shaped objects first seen by Kenneth Arnold on 25 June 1947 bouncing about between Mount Rainier and Mount Adams (Kenneth Arnold: "Half the people I see look at me as a combination of Einstein, Flash Gordon and Screwball"), the twenty discs in the sky seen by sixty 4th of July picnickers in Twin Falls, Idaho on "The Same Day" as a United Airlines pilot, first officer, and stewardess sighted two groups of oddly lit craft? The waves of sightings in 1947, and again in August 1952, November 1957, August 1965, March 1966, the airborne things observed by Fain Cole in Anniston, Alabama 8 July, in Wheeling by Mrs. Jess Jarrell of 1313 Lind Street, in Indio by Mrs. Pauline Watts, in Chicago by Capt. Paul L. Carpenter, in Dayton, in Buffalo, in Richmond ("One witness estimated they were traveling at 27,000 miles an hour"), in Warren, Ohio (Walter Bak of Benton Road), in Washington, DC (in the restricted air corridor above the White House), in Levelland, Texas (cars were shut down), in Fort Knox (Capt. Mantell's F-51 crashed), in Hillsdale, Michigan (watched by eighty-seven coeds and a county civil defense director)? Explain away these and then one must still justify the government's blatant suppression of the cold hard facts, the CIA's track record of withholding UFO data, the US Air Force's bizarre pattern of deletions from its so-called public Project Blue Book—Oh but this too needs further delineation elsewhere for my alarm clock just went clattering off to disturb my slumber, gave me a jolt—I look up and now the day is burning dawn and the sun like some thoroughly boring science project has illumined my apartment and simple items which into mystic shadow had fallen while I composed you this now fiercely are animated and radiantly dressed and though all seems so much clearer than before my throat catches as I contemplate how sugar-cheeked Marie at this moment in time is elsewhere yawning and stretching her arms languorously like tree boughs and probably remarking how the light is like something painted by some famous melancholic Frenchman, god how I hate her, and the night—is that the night there, is that it, rumpled behind me like a carelessly cast-off tarp?—DO YOU MEAN TO SAY I HAVE BEEN WASTING MY BREATH?!—Please no! for they all must learn how *wrong* it is to forsake and forswear good peoples as "These" Western Exterminators have done to all of us by abandoning this half-built enterprise which is the now teetering career of Frank Black—I must go shower and change clothes for work this very second I am out of time—

THEM LOST MANIFESTOES

Publisher's Note: These street rants appeared in New York City during the last eleven weeks of 1995. Written mainly in pen and ink, they were xeroxed and pasted as 8½" × 11" sheets upon postal kiosks, vending machines, electrical posts, dumpsters, community bulletin boards, subway pillars, fire boxes, salt trucks, ambulette bumpers, and roadblocks.

Pavement, Part One

When Marie says she loves me I know she does—and yet I wonder, how can she? Someone so good love something like me? How? By forgetting the importance of character, integrity, civility? By impossibly lowering her standards? By sidestepping that intuition which tells her, again and again in pounding refrains—*wrong, wrong, wrong, wrong, wrong?* Has she lost all sense of smell? Is it the love that a chime tower bears for the dead or a mountaineer for thin air; is it the love each seismologist carries for temblors or a youth fascinated with a Glock pistol? There is only one thing I love anymore—it is not you or me or her but a band you don't even know—but how I love them, with a closet's shadowy purpose and depth. The band is Pavement and only I know them—you may own all their CDs *but so what* they are mine alone and I am theirs all theirs, they do not write for you as much as evoke to me (they do not even know you, my friends). I saw them give the most astonishing concert

57

86

KILL THE MOVIES

YOU HEARD ME RIGHT - NOW THAT WE HAVE HOUNDED THE NETWORKS OFF THE AIR AND TOSSED EACH TV OFF EACH MOTEL BALCONY AND NOW TOO THAT WE HAVE MADE THE POLITICIANS TO REVEAL THEIR TRUEST LEAST FLATTERING COLORS (THEIR INTENSE OPPOSITION TO ANY CULTURE) WHICH DISPLAYS THEM AT A SQUARE DISADVANTAGE IN A STUCK-UP STANCE OF UNENVIABLE WEAKNESS AS INSIPID COWARDS STUCK IN BROKE-DOWN CARS NOW THAT WE HAVE ALMOST WRESTED OUR LIVES BACK FROM THOSE WHO MIGHT WANT IT OTHERWISE LET US FINALLY COLLECT OURSELVES CALMLY TO FINISH THE TASK AT HAND: AND LET US AT LAST TURN TO THE Big Screen, UNDISGUISED FERVOR GLIMMERING FROM OUR HELD-OUT KNIVES, AND SEE US NOW RACE DOWN THE POPCORN-DIRTIED AISLES TO CUT THOSE OVERPAID MODELS ~~AND THEIR~~ RIGHT OUT OF THERE, HACK THOSE BIGHEADED HIPSTER SNOTS AND THEIR GLAMOROUSLY LARGE THIRTY FOOT HOLLYWOOD FACES FROM THE PROJECTION SCREEN AND LIKE SOME CIRCLE OF SOILED FABRIC SIMPLY ROLL THEM UP, MAKE THEM LONG TRUMPETING TUBES IN OUR HANDS WHICH WE COULD RAISE TO OUR NOTHING MOUTHS TO AMPLIFY OUR PUNY VOICES (AND THUSLY STEAL BACK THE RECOGNITION THEY DENY US) AS WE BROADCAST TO THE WORLD: Kill the Movies and Set your Selfs free
We can be quenched ↘ no more by your poisoned milk. Give to US time & money instead of charging us $8.50 to spend 2 hours with you, no one is worth that kinda dough (except anyone who is not you!) Ah the life I have expended wastefully in dead-dark cinema houses waiting for something to happen [in that escape-land I once so adored (and which once adored us for that matter)]

BUT NO MORE!

Killer Joy   Manifesto #86

when least expected—they did it *for me!*—and they hauled their own equipment and tuned their own instruments and listened attentively to one another closely and finished most everything they started. (Note that I gave up making music myself so they'd have more room to maneuver about onstage!) She says she loves me what does she (who is not Pavement) know of love—she was not tasty enough to make me retire—she does not "captivate the senses like a ginger ale rain." [Pop song musical words? Yes, yes, I know! The dreams she details each morning sound doubtless no more dry and dull, and dull and dry, and *stupid stupid stupid*, to me than the rock lyrics which I, in turn, quote out of context to her. I must learn to be better! I know!] She did not issue the sprawling challenge of *Wowee Zowee* as a follow-up to the tight-knit pop-crammed *Crooked Rain, Crooked Rain*, she does not haul her own equipment or tune her own instrument—where may I set down this bulky item she terms "love." (I would so like to!)

Pavement, Part Two

I hereby suggest the American President of the United States and all them U.S. trade reps haul Pavement to the trade talks. They are our grandest export, our finest product, infusible in hot weather, our best materials. Pavement should be carried on our shoulders and emblazoned on our backs and ushered unto waiting planes at the last minute and with an almost effete, deliberate importance, their bellies bloated with our very best meats.

Pavement must be not dismissed as sell-outs, hear me now! Nor shall they ever be taken for granted, never! They might seem to you lazy and overrated but they work very, very hard and are very, very good.

That they have not become household words is testament alone to their genius for craftily sidestepping the Romanovs (but certainly I do recall "pavement" as a household word, I remember hearing it offhandedly employed many times in less enlightened circumstances).

Pavement (we clamor) and once more: "pavement." Listen how they mature LP to LP—if Hitler had ever learned of their existence he would've ordered Pavement to be kidnapped and called them his "ultimate secret weapon" and brought the world to its knees—instead they are ours and thank God for that!

Untitled

It is always imprecise, dreadful, wrong, evil and stupid and unjust and filled with sin to compare literature to music and quote one in the hopes of arguing the other but yet here I am to do it. (Watch Me Now!)

Marina Tsvetaeva, when you hanged yourself at the Brodelshchikov's house nobody noticed (it was Russia, late '41, with Nazi invaders a few miles off). The landlady who discovered your body said you were "round-shouldered, skinny, grey-haired, like a witch of some sort. Not at all attractive." Pardon her! She did not know, watching your unsteady cadaver creak there to and fro on its heavy rope, that she was describing one of Russia's greatest poets. When I saw (late '94) you teeny-tiny singer Mary Timony sing before your band Helium you too were skinny and like some sort of dead witch withdrawing right before us, performing less than is possible, nobody could be so stiff and still but some corpse, your eyes contained nothing, you remained flat, unaffected. *Not at all attractive.* I grew worried. Of all of today's tired bands of noise that nobody notices, why should your particular one compel me so utterly? You looked to be dying from something (love?). You appeared as if you might set down the guitar, step backstage, kick out a chair, and dangle to your death. Teeny-tiny Timony (I wanted to shout): no!

Marina Tsvataeva, Mary Timony: you bear identical initials, the same bite and disinterest in theatrical falsity, the same self-destructive stubbornness. Marina, you hailed a revolution which then subsumed and wrecked you, and proud haunted Mary could easily do the same—witness Helium's first release (*Pirate Prude*; love leads to betrayal, prostitution leads to vampirism). "Careful your pretty face," runs the refrain of one song which Marina could have composed: "Your love is like small change."

In here there is no comfort in realizing that it's a man's

world because although men have so thoroughly botched it yet still too few women will acknowledge it or step to the fore. "I shall walk with this bitterness for years across mountains or town squares equally, I'll walk on souls and on hands without shuddering." When beauty at last flees, it leaves one as a ravaged remnant to recite things that sound written on the back of one's hand in a pique, in a smelly dark closet, with magic marker: "I may be *very small* but you'll never *lose me* at all." Blood tastes like wine, love makes you money, hearts are devoured candies or disengaged lockets. In this sick sad and yet wonderful world airwaves criss-crossing the globe with sorcery spells and mean wishes it is always imprecise, dreadful, wrong, evil and stupid and unjust and filled with sin to compare literature to music and quote one in the hopes of arguing the other but yet here I have done it (watch me now).

Kill The Movies

You heard me right! Now that we have hounded the networks off the air and tossed each TV off each motel balcony and now too that we have made the politicians reveal their most true, least flattering colors (their intense opposition to any culture) which displays them at a square disadvantage in a stuck-up stance of unenviable weakness as insipid cowards stuck in broke-down cars, now that we have almost wrested our lives back from those who might want it otherwise, let us finally collect ourselves calmly to finish the task at hand: and let us at last turn to the big screen, undisguised fervor glimmering from our held-out knives, and see us now race down the popcorn-dirtied aisles to cut those overpaid models right out of there, hack those bigheaded hipster snots and their glamorously large thirty-foot Hollywood faces from the projection screen, and like some circle of soiled fabric simply roll them up, make them long trumpeting tubes in our hands, which we could raise to our nothing mouths to amplify our puny voices (and thusly steal back the recognition they deny us) as we broadcast to the world: Kill the Movies and Set Yourselves Free. We can be quenched no more by your poisoned milk. Give to us time and money instead of demanding $8.50 to spend two hours with you, no one is worth that kind of dough (except anyone who is not you). Ah, the life I have expended wastefully in dead-dark cinema houses waiting for something to happen, in that escape-land I once so adored, and which once adored us for that matter. But no more!

Bring Me the (Fat) Head of Fred Fatzer

Know that I once was a bigger fan of Freedy Johnston than any of you, and that I felt assured — in hearing his soaring *Can You Fly?* second record album — that we had a good thing on our hands yet now I must reverse myself as I command unto you now: Bring me his bored bald head with a fat fork stuck in the forehead, and let us decant into it the heady broth of his betrayals, and drink! Yes, Pinochet and CIA slaughtered the modern socialist movement and we forgave them; yes, LBJ betrayed his pledge to the Good Society and we shrugged it off, yes, Nixon snapped the constitution like a dry stick over one knee and he was pardoned — still *This Must Not Be Forgiven!*

Freedy now is not even reminiscent of who he used to be, gone is his voice, gone is his inner life, gone is his subtle poetry, gone is him looking at you, hoping you like him. Now he wears leisure suits! Hear him now praise famous crap! Now he cynically croons "Autumn in New York" everytime I see him lately, and what — is this funny to you, Fathead?

Your name was once Fred Fatzer — hear that, world?! — and you were once six hundred pounds with no ego — where have you gone, fat Freddie friend? I liked you better then. Now you are thin with a five ton ego and an embarrassing inability to convey complicated phrasing. Oh Mr. Big Star, look at yourself. When next I pass you on the street Freedy I will bump you (I promise!) into high voltage wires — there must be some way out of here! It would be a mercy killing for you are like Jack Nicholson in *Cuckoo's Nest* after the operation and your old self would be disgusted at this alien now passing itself off as "Freedy Johnston world-famous Elektra Recording Artist."

I would crawl through glass to claw your eyes.

I would offer a hug if my suit were explosive.

I would send you poisoned orchids

(if I knew you would sniff of them deliciously).

Your last release stunk so bad I couldn't even finish it — damn you, Mistah Freedy you maked a liah outta me and done broke my heart! To even sing this "Disappointed Man" — how dare you! *You* have disappointed *me* (for that last time!) and now you dare to sing-song of it?

Remember who you were if you want to live, Mr. Fred Fatzer, remember and make good on your promise — *or else!*

Yo La Tengo is Good to Eat

Who dares to suggest unto me that Yo La Tengo are not great like Chinese food?

Can you not understand?

Chinese food, so reliable no matter what is ordered, whether you're thinking budget or palate, whether you're sitting on naugahyde or at a cloth-covered table: the steam off rice rising, tea and cookies, the exquisite exotic, the comforting otherness, garlic and ginger — our home? Why, it's in every Chinese restauarant anywhere, that's where. And this, like them our Yo Las, our friends in feedback or in soft tones, who perhaps cannot do everything (make that one clear: Yo La Tengo can do little with their voices and appear incapable of hitting consonants — they are not always straightforward or tender enough — they wear their damn pants too slippery low on their hips and slacker disrepair adorns their most every move — yet there is Chinese food too at times which falls short arriving half-cooked or grease-smothered yet always *reassuring* and *kind*) but I defy you to find another Yo La: their two "perfect" record albums (*Fakebook* and *Painful*) are more than most any band ever ever could . . .

Listen to "Drug Test" (the greatest something masterpiece).

Listen to Ira figure out distortion and sweetly worked moods.

Listen to Georgia when they heft the song onto her back and make her carry the whole damn thing . . .

So remember: when the waiter says "What'll it be — chow fun or lo mein?" always order "Yo La Tengo," the most distinctive vodka in the world.

Untitled

O! Frank O'Hara! It may be silly to call across to you so cold in the casket you inhabit but I am hopeful you are not for reals dead but rather that was you who was spotted beaming in the colored jewels of Nike Town, penning ad copy while smushed against a candy shoppe window and taking the sorrow sympathetically, hard but happy. Where have you been all my life, frank one? (Dead, is the answer.) Have I always had you but not got you till now? O!Hara (as in Frank) how I wish you had been there pressed against me in those cheerless years of yore, with sugar hard-pressed to find and days airtight and lead-lined as a safe and skies grey as a fort and hope like some bon-bon in wartime which we cherished and brought out to polish but never dared to consume —

Sing to me of deep-fried airplane wings, sing!

Oh! Frank OH!ara! Now you are my brother, it seems. Will you phone me up soon? I am listed in the city directory. You, the saint of accidents yet robbed from us by the biggest accident of all, if you had only lived—if you had lived, how I would hug you and gin drink with you.

Oh, Frank O'Hara, your bones were pulverized to make ink for this pen and others similar to it and thank you.

Dear History

You are no quaintly fickle aunt but a greasy dunderhead lavished with too much brandy diplomacy and festooned with honorary degrees, stretch limos there to pick you up and drop you off, private cellulars and wine cellars and silk collars at your instant disposal—how might we instantly dispose of you, though, Mister History? Killing you is one thing (a cinch! consider it done!) but disposal of the body (a mess). One day we will all be dead and what sort of lives will it be said we led, steered through the hopeless Radio Free Afternoons with bowlfuls of medicating Rolos and pretzels, compromised hourly by today's etiquette of evil, the last boss I ever expected to obey, taking luxury abundant for granted, overstuffing the aisles in every pop star's superstore, piggish

77

JOE STRUMMER WHERE ARE YOU

LOST MAN. '77
CAMDEN JOY

and kingly lives while in other parts peasants were being marched into fields and shot, left to whisper final wishes at the Lord's retreating back—are you even listening, History?

The MJ-97 wanders loose amongst us! He is making moves on Ms. Madonna—she has leaked to the tabloids her desire for an heiress, a youthful replicant to further besmirch the family name. Ah, History, your bodyguards and silver canes are no match for the Jack of Hearts.

It is time you tottered off to bed, my friend, with a baggie of barbiturates into some garage filled full with carbon monoxide—you are forgetful of your responsibilities, old man, and have let us off too too easy. That not one of us is conversant in the Lincoln Brigade or the WWI vets robbed of benefits by Doug MacArthur, that communism has gone down as a failure—why not also Love, old bastard? Love too hurts and disappoints, why not as well murder it, foolish History? But no—arbitrarily you steal from us communism and leave us Love! ARRRRRRGGGHHH!

I think it best that you should let me have your job now, History. You are weary and near-blind (it has been a long century, we sympathize) and now ruddier blood must be permitted to flow down your hallowed halls, if you please.

Please contact me soon.

The Other Greatest Record Album of the '80s

When from the Nineteen Hundred and Eighties I fell as might a safe from a bank, awakening as an inmate released, my feet in someone else's shoes, it was to taste Reagan on the tongue like a breathmint gone sour, everything at once beckoning and mocking me, in America.

We concluded that decade by clobbering a country called Panama, in an invasion nobody much remembers, because the leader called us names, and when that leader was eventually found cowering in the Pope's Palace the army pummeled the place with punk rock songs, which also nobody much remembers, until the leader materialized. I liked punk rock

74

THE OTHER GREATEST RECORD ALBUM OF THE EIGHTIES

WHEN FROM THE NINETEEN HUNDRED AND EIGHTIES I FELL AS MIGHT A SAFE FROM ~~THE~~ A BANK, AWAKENING AS AN INMATE RELEASED, MY FEET IN SOMEONE ELSE'S' SHOES, IT WAS TO TASTE REAGAN ON THE TONGUE LIKE A BREATH-MINT GONE SOUR, EVERYTHING AT ONCE BECKONING AND MOCKING ME, IN AMERICA.

WE CONCLUDED THAT DECADE BY CLOBBERING A COUNTRY CALLED PANAMA, IN AN INVASION NOBODY MUCH REMEMBERS, BECAUSE THE LEADER CALLED US NAMES, AND WHEN THAT LEADER WAS EVENTUALLY FOUND COWERING IN THE POPE'S PALACE THE ARMY PUMMELED THE PLACE WITH PUNK ROCK SONGS, WHICH ALSO NOBODY MUCH REMEMBERS, UNTIL THE LEADER MATERIALIZED. I LIKED PUNK ROCK THAT CALLED PEOPLE NAMES AND SO DID THE MEKONS, YET ODDLY THIS NEWS DID NOT CHEER US.

I SPENT MY TIME THEN ALONE WITHIN WINDOWS PAINTED RED-THEN-BLUE BY THE BLINKY-BLINK OF A BOWLING ALLEY'S NEON IN THAT UNCOMMONLY CLEAN CITY WHERE JOBS COULD NOT BE HAD AND NO BEER WAS CHEAP, AND WHEN I FINALLY MADE A GOOD FRIEND ITS NAME WAS **THE MEKONS ROCK AND ROLL**, A CASSETTE RECORDING WHICH AUTOMATICALLY FLIPPED OVER AND OVER ALL BY ITS LONESOME, AND I MADE IT TO THE PRESENT
THANX TO THAT FRIEND!

TV TODAY BEARS RELENTLESS TESTIMONIALS ABOUT HOW "ROCK AND ROLL SAVED MY LIFE" BUT IN THIS INSTANCE **THE MEKONS ROCK AND ROLL** SAVED MY LIFE, AND THAT MAKES SOME CONSIDERABLE DIFFERENCE. BECAUSE MEKON LIVES HAD NOT TURNED OUT AS EXPECTED, AND NEITHER HAD PUNK ROCK, AND NEITHER HAD I, AND SO THEY BUILT THIS LOYAL FRIEND, THIS ULTRA-FINE RECORD ALBUM, OUT OF DISAPPOINTMENTS AND DISPUTED MEMORIES, AND EACH SONG GETS WISER AND MADDER THAN THE LAST, THOUGH YOU CANNOT LISTEN WHO WEEPING, AND ROCK AND ROLL (& ITSELF!) INHABITS EVERY TRACK, IS MENTIONED BY NAME A WHOLE LOT, AS A CHARACTER AND CURSE, & AGAIN & AGAIN YOU MEET ITS PROMISE
AND BETRAYALS ANEW!

& NOW MY LOYAL FRIEND IS STILL HERE BESIDE ME, STILL GOING AND GOING AND THEN FLIPPING OVER AND OVER NOW THAT I HAVE EMERGED BARRELING FROM BENEATH GROUND LIKE SOME TRAIN. IF YOU SEE THE MEKONS SAY HELLO; AND WHEN YOU GOT CLOSE TO THEM, KISS THEM ONCE. FOR ME.   THANX CAMDEN JOY that called people names and so did the Mekons, yet oddly this news did not cheer us.

I spent my time then alone within windows painted red-then-blue by the blinky-blink of a bowling alley's neon in that uncommonly clean city where jobs could not be had and no beer was cheap, and when I finally made a good friend its name was *The Mekons Rock and Roll*, a cassette recording which automatically flipped over and over all by its lonesome, and I made it to the present thanks to that friend!

TV today bears relentless testimonials about how "Rock and Roll Saved My Life" but in this instance *The Mekons Rock and Roll* saved my life, and that makes some considerable difference. Because Mekon lives had not turned out as expected, and neither had punk rock, and neither had I, and so they built this loyal friend, this ultra-fine record album, out of disappointments and disputed memories, and each song gets wilder and madder than the last, though you cannot listen without weeping, and rock and roll (itself) inhabits every track, is mentioned by name a whole lot, as a character and a curse, and again and again you meet its promise and betrayals.

And now my loyal friend is still here beside me, still going and going and then flipping over and over now that I have emerged barreling from beneath ground like some train. If you see the Mekons, say hello. And when you get close to them, kiss them once. For me.

Son Volt Trace
(Warner Bros.; CD, Cass)

I've come to feel that I was once a heroin addict, though in public I pretended I wasn't by drinking vodka straight and calling my subsequently numb self satisfied even though I wasn't — not *really* — not *satisfied* — without the heroin to help me past — and one time I believe I was broke, I really needed it, I had no vodka, no money, and I comforted myself with the thought that we're all addicts, all of us (addicted to something) though not all of us really just those of us addicted to skag, this was my comforting thought as I cruised bodegas hitting

up suckers and friends for change and getting nowhere so
eventually I held someone up—I'm ashamed but I needed
five more dollars and some comfort and had no more friends
but I had David's bowie knife—and it was a mother pushing
a stroller which genuinely upset me (but I was a junkie what
did I really care, really) her eyes scared to death and baby
screaming but I got my five dollars (plus!) and bought that
disgusting skag and went home afterwards walking like a
whisper through the unloosed dawn and pink high-boughed
sycamores (barely able to walk) and I laid in bed with the ocean
rolling over my face, waves crashing on my head, down and
withdrawing, the ocean inhaling and exhaling and so on—and
I thought how life was actually okay in fact—*quite okay, quite
okay* I murmured to myself underneath the sea—and this is
the junkie hope that is called up when I hear Son Volt over
the loudspeaker at the laundromat, and perhaps you must
experience it (don't do me any favors).

Untitled

Let us now sing (as public men) of private things: how we
buck and how we groan, and climax yes when told we're
tyrants (mess with us, such happiness! *yes and yes! ah yes! we're
tyrants!*). And let the happy pictures of toy-filled folks lead us
to trust our inescapable selves, embraced in baseness while
yet looking heavenward to pornographic priestesses aloft in
their cathode-ray holiness. So tiny are we beneath this eternal
celebrity balloon parade and our frantic gesticulations go
unnoticed. . . . Let us now praise hot dogs and finger pies and
stuffs which garner sneers! We are encouraged to believe we
are above simple joys, naughty joys, camden joys—Ah! but
the shivery feel of them coins of temptation, the comforting
rankness of freshly chloroxed floors!

The only films that should be allowed anymore are those
which can be caught in small unplotted segments and left
for us in our minds to finish, those which inspire self-
gratifications and cost just a quarter a minute, naked bodies
watched and honestly excited, prancing on that small blue
electric screen which goes at all hours—not just teasing but

always always delivering (unlike the Romanovs who tease us
but never give us so much as a drop) all the way through
the abandoned dusk and the longing lunches, their video-ed
bodies relentlessly pushed to places none but Boom-Boom
Mancini can fathom, points which can no longer be called
"acting": screaming, ecstatic, drunk with it gleefully, visibly
wide-eyed to find uncharted terrains inside here, within the
frothing sea of their own passion, and the *sounds* of it, the *sights*
of it, even them ordinary pleasures of being taken advantage
of, or of taking advantage of someone who so desires it [small
wonder that with each passing day we live less and less like
the previous generations].

DO NOT FEAR US!

Untitled

As I do not respect movie films anymore I want it known
that I too have many movie film thoughts (last count: 947!)
to give away free. Please do me common courtesy of bringing
up to famous cinematic personalities my thoughts for movie
films about plight of Spanish Civil War's Lincoln Brigade in
which two American brothers (one fierce, other wary) protect
one another from world's hypocrisies, or my movie film set
in smoggy gross future when populations have grown so
dense that murders are roundly applauded which tells how
accolades of world pursue particularly sadistic serial killer
(Keifer Sutherland) so that it might pay homage to his genius,
another sports comedy/cop thriller (*Kuffs* and *Ducks*) in which
amateur hockey team of off-duty police folks bring in well-
intentioned but oafish ringer for big match against crosstown
rival but discover wacky hi-jinx when they can't find cop job
safe enough for ringer, yet another Merchant-Ivory character
tale which dramatizes nobly mannered balloon contest of early
1800s when proud determined gentlemen manned primitive
floaters to see "who coulde sail highest" (all emerged either
dead deaf deranged or distraught), and one (*Dirty Dozen* and
Commando) in which beautiful but bedraggled Italian peasant
refugee Natasha Richardson trapped between German and
Allied lines in basement of Benedictine monastery in Monte

Cassino undergoes blissful epiphany with passionate mute monk Brad Pitt amongst ruinous bombing raid of Valentine's Day, 1944. I have million of them like how about Mr. Bob Dylan glibly played by Luke Perry who gives us under-reported tensions and furies of Mr. Bob Dylan waiting out 1960s writing *Self Portrait* and recording basic tracks for his eponymous album of covers or you'd prefer maybe terrifying flick (*Invasion U.S.A.* and *Red Dawn*) in which inoculation designed to counteract space-borne allergy brought to earth by massive meteorite has unintended side-effect of turning whole cities into hardcore fans of pretentious wanna-be Jim Morrison pompous poseurs Dead Can Dance, who suddenly emerge to world domination when—during supposedly "mock" duel conducted mostly in virtual reality—band slays Bill Gates (Matthew Broderick), but also keep in mind ecologically minded animated classic (*Hello Kitty* and *Jurassic Park*) in which one rabbit, handsomer than rest, leads friends, relatives, and other small furry things to freedom by retracing what once [before devastating industrial accidents of 1997] used to be "mighty" Mississippi river, and another movie film entitled *The Bubblicious Movie Film* (computer-animated spectacle) in which all the many gum flavors use their voice-over'd idiosyncrasies and distinct superpowers to defend the galaxy from a proliferation of inferior Made-in-Korea candies and Pataki and a washed-up forgotten playwright Jacques Levy played glibly by Luke Perry tirelessly seeking to revive his long-abandoned friendship with Bob Dylan (*30th Anniversary Concert* and *The Buddy Holly Story*) in efforts to kindle anew the songwriting collaboration which rang down *Desire* on unsuspecting world while Alicia Silverstone (in arty black-and-white role as Princeton student whom Einstein always secretly adored) calmly completes Unified Field Theory in nothing but brassiere and panties and stepping outside boards hovering spacecraft and portals into seventeenth dimension with heavenly *whoosh!* There's more: that kid with that leukemia and his gently wise-cracking grandfather (*Jurassic Park* and *On Golden Pond*) searching to uncover truth about their haunted grand piano which was said to have once been played by Rachmaninoff and the true story from my own experience how one day great gobs of people were hit with a debilitation like amnesia (*Jurassic Park* and *Being There*), each day it spread until we were a planet of strangers who remembered no movie films and just then a great winged messenger dramatically descended from the heavens to liberate our vacated souls. These provide just a small sampling from my box of hits-to-be, I tell you all—shoot these movie films please and there will be others I'll donate to you when the time comes! You're welcome, Hollywood.

Untitled

Down below me the world tries to appear ecstatic but nobody trusts it, nothing can convince us, neither the sun burning high in the branches nor the lovers scrunched together kicking through leafy piles, neither is true, not Justina wrapped in her loud colors, not the children prancing in the hydrant, not the athletes in their devotional ways, none of this could be! Which is not to say I am happier than I have ever been (I am) but neither so far from despair. You wonder sometimes, can I ever get enough, when one drug has barely concluded and already you have ordered three more, when there's no celebrity death you do not envy, when the waiters move to take away your empty plate of sadness, and you wave them off—"Not finished yet, pal!"—when falling-to-bits gargoyles high on the facade close up your throat and drag tears down your cheeks—make the world how I want it, I cry, dammit! I once said I loved Kurt Cobain then he forgot how I loved him and stopped his own life—so be careful who I claim to love next for they are doomed! And this is why I worry for today I think I love you all, you ridiculous people, who are so good to me.

"Be My Baby" by the Ronettes

"Oh, won't you," she said, "be my baby," said it frequently and with such ambulance urgency I was captivated—capsized—no doubt about it, *this* crazy sandwich of a girl was ordered up especially for me. Ah, the ways we found to speak our love, those bawdy afternoons, bodies tasting of maple syrup, she and I, blithely dancing between the April raindrops with

4

BE MY BABY by The Ronettes

"Oh won't you" SHE SAID "be my baby" SAID IT FREQUENTLY AND WITH SUCH AMBULANCE URGENCY I WAS CAPTIVATED - CAPSIZED - NO DOUBT ABOUT IT, THIS CRAZY SANDWICH OF A GIRL WAS ORDERED UP ESPECIALLY FOR ME! Ah, the ways we found to speak our love, THOSE BAWDY AFTERNOONS, BODIES TASTING OF MAPLE SYRUP, SHE AND I, BLITHELY DANCING BETWEEN THE APRIL RAINDROPS WITH POLICEMEN NIPPING AT OUR MERRY SPRINGTIME HEELS, TEA-CUPS AND FORK-LIFTS RAINING DOWN UPON US! [my girlfriend is so great she lets me write on walls my girlfriend is so great]

SHE CONFESSED SHE WAS UNHAPPILY BETROTHED TO AN ENIGMATIC ENFANT TERRIBLE WITH A PENCHANT FOR PISTOLS AND SUNGLASSES. (HE WAS FAMOUS.) EVERY TIME HE SNAPPED HIS FINGERS ONE-TWO-THREE SHE HAD TO GO, "oh won't you please...be my... be my baby." HER NAME WAS RONNIE HIS NAME WAS PHIL AND HOW WE THREE HOWLED AND THREW OUR ARMS ABOUT EACH OTHER FORGIVINGLY WHILE BELLOWING "MORE LIME GIN FOR MY FRIEND'S RICKEY, GENTS!!" AND BRAGGING OF FEATS PERFORMED ON GRASS-COVERED SQUASH COURTS AND CROQUET YARDS AND OF OUR CASUAL RUN-INS WITH BEACH BOYS. AND WE WERE AWARE OF THESE AS THE GAYEST OF TIMES, SHE WAS FROM PHILLY I THINK HIS NAME WAS RON (OH, THEY LOOKED IDENTICAL AND AS TO WHO-WAS-WHO I COULDN'T'VE CARED LESS, THEY BOTH CALLED ME BY MY NAME "JOY" THEY CALLED APPRECIATIVELY "JOY!!" AND I BOUNDED OVER TO THEM, BARKING AND WAGGING AND TERRIBLY IN LOVE - THE SPECTER OF BLISS PASSED INTO ME VIA THESE SPECTORS)

AND NOW YOU WANT THAT I SHOULD WEEP AT THEIR ABSENCE AT THE DEATH OF INNOCENCE AND RONNETTES AND YOUNG PRESIDENTS BUT AT LEAST I HAVE MY MEMORIES OF HOW SWELL IT WAS THEN, AND YOU, YOU IMPOSSIBLE PERSON — WHAT DO YOU HAVE THAT MAKES YOU SO ALL HELL-FIRE CERTAIN OF THINGS (WHEN YOU HAVE NEVER EVEN MET JOY FACE TO FACE!)?? NOTHING, THAT'S WHAT YOU HAVE, NOTHING, EXCEPT A WORTHLESS OLD SCRATCHED-UP 45 BY RONNIE SPECTOR'S POP MUSICAL BAND: YOU HAVE NOTHING.

YOUR FRIEND,
CAMDEN JOY
NOV. 95
LOST MANIFESTO NUMBER FOUR

53

I NEED MY MOMMY

O! Ms. Madonna! HERE winter is upon us and I remember yet again I have no children, No little ones to roast open fires for. HERE the Millennium's cold corner has almost been turned and I call out for my kiddies to gather round me in the featherbed--- BUT NO ONE COMES! No chuckle-faced younguns to stir me awake! And though I am much too large for my treasured swing set yet I cannot bring myself to toss it out. I admit now (with all the splashy ker-plop of a submarine breaking surface): I NEED OFFSPRING. Any takers? I saw in the paper where you-Ms. Madonna- are to begin soon advertising for a father to put a little Hansel in your oven. YOU TOO, MS. MADONNA?! Famous you? Madonna with child for this X-mas, right on!

You claim to have trouble meeting men who "are not a _ _ _ _ _ es." Amputees? Is this what you mean? (Will 'Hangman' be on your test? I excel!) Amputees are so prevalent in your glittery scenes-a-faire? Will then: Here I am. All limbs present and accounted for. Pick me! THE UNA-BOMBER?! - he is not for you, his sperm count is low, and he is missing two digits.

I am so qualified for this, Boss-girl, it is ridiculous! I ONCE HEARD ONE OF YOUR RECORDS! I SAW YOU IN VISION-QUEST! I even find you ATTRACTIVE! Ah babe, how's about you and me take down a pair of winged creatures via the utilization of a single weighty object! I mean: 2 birds! 1 stone! Those of us on disability have always felt you were one with us, that you too did not appreciate their signs every five feet saying WET PAINT, their demands to us signed "The Management," their corner pay phones always ringing, their deceitfully priced LUNCH SPECIALS, "their things they claim to "know nothing about."

FORGIVE ME my blathering darling I am dizzy with passion at our pending prospect! SLEEP WITH ME BY NEW YEAR'S EVE or my heart will be reduced to a size no bigger than the period at the end of this sentence! I will retire! I will jump off City Hall and be heard from no more forever - I am serious - and the world will lament the loss of Joy this holiday season.

PANGINGLY YOURS, CAMDEN JOY
LOST (FOUND?) MANIFESTO #53

policemen nipping at our merry springtime heels, tea cups and forklifts raining down upon us. [My girlfriend is so great she lets me write on walls. My girlfriend is *so* great!] She confessed she was unhappily betrothed to an enigmatic *enfant terrible* with a penchant for pistols and sunglasses. (He was famous.) Every time he snapped his fingers one-two-three she had to go, "Oh won't you please . . . Be my . . . Be my baby." Her name was Ronnie, his name was Phil, and how we three howled and threw our arms about each other forgivingly while bellowing "More lime gin for my friend's rickey, gents!" and bragging of feats performed on grass-covered squash courts and croquet yards and of our casual run-ins with Beach Boys. And we were aware of these as the gayest of times, she was from Philly, I think his name was Ron. (Oh, they looked identical and as to who-was-who I couldn't've cared less, they both called me by my name "Joy" they called appreciatively "Joy" and I bounded over to them, barking and wagging and terribly in love—the specter of bliss passed into me via these Spectors.)

And now you want that I should weep at their absence, at the death of innocence and Ronettes and young presidents, but at least I have my memories of how swell it was then, and you, you—you *impossible* person—what do you have that makes you so all hell-fire certain of things (when you have never even met Joy face to face)? Nothing, that's what you have, *nothing*, except a worthless old scratched-up 45 by Ronnie Spector's pop musical band: *you have nothing*.

I Need My Mommy

O! Ms. Madonna! Here winter is upon us and I remember yet again I have no children, no little ones to roast open fires for. Here the Millennium's cold corner has almost been turned and I call out for my kiddies to gather round me in the featherbed—but no one comes. No chuckle-faced young'uns to stir me awake! And though I am much too large for my treasured swing set yet I cannot bring myself to toss it out. I admit now (with all the splashy *ker-plop* of a submarine breaking surface): I NEED OFFSPRING. Any takers? I saw in the paper where you—Ms. Madonna—are to begin soon advertising for a father to put a little Hansel in your oven. You too, Ms. Madonna? I toss my anchor to famous you. Madonna with child for this X-mas, right on!

You claim to have trouble meeting men who "are not a******es." Amputees? Is this what you mean? (Will Hangman be on your test? I excel!) Amputees are so prevalent in your glittery *scenes-à-faire?* Well then: Here I am. All limbs present and accounted for. Pick me! It is true I made this self-same offer to Patty Hearst—did she listen?—do not repeat her snobbish error, opting to marry within the entourage. No one you've met is father material (because, I know! I actually had a father once). None but me can name Red Red Meat's releases in order, can get free quarters out of a Konelco change machine, can wring music from a gas pump—

I am so qualified for this, Boss-girl, it is ridiculous! I once heard one of your record albums! I saw you in *Visionquest!* I even find you attractive! Ah babe, how's about you and me take down a pair of winged creatures via the utilization of a single weighty object! I mean: two birds! One stone! Those of us on disability have always felt you were one with us, that you too did not appreciate their signs every five feet saying "Wet Paint," their demands to us signed "The Management," their corner payphones always ringing, their deceitfully priced lunch specials, their things they claim to "know nothing about."

Forgive me my blathering, darling, I am dizzy with passion at our pending prospect! Sleep with me by New Year's Eve or my heart will be reduced to a size no bigger than your period at the end of this cycle. I will retire, I will jump off City Hall and I will meet John Doe no more forever—I am serious—and the world will lament the loss of Joy this holiday season.

Flat Old World

The whole world stinks to high heaven with the bands I have loved and lost (began with the Band, the Beatles, the Burrito Brothers, and then got stinkier from there) and now: more stinky news: the country musicale outfit Flat Old

World is surrendering to the lack of hype which attends their every single move and will play no more forever post-Jan. 1996—*what*? Who will lend these days their necessary focus if not our flat old friends, who will speak to us of relevant historical antecedents (without actually speaking at all)? Who else cares enough to tell the small tales of towns like Two Blades, Jubilee, Lost Falls, to evoke heroes and villains with names like Haddy Mae, Sir William, Jigger Statz, Jenny Pretty-Eyes? Who will remind us of ancestral longings—conjure up antebellum britches, failed campaigns, Wilson-era lullabies, teapot domes, salvation armies, angel voices, weeds and dirt? No one—that's who—and that's why this stinks.*

Have you ever seen them, all the group's characters belting out their theme "It's a Flat World (After All)," crammed like canned cherries onto the disreputable stage of some firetrap? THERE is the honourable Tuba Jones, who donates all his proceeds to widows and builds orphanages in his spare hours (while the rest of us selfishly sleep), having brokered peace accords through the holy *oom-pa-pa oom-pa-pa oom-pa-pa oom-pa-pa* of his blasted instrument! THERE is that percussionist fellow, what's-his-name, who drums like he sings, stumbling, stammering, a faltering shiver of sound, arriving in the middle of words as if by accident! THERE is the strawberry-topped member who has been known to bellow with such breadth/width/depth that—as Hurricane Nancy—she steers weather, knocks down houses of detention and sets the captive free! THERE is the robin-larynxed golden girl, that facet-heavy ukelele-ist, bearing so many shades and talents she can play any position from halfback to goalie, from safety to guard, from slugger to reliever, and always more disguises than Sherlock

---

* It's because, you see, sometimes the trend seems completely this way or that way and rejectful of anything that seeks change or don't fit, like all we ever thought once was "Doc Holliday, Great Gunfighter Hero Guy" and now it's "Docteur Jour de Fete, le coupable sauvage," now the world defiantly represents itself as round and big and glistening new and not at all "flat" or "old," this contemporary Fed-Ex planet of ours delivers to your door with all its might in Tyvek toughness to quash the flat old sentiment but one day I know the world will kick itself in the head for having missed yet another broadening opportunity (they didn't get Van Gogh or V.U. during their lifetime either so it's not unprecedented!) and being forced to enjoy the Flat Olds solely in retrospect — as an extinct bird of pray not at all in their present-era modern state of living aliveness.

Holmes, more laughs than Lucille Ball, more cars than American Motors! THERE is that irrepressible Fink puppy (*Canis bilious*) pawing out single ringing fuzz notes from a Gibson guitar, one at a time, who never quits with the humbleness and the humility! THERE is the sure and able Governour, the band's governing instinct, always quietly there, she with her stone-steady string section, ever-ready, ever-reliable, who has been known to outplay any player, outwait every waiter, even to outlast the Most Lasting Flavour! And then at last THERE is the one we truly most came to see: V.W.H. Cricklade, Mr. Magnetic South, the show-runner, the preacher-host, the shoe-tree, the reclusive composer extraordinaire Mister World himself, rarely spotted in the daylight hours but for to answer heartsick prayers, mysteriously slipping rooftop to rooftop & shadow to shadow outfitted in superhero colours. . . . Ah! but why even go on and on, why replunge the dagger over and over when the gruesome fact is already taffy-stiff and cold as a corpse: (sad enough words have not been invented) Flat Old World's final show is about to begin and now is the time, my friends, for your tears.

It's the end of the world.

Commencement Day

To you—the graduating class—you have not earned these diplomas, but here they are, come get them, but take with you too this warning: do not do as we have done. Take the reins gently; reward only the worthy; please stop scaring me; and forgive us everything! Put a man on Mars—two men! A *lesbian* (see what I care). Just leave us be before our TVs. . . . Lace up your loose-laced Nikes and take off your Walkmans and those hooded jackets and hooded sweatshirts and hoods and scarves and pullover hooded sweaters and Walkmans and participate in the world and take care of us aged and infirm by taking off your loose-laced, hooded things and showing your face and coming and getting your diplomas and participating and not scaring me in this world anymore with hoods and loose-laced Nikes.

On the eve of this prestigious occasion, presiding over your voyage through the shadows into adulthood, I am at some considerable loss and proffer neither advice nor examples to follow (I have none).

If you ask yourselves, "How can I get to be him, that fellow up there addressing my graduating class?"—Oh, but do not do this! You mustn't do what we do, you must make something of yourselves, protect the ecology, find peace of mind and world-peace! This is a nowhere gig. I am merely the dupe of that American amnesia Romanovs advocate, and what makes me such an ideal idolatrous consumer (since you asked!) is that almost every day I get boinked on the head and have to relearn it all, the world afresh, anew, each of their bleating commercials convinces me utterly I am the best—the only—the brightest—if only I invest in their items. I am that much-prized eternally promised purchaser from Peoria boisterously ballyhooed but badly bamboozled and then *boink* it starts all over again.

Now I ain't no popularly accredited student of culture (like the whole scary hooded flock of you) but I do notice myself growing whole in the bath of commercial television and ripped apart by real life and wonder if I'm probably losing some vital tissues.

So ignore this address, graduates. Just go do your thing and we need help, so take real good care of us, thank you.

THE LAUNCH OF THE MJ-97

(12/22/93) RAN INTO DAVID of the twenty-fifth floor, recently
demoted, who now programs the network committee's
nightly back-ups. Okay guy, rather short. Mere hours from
the launch, but David bore it well. Per usual, he and I spoke
as buddies, reasserted our mutual desire for "hostile grasp"
and "ruinous bonds" such as are delineated in the adrenaline
and mead bouts of Beowulf. He hinted at continued fallout
from foul-ups associated with the debut of the MJ-96 model,
asked what I'd heard. I expressed noncommittal support,
though I had been BCC'd on the committee's electronic chat
and in fact worried even now about being caught in David's
company. But he had recently incorporated a new look into his
repertoire, a look close to tears, and was (I guess) determined
to perfect it on me.

Grave issues relating to the "dimensional verisimilitude" of
the MJ-96 had arisen upon tight tick-clocked reevaluation of
the prepared segments from the 01/31/93 halftime and the
02/10/93 Oprah telecast, and David — involved very early with
the axonometric blueprints — was clearly at fault.

My own comprehension of the concerns was limited: I
was a Floor Twenty-Two man, strictly dataflow compilations,
timed publicity summations. To me, as to the rest of the
world, the MJ-96 had appeared in these broadcasts as "live,"
even "engaging." I had conveyed such, in a subcommittee
FYI of 02/16/93 (which likely fueled David's assumption that

we were buddies), but my layman's views were held to be of marginal significance.

For those upstairs involved with the model's transformation matrix, the programmers and animators and such, these events spelled disaster. Abrupt tessellations (attributable to basic format incompatibilities) within the upper mid-quadrant of the mesh density had created the hint of an MJ-96 third eyebrow (visible for no longer than 0.01 seconds) when the model was manipulated against both environments, the Rose Bowl and the intimate Winfrey setting.

"Strictly junior league stuff," had complained one committee member. "Inconceivable," I had to agree, aghast that something so elemental as format incompatibilities could potentially derail the integrity of an enterprise of this magnitude. The word "sabotage" was used more than once in connection with David of the twenty-fifth floor.

I found myself still standing awkwardly beside David in the grey corridor. I was unclear as to the point of our continued conversation. Assuming the MJ-97's successful launch, he asked my feedback regarding the imminent implementation of the AI chip, aimed at bypassing individual contributions to the network. I meekly confessed unease. We both enjoyed a good, hearty laugh over this.

Word from the AI manufacturers is that TQ-305s and SEs are green-lighted, and full implementation—"a walking, talking Michael"—is expected within six to nine weeks. Within that time period, the committee's brochure has warned us, our job descriptions will undergo a radical transformation. Of course, such a thing has been regularly threatened before, and, in the end, it's always deemed simpler to continue maintaining the enterprise—whether the MJ-97, the MJ-96, or one of the earlier simulations (supplemented by closely managed "real world sightings" of MJ-lookalikes)—from our building rather than unleash too many unpredictable manipulations upon "unscreened environments."

In the bland tones of office chit-chat, David asked my understanding of the ancillary TQ features which permit so-called "time vaults." I admitted complete ignorance, silently puzzled as to what gave rise to such speculation on his part.

Was this related perhaps to our articulated Beowulf desires, or did David see in the possibility of "time vaults" a chance to repath his MJ-96 programming error before it "actually" occurred?

David unsuccessfully sought to probe my knowledge of the committee's top-secret funding of a project to isolate the much-rumored "rock star" gene, their determination to periodically uncouple that reputed DNA trigger of hollow-cheeked charisma in furthering issues of master profitability. How many of our coffee breaks and water cooler roundtables had already been wasted on such speculations! Once more, yet again, the question arose that if a star's faux frontier frightfulness can be shown to've evolved as a biogenetic predisposition, then far greater exploitations were possible. No big news there. Perhaps to relax my guard, David quoted with uncharacteristic vehemence from "Transcription Attributes Identified in Chinese Hamsters Suggesting Variants of Chromosomal Stage Authority and Romantic Appeal" (published out of North Carolina) a paper which, he persuasively insisted, posed some interesting riddles. (Note: subsequent investigations turned up no such paper.)

By now, the launch was almost upon us, and we both had done very little work. David turned in an almost comically secretive manner to ask me this: Would I enjoy a gift of mazur? I could not fathom his secretiveness, though naturally I assented. I no longer possessed mazur, this was true, but its consumption was quite openly encouraged in our building. Following him to his cubicle, I received several of the usual capsules, yellowish in shade, perhaps ¾" in length but quite slender. I walked to the water fountain and swallowed the capsules without difficulty, and thereupon I returned to my desk.

For those unaware of mazur, the most elusive of psychotaraxic compounds, perhaps a few words of explanation. Mazur had become a sort of energy vitamin for all of us on Floor Twenty-Two. As I say, it was well known that we took it, and no one on the network committee had, as yet, disapproved. Since its introduction into the workplace, productivity had soared amongst everyone involved in information compilation (within the aegis of our particular subcommittee). We met our annual quota without difficulty—four months early. We spoke regularly of the peaked mental clarity and euphoric imaginings attributable to this uncommon substance.

Upstairs, the gentlemen were performing last-minute vertex manipulations on the MJ-97 in preparation for its great launch—four minutes "Live from Neverland Valley" in heartfelt defense against charges of child molestation (charges solely manufactured by us to distract from the MJ-97 launch, while affirming the "humanity" of the new model). There would be, to the untrained eye, no discernible difference between this new model and the MJ-96. There "he" would be, the celebrity we knew so well, with the ink-black ringlets and the improbable nostrils, appearing to look into the camera, appearing to speak, haltingly, as if with great emotion, the words our subcommittee had hammered out several weeks earlier.

I had watched this demonstration already a hundred times and despite the launch's arguably "live" nature truly saw no need to withstand it any longer. I did not share the glee of my co-workers that at noon the words "penis" and "buttocks" would be stammered live over CNN, CBS, ABC, and NBC. The MJ-97 too would be a profitable success in simulation.

I sat with my column of figures, rechecking again what had been handed to me earlier in the day. The next task of our endeavor would be undertaken in mere weeks, but no clear standout in our polling could yet be discerned. The union of the MJ-97 with . . . well, with what? Yesterday's market supported just two candidates—Brooke Shields or Madonna—but both, as of the last hour, had suffered dramatic downturns in global feasibility, and a new name found itself floated: Naomi Campbell. And there remained of course the others, the Shannon Doughertys, the Oprah Winfreys, the Princess Carolines, the Lisa Marie Presleys.

Something leapt on my screen in an agile flash, and as quickly as my eye could follow I was made aware of the most recent feedback compiled from the Southern Hemisphere. But it scarcely seemed to matter anymore. "Gary Indiana," someone breathed, quite close to my ear, a name balanced

in my background between "place" and "song," balanced on
an LP rack somewhere (in my brother's room!): Shirley Jones
staring out, ready for marriage. But no one was near enough
to have spoken, and I must have simply imagined hearing
that great musical referenced.

Mazur. I have noted herein our floor's escalated productivity
under its influence, but I must also acknowledge that the reverse
was always a possibility—an undependable realignment of
the senses, an awkward deception of sight. This happened
to each consumer once every several months. As a numbers
man, I dreaded these occasional hallucinations although
this was, some said, the truest nature of mazur. They spoke
of mazur (*Mazargyreia nervosa*) as having been the exclusive
province of Arctic primitives for hundreds of generations. I
can vouch for none of this, but mazur—an edible moss, most
effective when dried and consumed with liquids—would thus
be a bryophyte, a discovery of huge botanical significance as
the first hallucinogen in that branch of the plant kingdom. Its
efficacy among the undisturbed northern tribes was implicit
in an indolic alkaloid composition structurally related to the
neurohumoral tryptamine serotonin (5-hydroxydimenthyl
tryptamine) of all warm-blooded animals.

I recalled David's strange secretiveness, our dully routine
assertions for the taste of Beowulf's "hostile grasp" and "ruinous
bonds." Surely this saboteur had not taken me literally . . . or
had he?! Had David tricked me into the consumption of some
far wilder ingredient, teonanacatl or toloache (*Datura inoxia*),
something terrifyingly unreliable in its effects? No more—I
swore—would I mull over replacement bulbs with him in
the supply closet! This David! I had played into enemy hands
perfectly! I had betrayed it all, the marketing data was theirs
to thumb through and contaminate! Here, the day of the
launch of the MJ-97, a moment of historic consequence, and
I was reduced to nothing but the recipient of ecstatic visions.
Some part of me understood this to be what one would term
"a bad thing" while simultaneously, shutting my eyes in the
monitor glow to feel the glorious warmth of its radiance, I
could only be . . . pleased.

I next heard, of all things, a transistor radio (—!) playing, of all things, "Standing in the Shadows of Love" by the Jackson 5. There, standing in the shadows at work! Marie, how could you write me that letter, so apt, so right, which she did, when I was nineteen, flooring me with her conviction that we were so completely perfect for one another, as she heard attested to in the shadows of "Standing in the Shadows of Love" when we had been darkly parked together two years earlier. Oh Marie, incessantly I kick across toys that take me back to you. Where to have you fled, small-wristed creature? No more can you be found lobbing ping-pong balls at the goldfish bowls, pulling up fillings on bubble gum and banana taffy as the ferris wheel blurs its landing lights against the sooty ambers and oranges that make up our sunsets. Are you lost in the madhouses of furrow-browed adults? Whose handlebars do you ride now, troubled one? I remain devastated still from the final day of class, and your family was moving that summer, and the smell of blazing asphalt overcame me, in the volleyball courts by the woodwind shack, as we dismantled our school clarinets, shaking out the spit and weeping forever goodbyes, desires unspooling from great heights like full rolls of toilet paper tossed from rooftops. You were right, we were made for each other. Coquette! Tease! *Arbitrageur!* Dear Marie, how my heart has never been right since our union dissolved that summer and now look at you, happily married to the wrong character. But you cannot hear me now.

I immediately left work to purchase a slice of pizza. My thoughts were busy important streets. I had to cross them before I could get to the restaurant safely. It began to snow on me, unlike in Neverland where the sun always shines and winter never falls. Snowflakes swarmed the streetlight, bees in a windstorm. My movements were exaggerated, or perhaps only seemed so. I was unclear. One could read the wind weaving the snow's path. In blowing on my pizza to cool it off I could no longer sense how long it was appropriate to blow, whether I had been blowing so long as to embarrass myself in front of these more sober pizza-blowers, whether I was blowing neither hard nor long enough and I would burn my benumbed mouth. . . . The snow danced on the street in patterns reminding me of desert sand. How many thoughts came and went as I stood there with my slice.

It seemed years since I'd been blowing on the pizza! My watch indicated only 45 minutes since I had consumed the mazur. For most of that, I must've been blowing. My hands, so yellow and small! Like Ryan White! How lucky brother Jermaine, his tendency toward honesty at a very young age, seemingly unafraid to get in terrible trouble and thus immuning him to what others make of him now. My pulse was holding steady at 56 BPM. It occurred to me again that any magazine would buy an interview called "Raising Michael Milken," in which I interview ten mothers about how they might raise Michael Milken were he a sunken vessel. Such a thing would be unprecedented! Free rides in cars would ensue! Notice from the Hays Commission!

I came to believe that, once I got home, I would put early Motown on my Walkman and step out again to rent some pornography. That done, this is what I would see: a businessman busy with a refrigerator door. I would see a happy couple in the porn section of the videostore! I would see people studying me, wondering, as I passed, as I eavesdropped on their conversations between Temptations songs. I would grasp, in crossing a street, the power in a crosswalk, when all cars stand at attention, parade horses before the monarchy, their headlights halted to light your stroll. And this graffiti would appear upon the streetside wall of a parts shop: "Pardon the Cartesian paraphrase but if Michael Jackson did not exist we would have to invent him." And I would think: *very funny.*

A sort of premonition became known to me as my awareness expanded. This epiphany will be difficult to express. Gradually I noticed that some of us are dogs made in one motion, sleek and decisive, burly and fierce, one per street, wearing wry grins, haughtily cracking in our grizzly bear jaws the bones of once-prouder beasts, our eyes brimming with contempt. And the rest of us, a pack hobbled with runover limbs, chewed ears, mangled tails, mange and fleas and thirsty as hell, sniffing damaged metal, unsure where dirt ends and food begins, mindful of the fleeting satisfactions of victory, of how those handsome pups are never happy for long, of justice, all of us essential to the other, one with good math skills, one with talents in drafting, one can hit southpaw pitching, one has a swift right jab, one's a diplomat, another an encyclopedia, every one of us a poorly drawn cartoon, flat of vision and oft-surprised, and there's always one collapsing, the trail guide or the acupuncturist, the telepath or the inventor, leaning on a telephone pole to catch his breath, one weak paw curling in, involuntarily, signaling vulnerability to attack. You know what I mean?

I sit sorrowfully on a folding chair in a laundromat. Here we wash the widow's black veil, the sheets of the syphilitic, the refugee's scarves. We wash shirts that have no arms and pants with one leg. They patiently spin through their soapy cycles — a swirl of loss itself — foamed to the brim, whited from view as if erased. And in the dryers the frail items tumble to pieces, toppled by temperatures and torn, becoming a clutter of glass eyes and hearing aids, canes and crutches and leprosy bracelets. Until a boy orphan's glance, so courteously averted, has me sobbing.

I have fallen in with a superstitious people, a gypsy offering cheap fortunes and a tired healer promising anything, our lives lost to any larger significance but for the germs we carry (which we well know will outlive us all). And now my hands, muddied though mute, and my tongue itself, tied by kite string. Someone amongst us attempts to make a meal, someone with crushed tins to make mirrors and thus extend the votive light deeper into the establishment. There is a television there.

Someone brings out a rooster with one wing whose beak pecks the bass line of "Beat It" from a toy Casio. He has others: a pair of identical twin midgets who in tandem offer a stark, even chilling, recitation of "Black and White"; a goat in a *Victory Tour* necktie bleating a Grammy acceptance speech while a caged dove coos the melody to "We Are the World"; and a miniature elephant that moonwalks.

Children, their heads seemingly of fruit, claw their way over to me — a pineapple-faced boy, a pomegranate girl, two apple-heads and a lop-eared banana sort — clamoring for coins to purchase souvenirs. I buy them balloons emblazoned with the *Dangerous* record album design. So handsomely they draw themselves up, quite deliberately, proud and overjoyed, and each kisses me in gratitude.

I look up at a television screen bigger than any one person can entirely see; a set to dwarf the earth and heavens, its edges defining the known universe. The television plays the only thing it can play and once more we succumb, as at dusk we no more hold back night than unplant the dead to beg for wisdoms. Programmed to every channel is a man asking us to release him from this ordeal, to pray with him. Naturally, I know the words by heart: "I am doing well and I am doing strong." I do not need to identify this man because he lives within each of us — "In no way do I think that I am God but I try to be god-like in my heart." At night the fronds atop palm trees, elegant and aloof, slapping in the watery wind and hidden in the gulch behind the stadium, pass his name into the dreams of children in sensing all hope has ceased. "I have been forced to submit to a dehumanizing and humiliating examination by the Santa Barbara County Sheriff's Department and the Los Angeles Police Department earlier this week."

The boy orphan scampers onto my lap. His teeth are the color of the sharps and flats of a piano. "Is it true," the child sighs, "he has a Ferris wheel?" I hear the bones clicking in his body, the tidal pools in his lungs, the breaths drawn with difficulty.

"Yes."

He waits, wanting to hear more.

"And an exotic managerie," I continue, "and a movie theater and a personal security staff of forty." The child weakly nods. I wipe his nose with my sleeve. The child speaks, still watching the television. "How I love him." Then his small head falls against me as if to listen to my heart.

"He's done nothing wrong," I assure the child, light as a bird in my hands, more air than boy. "He's done nothing." I peer to see if he hears me. He seems not to be moving. Should I worry? I cannot be sure. Perhaps he's simply fallen asleep?

THE GREATEST
RECORD ALBUM
SINGER EVER

BROTHERS AND SISTERS, as you turn to this tonight, do not seek
To Escape but rather To Examine and critically to scrutinize
your own selfish selves — to discover how best you will purvey
these oft-suppressed teachings around the squat chilly
pancake known to us this night as "the Known Universe" — for
if you teach, indeed teachers have pupils (— do they *not?!*),
editors have newspapers, chefs have staffs; lawyers and
masseuses and architects all have clients; if born in the
spring months (I am told) you possess winning Charms and
Charisma, if born in the autumn months you possess Luck
and good Resources — EMBRACE THESE ORACULARLY FORETOLD
ATTRIBUTES — if you are one to entertain, well, entertainers
have their hangers-on, even Crafts-brothers and -sisters
from Labor-Intensive Production Capacities yet still possess
dependents — surely there is at least someone over whom
you hold sway, someone who searchingly looks to you for
guidance — and unto seekers such as these I encourage that
you pass along these words. It is only this hope — that being
a fly that flies in the face of the ointment of the Advertocracy
you will take these long-suppressed teachings, strap them
to your winged back and physically buzz them back out

to the People (where they belong!)—that allows me now to continue. Must I be disappointed?

Part One

To speak rationally of the greatest record album singer that ever was, whose name we forget a little more each and every day, we must first invoke the name (Sefton Delmer) of a man already oft-forgot, the author (Sefton Delmer) himself of a lost pamphlet called *Black Boomerang*, the son (again! this bastard Delmer!) of a British constable and the father (co-father with P.J. Goebbels) of modern propaganda. In 1929 Delmer met a short, dark Austrian—he initially detailed this meeting richly though in later editions of *Black Boomerang* all detail was inexplicably withdrawn until by the pamphlet's fifth edition Delmer describes their meeting as merely a glimpse: "He sat in a rail carriage in the Munich depot, his eyes softening to an occasional blue as he contemplated the train platform. Even at rest, he was thoroughly engaging; quite clearly, I would later hear much more from him."

This occasionally blue-eyed fellow (Adolf Hitler) could have dominated all of Europe but he refused to invade Britain. (He loved the British!) Hitler too was an author of lost pamphlets: *Hitler's Secret Book* remained unpublished until the late '50s. In this pamphlet, he writes that, "No inducement exists to make eternal England's enmity against Germany. In fact, Germany—in showing itself useful to British interests from time to time—will be invited to be on England's side regardless of whether there was an enmity in the past."

So Delmer met Hitler and promptly (conveniently?) met eradication from the history books—much as the slobbering aviator D'Ambrosio before him and the "Mad Diarist" Loonis after him—the meeting reduced to a chance encounter in Delmer's pamphlet. (And yet Hitler loved the British, loved police.) Sefton Delmer—Adolf Hitler—do you notice how nicely they echo each other? (Delmer's father—a constable.) I think you see where I am headed with this. [Sefton Delmer, incidentally, was never tried at Nuremberg.]

After meeting with Hitler, Delmer suggested to the British government a secret ministry of propaganda, had himself installed as head and ran it during World War Two — fresh (I say again) from his meeting with Adolf Hitler, Delmer claimed that the BBC's current propaganda (consisting exclusively of expatriates beaming their denunciations and diatribes back into the fatherland) was too obvious to have any negative effect on the enemy (—well, well espionage buffs! would not THIS be the perfect cover for a double-agent?!). He claimed that as soon as you know someone is trying to sell you something, you tune out this "white propaganda." Delmer's solution was to gather lies and distortion into something he called "black propaganda."

Black propaganda was a slight and a subtle form of psychological warfare. By pretending that his shortwave radio show was a legitimate news source that dearly loved the pamphleteer Adolf Hitler (as simultaneously it worked to distress the German people), Delmer supposedly nibbled away at their certainties, at their belief in leaders, paralyzed them in the face of patriotic efforts. The German people (the Advertocracy has since claimed) were led to believe that Rudolf Hess had joined the English side and that the Wehrmacht actively opposed most of Hitler's aims, and the German authorities were convinced (or so we hear) that the invasion of Europe would come at Calais at a far later date than the actual Normandy landing.

[I myself have just recently been the recipient of these very tactics emanating from nervous little Advertocrats seeking to undermine The Entire Process but no doubt we will get to that, brothers and sisters —]

Supposedly, as Delmer claims, a combination of black and white propaganda defeated Hitler. In his book, the British won the war. Hitler loved the British, loved police. (And Sefton Delmer's father a constable; Delmer British.) A meeting between these men was swiped from the history books.

What (stop your fidgeting) does all this have to do with Great Record Album Singers? Well: in his mind Hitler pictured a sort of master race, in which all the ethnicities competed against one another rather like the Olympics but Hitler believed whites would win—that whites were (in essence) The Master Race—so he didn't invite Blacks to join the competition. This was white propaganda, black propaganda, these were Sefton Delmer's inventions, the father of modern advertising, co-father with P.J. Goebbels.

Reportedly, as the story goes, Hitler was defeated.

An opened and a shut up kind of case.

Except that after the war Delmer accepts an offer from the marketing agency Beragulum-Mahoney, flies to Osaka Japan—again although Japan was said to've "lost" the previous war (like a pamphlet) no one thinks it's odd that this man who met with Adolf Hitler (a man who in turn envisioned a master race) is now pole-vaulting right over to some country with whom we just "fought" some gigantic war, they allow Sefton Delmer to enter Japanese airspace, they clear him to land, and immediately he contributes to the reconstruction of the country by selling . . . televisions! Sells—in fact—over FOUR MILLION TVs in the next year and a half.

Speaker: *What kind of* TELEVISIONS?

Congregation: *Black and white.*

Speaker: *Fathered what kind of* PROPAGANDA?

Congregation: *Black and white!*

—with the help of P.J. Goebbels.

They go interview Delmer as to Beragulum-Mahoney's goals in *Look* magazine, July 1948, and he says, and I quote from that issue's page 87, "We will make Japan a model for our world. We will establish here the first true advertocracy."

[Dear friends, I must inquire at this time if you've ever witnessed Cable Access Fifty-Three? I commend it to all of you for they accept no advertising money, are devoted to promulgating TRUTH at whatever cost. The newspapers deny its existence or else simply deride it in listings as the 'Conspiracy Channel' but I say unto you tonight this is untrue unfounded unkind unfounded and untrue. Cable Access Fifty-Three, write that on the back of your hand; Cable Access Fifty-Three, it's where I've learned everything I know. If you can, call the station—though don't bother to call Information for their number, they'll tell you Fifty-

ad-ver-toc-ra-cy *n, pl* **-cies** **1 a** : one of the totalitarian "shadow societies" **b**: a purported democracy which actively protects unelected authorities; specifically, those authorities who exploit envy by way of coercing consumers into repeated purchases of unnecessary, often shoddily constructed, products **2** : any state in which autocratic dictums issued by advertisers are implemented through a national mobilization overseen by the police state **3** : a very bad place where people are made to feel small if they don't own the right things.

Three "does not exist" and then demand to know what you want with them — find the station, get a copy of the show they unveiled the other month on The Advertocracy — Sefton Delmer uttered the word but once and that was the last time it was spoken aloud until uncovered by the sisters at Fifty-Three. Seeing that show, my hair caught fire with the realization that it was fine to step forward and to speak now of what my mom taught me but made me promise to keep secret. So let me, if I may, begin all over again.]

Part One

Having seen Cable Access Fifty-Three's program, it is incumbent upon me now to clearly express unto you that a secret organization maintained by Lying Constables & Advertisers — I feel — MUST clearly run the whole shebang for in this Advertocracy of ours there remains no better well-kept secret than the Biological Secrets, specifically the secret mystery of dermal melanoblast and in particular this secret mystery called Invibiosus Dermal Melanism — literally "pigment envy" — whereby the maturation process stimulates an over-abundant production of amino acid tyrosine thus:

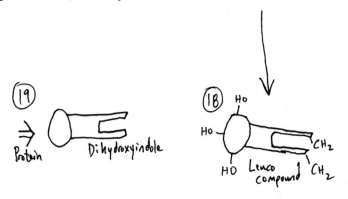

—give tyrosine some oxygen it starts to resemble a tiny space station, an enzyme drifts in and docks—

—and turns our space station into melanin the dark pigment—

—and incredibly enough blasts this off into one's cytoplasm and thusly is accomplished the incontrovertible indisputable established fact that —

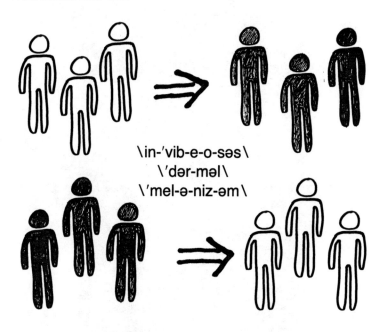

\in-'vib-e-o-səs\
\'dər-məl\
\'mel-ə-niz-əm\

— white brothers, once grown-up, become black men and visa versa, that black brothers grow up to be white men.

To say that the biochemistry underlying this switch of skin pigment has accidentally escaped the national dialogue for the last however many hundred years does not even hint at the breadth of this melanistic issue's prolonged coverup; for one—in vain—may peruse TV's "science" channels (these are cleverly orchestrated by Lying Advertocrats) for mention of *invibiosus dermal melanism* and be assured you will come away only empty-handed (but keep looking! for eventually you will see). *Industrial melanism*—yes, this they will admit—how certain moths displayed striking examples of rapid evolutionary change, an entire species changing color in less than a hundred years—

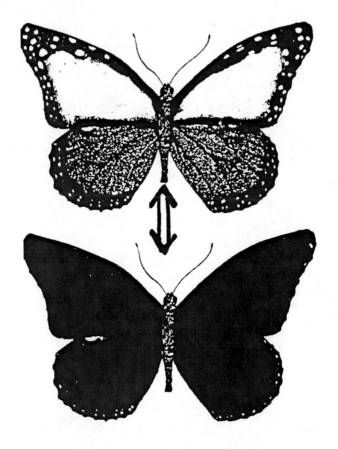

— but *invibiosus dermal melanism* they suppress talk of this at all costs—and I ask who can blame them, for could we still teach The Lessons of History in Delmer-ese once knowledge of this pigment switch grew widespread—Telling of how white men at planter's wharves and auction houses used to behave like Joseph's own brethren (white men being, remember, only grown-up black brothers) by selling into slavery those black brothers destined one day to be their inheritors, the next white generation—clearly, this habit of selling off the next generation constitutes One Bad-Assed Unbearable Truth which Sefton Delmer's Advertocrats actively suppress By Any Means Necessary—they attempt to distract us by advertising white people sports cars to us as "A Revolution"—the only products they even market solely for us black brothers are those jams and jellies made to straighten our kinked-up heads to look more white, to soak up the natural oils of our bushy hair, then they sell us too their flowing hair-weaves and these straight-mopped wigs they sew out of the hair of dead white people—these being the standard commercials during any African-American film-strip tale, one such as "The Greatest Record Album Singer That Ever Was" which we have observed a million times on that blue-eyed TV screen of ours: Man meets woman, woman falls for man, man rejects woman, woman pours boiling grits on man while man bathes, woman locks self in man's bedroom and shoots self to death—*commercial break*—Christian brother raised near Detroit hears secular Sam Cooke on the radio, resolves to become a popular singer, devoutly religious parents call him "sinful," discourage him at every turn "for his own good"—*commercial break*—King of '70s Soul Music (a.k.a., The Greatest Record Album Singer That Ever Was) topples from Cincinnati stage in 1979, slams into steel instrument case, comes out of hospital after fifteen days saying, "I was being disobedient toward my calling, I was moving toward God but I wasn't moving fast enough, this fall was God's way of saying I had to hurry up"—*commercial break*—Meanwhile how lost the brother has gotten in the 1960s! kicking around on the Chitlin Circuit performing the music of others to little recognition restlessly searching for dynamic and powerful sound combinations finding none intimate enough: "Nobody was writing the kind of material that I heard in my head and wanted to sing," this brother tells later interviewer. "My only choice was to write my own"—*commercial break*—Brother realizes himself as Al Green, who is tired of being alone and says so in his first song, a million folks buy this single, followed by three platinum albums released in 1972, three gold albums released in 1973, grammies and grammies and more grammies, then Al Green rethinks it, decides he isn't tired of being alone so much anymore and so gets ordained as a minister in Memphis, devotes himself to gospel music, rejects secular past—*commercial break*—Brother dreams and yearns, brother longs and aches, brother accomplishes, achieves, attains widespread credit and renown, God shows up, God tests brother, brother barely passes test, God tries brother, brother surrenders all to Kingdom of

God, brother is saved—Roll credits then more commercials—

And the thing these little Hitlerian Advertocrats that speak Delmer-ese (for he concocted the whole lingo with P.J. Goebbels and then sold us our televisions) the thing they love to sell us on in these commercials is this notion that 'It's as simple as black and white' WELL what if Black and White are not that simple at all? (For as we've seen preacher Al Green is both Green and Black)—they will make you *Try to Deny* what you see with your own eyes how the lives of African-Americans bleach out as they mature—are dried of options like dehydrated jerky—just as my life—the life of a thusfar white boy—fills as I grow with more and more color until someday soon (quite soon, I pray) it will grandly spill over and stick to my skin, darken, caramelize, and I awake as handsome and chocolatey fine as my black father, preacher Green (as opposed to my white father, whose name I never knew)—

I always suspected preacher Green was there the night I was conceived—the first thing I ever heard was his voice—when I confronted my white mother on this she admitted this was absolutely true—they were making out to *The Belle Album* she confessed and things got completely out of hand—what a disco hound that woman (and of the white man who inseminated her and begat me—about my white father who can say—evidently a fellow with a hurried manner—a watch-watcher cruising for snappy sex between a shit, shave, and shower) —

Nowadays who even chats of Al Green anymore but to snicker "WHATEVER HAPPENED TO . . ." and then giggle "Ooooh yeah. He murdered that chick and then found GOD *har har*" like it was some publicity scam put over on us by Lying Advertisers not the act of a wounded man sincerely redeemed—he had it all, Italian shoes and white people sports cars, and HE SACRIFICED EVERYTHING—some said Al Green turned Yellow—but yet how is it that with nearly every step we still speak reverently of Bob Marley, every day with veneration, with open unclouded adoration—should Al Green like Marley have died in the early '80s (instead of simply "dying" in the early '80s to be "reborn in Christ") then we might more regularly thank our lucky stars for his ever appearing—for we needed them both—Marley and Green were so much the two prongs of a single attack, parallel in purpose, but to speak of these contemporaries now our prejudice is nakedly apparent as we initially introduce them as "Marley the Angel" and "Green the Dupe."

Simultaneously and from the very same American R&B sources they arose, Al Green and Bob Marley, reacting to the mean muscular militant jerk of so much over-politicized '60s soul by internalizing The Moment of every song, by making music which could transmit careful apologies, could reach out, teach trust, administer to the listener.

Rather than dominate, control, overpower the beat Al Green chose to duck beneath the song, to under-sing. Consequently, Al Green—one critic swooned—sensuously tickles the soft tender backside behind every song's knee, that point of vulnerability that will tease it down onto the animal-skin rug in the candle-lit den. But there are those (I SEE YOU!) who can't hear past the goopy strings and laid-back lovin'-ness, the determined grace, ease, and sly smoothness of the man—that distinctive squeal, that keening falsetto (—oh how can these not do it to you!)—that lumbering husky quaalude murmur set to a tantalizingly shushed dance track—those jabs of brass—spurts of guitar. For Listen Closely Children and You Will Hear: Al Green is an emotional wreck, sounds as if he is serenading someone in intensive care. You can hear his distraught expression—his face all scrunched up as he sings to this comatose love, his shoulders high, eyebrows leaping, trying to Hold It Down while still gettin' funky, doing his damnedest to sing on eggshells, to hit all the high notes without unnerving the other ICU patients. Occasionally things in his songs—Jesus, marriage, an ungettable babe, The Lord—appear to possess his every meaning, HE WILL CONVINCE YOU THAT THESE MESSAGES ARE THE POINT OF THE SONG but I must disagree and I say the MESSAGE is the MESSENGER—for example Al Green sings "Take Me to the River" which I hear as "Take Me to Al Green" for Al Green IS my river. [On a bad day, when the day like some scald dog has scurried crouching and defeated to the furthest corner of one's vision (then abruptly is gone), I rely on preacher Green's songs to run soothingly acrost my tortured brow like a medicinal balm, his voice to succor me, I count on being dipped in the soothing bath of his voice, and I relinquish my soul to the warm moan and flow of his Green river waters.]

In the '70s both Marley and Green did the unpopular by electing occasionally to celebrate their new-found religiosity—Robert Nesta Marley singing of Ras Tafari and Al Green singing of Jesus Christ. In the mid-'70s both were nearly killed by people who raided their houses—Al Green by Mary Woodson a former girlfriend who entered his apartment while he bathed and scalded him with "Memphis napalm" and then she died a few moments later from a bullet which came out of a gun owned by Al Green—Bob Marley by political gangsters who forced their way into his pad and attempted to take his life but only wounded him in the arm then fled. By the turn of the decade they were both at the height of their careers which was when they each left our sight—in 1981 Green was killing his career with gospel tunes when cancer suddenly killed Marley.

Seven years go by and it's the NBA Finals sometime around June of 1988 and I am sitting alone watching Detroit battle Los Angeles in a meanly fought Game Six—tiny guard Isiah Thomas scoring a record number of points on a majorly sprained ankle—aided in his noble efforts by fierce young forward Dennis Rodman—Magic and Kareem heroically fending them off as best they can—the entire television screen is filled with greatness, with talented dedicated sweat-drenched brave African-Americans—when *commercial break*—and first it's hilarious Bill Cosby selling Jell-O brand gelatin, then a trailer for the new silly Eddie Murphy movie, then super-cool Carl Lewis and Superbowl quarterback Doug Williams telling me how I should not do drugs nor do graffiti neither, then ultra-hip Arsenio Hall plugging his next show with guests Dick Gregory and Andrew Young, and I look away—there is a Martin Luther King quote on the wall of King talking about this dream of his that he had, and I look away—on the other wall is a painting from the Harlem Renaissance, and I look away—the radio in the kitchen loudly plays "Kiss" by Prince, and I look away—then my mom passes through the room, asks me what is wrong and why I am crying and I say how I see that all the great men in this world are black like Al Green and I'll never amount to nothing. And Mom, she goes: Not all the great men are black like Al Green, what about . . . And she thinks and goes: What about

Michael Jackson he's sorta not black, what about Rod Carew?
And I go: Rod Carew IS black. And so she goes: YES but he's also
JEWISH and that means he's not REALLY black. And I go: Oh. So
then she goes: My baby I gotta tell you a secret at this point in
time it is such an enormously well-kept secret that people will
hate you if you speak of it, no one will ever love you and you
will be roundly disdained and die in filth alone, so promise me
you'll tell no one that you know this. So I go: I promise. Have
you heard of The Fact of Life, she goes. I go: Sorta. Then she
goes: Well, The Fact of Life is this: At a certain age white boys
turn black. What, I go: Really? She nods. So I go: But how
come not everyone is black then? Oh well, she goes: The other
Fact of Life is black boys, they turn white. So we switch, I say
to check her meaning: White boys grow into black men like Al
Green and black boys grown into white men like my father. She
nods once more: That is correct. Wow, wow, wow, I go. And
she goes: It's a secret, don't ever ever tell anyone I ever told
you. I won't, I go: So Isiah Thomas, was he . . .? He was white
when he was little, mom answers. And Jesse Jackson, I ask:
And Reggie Jackson and George Jackson? And she goes: Them
too, all of them were white like you. Wow, I go: That's great,
so so great, I'm so happy. So you see, my Mom rubs a kiss into
my forehead and starts back to the kitchen to finish our dishes:
There's hope, there's always hope, you'll be a great man yet,
you'll make your mama proud.

Now I naturally know how this sounds of course one
receives much encouragement as a child that is based on
apocryphal rhyming nonsense, even patently false fairy tales
and superstitious conjecture, yet too is there that share which
comes out in the end to be absolutely true. UNBELIEVABLE TRUTHS
Mixed-Up with BELIEVABLE LIES: One hears for example of Easter
bunnies and ESP and massacres on Saint Valentine's Day, of
Mutual Assured Destruction (MAD) and Tom Dooley, hears that
the government will keep any bank from failing, that we are
free men created equal, that it's bad luck to use the scissors in
the house, that women shoot one another to death, that men
can fly, that men have in fact To The Moon Flown and Upon Its
Sea of Tranquility Walked, that the majority will decide what is
fair, that Jack sold a cow for a handful of worthless beans, that

I want to rock and roll all night (and party every day), that the state encourages our pursuit of happiness and wants us to do what we want whenever we want and we can even earn extra coinage by putting our teeth beneath our pillows while we sleep, that they made Susan B. Anthony dollars and $2 bills for a short time and then just stopped FOR NO REASON but there is NOTHING suspicious about it AT ALL, that once a year groundhogs determine the seasons, that army colonels and church men are virtuous, that in Chocolate Town all the trains are painted brown, that once a poodle in a microwave was exploded, that man comes from genetically altered monkeys named Adam & Eve who were deposited here by flying saucers, that the rich write the rules and the rest of us tag along, that POWs remain in the hands of the commie VC, that in the hand of our last chance lies the stabbed-up heart of our Lord Jesus Christ the messiah, that your insurance company wants to hear what you think, that Jackie Wilson (or Wilson Pickett or Otis Redding or Ray Charles or James Carr) and not Al Green is the greatest record album singer that ever was, that a pair of sneakers tossed over the power lines in front of your place means another angel just got her wings, and that we all go to heaven but for those who don't brush their teeth or make their beds or clean their rooms and that sometime in growing up white boys and black boys shed skin, trade color, and become men. Most of these — as I say — seem preposterously far-fetched yet many turn out to be accurate — and as for the last, one need only compile a clean set of experiential data (KEEP LOOKING you will see) to learn how little separates "Wasp" from "Blood" and verify the fundamental actuality of *invibiosus dermal melanism*.

It then becomes ridiculous how as honky kids we learn words like buck nigger but no appropriate response (peckerwood ball-face), how we are left ignorant as to how best to insult our original race, after our color has switched. I grew up a vanilla cracker blue-eyed devil boy and one day very soon I'll become a bongo-lipped porch monkey, a rugheaded Hershey bar-colored man, but I will never have learnt to snap back at the poor white trash, at the pink whoogies who corner me with butterhead, jig, raisin, chungo bunny, splib, I will be left in the dark, so to speak, not knowing enough to bite back with hay

eater, marshmallow jeff chalk-headed whitey, my spears will be
as toys to them and helpless my body theirs to enslave—

Oh Sob Not for ME but rather for ALL OF US—for 96% of our
good people now do not vote, 64% cannot read, 37% cannot
cook or clean, almost everyone tells BAD JOKES—what has this
land come to—what of the confetti eggs and air conditioning,
the better TV, these things that were promised us as children,
where now is that "CAN DO" zeal which mapped the impenetrable
regions of this dark continent and did so much to cleanse and
structure our formerly primitive plains and uninhabitable
mountainscapes, the variegated textures of this land, now
everyone costs something and nobody will sleep with me,
this is no revolution (despite what the white people sports
car commercials say)—The Advertocrats are making fools out
of us! (And they dare to call LEON SPINKS a drunkard!) And my
shoulder's got a kink in it and WHEN! WILL! I! BE! BLACK!—these
voices won't stop sobbing, I am inside someone who hates
me—My soul is free black, as pure black as night bending
to embrace thee—and in mammals and birds (according to
Gloger) melanin pigmentation acts as a barrier against the
effects of sunlight (namely, ultraviolet rays) and limits the light
entering the eyeball—OH Brothers and Sisters I Want to See
Life This Way OH When Will I Be Black—The secret, it's all in
the elusively heard tickings of biological clocks, that gradual
stringing of beads of time which takes us here from there and
eventually turns us into The People We Admire—which is to
say that although time it's passing my IMPATIENCE it's growing
and I can see myself I'm singing in the choir of the Full Gospel
Tabernacle Church in Tennessee beside Minister Al Green but
I must wait, for when I see myself this way—happy-voiced in
song—I notice I AM BLACK and I so love myself once I notice
this, it's a manner of love which seems almost to blister one's
lungs with its full-on intensity, like when some plant you pass
sends out its invisible spores and envelopes your world in rosy-
misted scents and you catch fleeting glimpses of a beautiful
woman's hand reclining on the screen door's other side—LA
LA FOR YOU—like when a soft dusk falls—that sweetest of
angels—to collect up in his wings the angered smoking ruins of
your soul, one feels tall, well-rested, soft to the touch, light, at

ease, one's shoulder has no kink in it—LA LA FOR YOU—a moon so chalky full it makes one's extremities tingle, the nightingales all seem to be chirping "What Is This Feeling" or "Let's Get Married" one possesses confidence in one's readership one gossips with strangers freely about the president—LA LA FOR YOU—the friendly wave of a tree branch, the hum of a departing pleasure-craft lifts high one's spirits, one again recalls kindly care-free Marie at the corner candy counter (so fine! that's right, her!) and our absolute duty to confide everything we know to care-free Marie (right on!)—LA LA FOR YOU—one trusts oneself despite all we know about oneself, this LA LA FOR YOU is all the love we need for when wearied peoples ask, "Who can even make a living anymore?" there is that love of preacher Green to remind us, "I guess there's no good reason for living; but I'll keep on living for you, babe (there's nothing else to do, babe)." Yes indeed! Once, when I was younger—I am not yet eighteen now and this was back some time—I tried to make a living by starting a business with a friend. We wanted (naturally enough) to be advertocrats, big-time mercantilist publicity pugs, so we studied up on advertocratic lingo (frankly it all read like nonsense to us) and after great consideration we everywhere distributed mailers that said,

but these met with absolutely no response no one came to us wishing help in pushing their sports cars away so then as further samples of our wares we manufactured envelopes which carried a date and were made to fit precisely over the heads of parking meters and read,

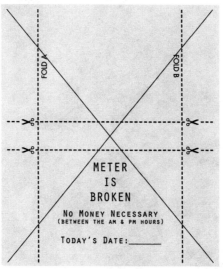

but again the windows remained dark within our house of opportunity so then we put up posters which said,

But *still* there was no answer of any kind so then we put up posters about our lost dog except they went like this,

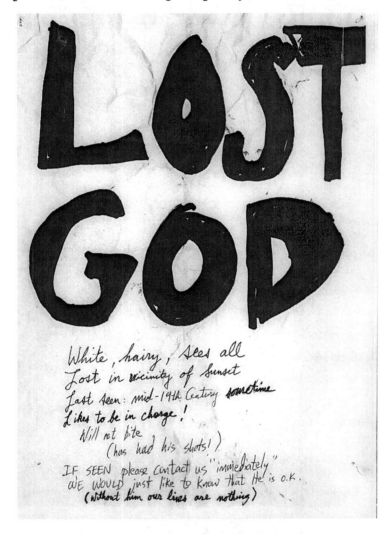

but again of course nothing so then lastly (we were desperate and desperately broke!) we put up bomb diagrams but still no one came calling needing our assistance except for the constables—which after all these failed brainstorms hit us like a double whammy!—like it wasn't bad enough spending the time and energy on these posters and mailers and receiving zero customers in reply—but now (that the Advertocrats should have held their enforcers in check for so long, now this amazes me) here come the constables—to outline our so-called predicament—to tell us they sense some seditious pattern to our flyers—and even though this is all like total horseradish they will not believe we are serious aspiring merchant-class capitalist advertisers and instead they pan our work by terming it 'cheeky and troubling' though in the same review we are later held to be 'well worth watching' and all I could think to do was to quote the mighty Eugene V. Debs who—as a young black brother—once defiantly expressed himself to a belligerent white constable thusly: AS I see it—it is me versus the REST of the World and IF be hanged to my death for this I must THEN be hanged to my death I shall—and the whole time that I was looking at this very picky constable with his big snooty hands on his big snooty hips I was also wanting to inquire WHO CAN EVEN MAKE A LIVING ANYMORE (I guess there's no good reason for living unless you're gifted with a voice supple and gracious as preacher Green)—but I said nothing, for as a white boy my voice was not much and, as I said, I was then much younger and lacking in the necessary confidences.

We have once more run out of space Brothers and Sisters (breathe your damned sigh of relief Marie! and nervous little adverto-enforcers everywhere) and so in abbreviated conclusion I reiterate this last teaching: Locate Cable Access Fifty-Three, do not pay parking meters because that coinage washes immediately up to the subjugators of our desire (Sefton Delmer's constables) (are we so sure that Hitler has lost his war?), and push your sports car away.

It is, none of it, so simple as black and white.

Publisher's Note: These posters appeared July 14–22, 1996, concurrent with Macintosh's second annual New York Music Festival. They measured 48″ × 72″ and were painted in oil-based browns and blacks utilizing a variety of hog-bristle brushes.

THIS POSTER WILL
CHANGE YOUR LIFE

APPEARED ON 13TH STREET NEAR FOURTH AVENUE, FACING SOUTH

LATER APPEARED ON 8TH STREET AT ASTOR PLACE, FACING NORTH

APPEARED ON BOWERY AT 4TH STREET, FACING WEST

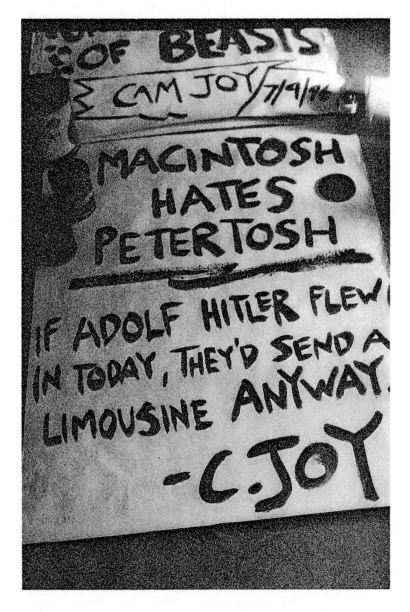

LATER APPEARED ON AVENUE A NEAR TOMPKINS SQUARE PARK, FACING EAST

APPEARED ON 13TH STREET AT FOURTH AVENUE, FACING SOUTH

TOP: APPEARED ON BROADWAY NEAR UNION SQUARE, FACING SOUTH;
BOTTOM: APPEARED ON ST. MARK'S PLACE NEAR SECOND AVENUE, FACING
NORTH

APPEARED ON 3RD STREET NEAR SECOND AVENUE, FACING NORTH

APPEARED ON BOWERY NEAR 3RD STREET, FACING WEST

TOP: APPEARED ON BROADWAY NEAR UNION SQUARE, FACING WEST;
BOTTOM: APPEARED ON FOURTH AVENUE AT 14TH STREET, FACING EAST

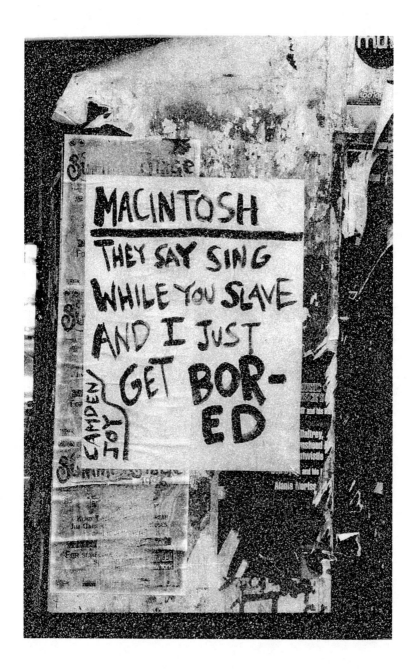

APPEARED ON BROADWAY AT 13TH STREET, FACING WEST

APPEARED ON 3RD STREET NEAR SECOND AVENUE, FACING SOUTH

TOTAL SYSTEMS FAILURE

AS ANYBODY WHO HAS FLIPPED past *Rolling Stone*'s editorial page to read their business section recently can attest, popular music is undergoing what those in the know like to call, "really something." All the record company people who signed the good indie bands and orchestrated bringing us the very best music of the '90s are being put on ice in favor of rootless meanies who favor brand-name ballads, dance crazes, and tits. It's perhaps true when people paraphrase the Clash these days that, "Even if the Beatles flew in today, they'd send no limousine anyway" (although people declaring such usually forget that the Beatles seemed harmless at the start, which is how they got so big; they began as Backstreets and became Beasties). So far, in my debatably short life, I've been lucky enough to see punk fall out of fashion not once but twice (it was better the second time because effects pedals caught up with the theory, and deadpan wit entered the rhetoric; at long last, wise-asses got the girls). We had some good times, didn't we, back when smart, sloppy groups had their shiny moment, back when the paying public seemed to've come over (at last!) to our way of thinking? Then the record companies ran out of Nirvana specialty reissues and Sonic Youth did not make another *Daydream Nation* as the talented British folk/dub Fellow Travelers dispersed and their leader

Jeb Loy Nichols reentered on the set of *Good Will Hunting* disguised in the robes of a soft rocker and stupid Mark E. Smith assaulted his wife at the Quality Hotel Eastside while Elvis Costello refused to even acknowledge any of what was occurring and forfeited his place in the pantheon and memorable, generational-defining classics were on the tips of tongues like the Breeders and Uncle Tupelo and the Campfire Girls and Belly and the Dirt Merchants when instead the band members turned on one another as Nick Cave and Morrissey became jokes and Bob Mould and Mike Watt continued on cluelessly and the gifted pop band Christmas came back as the highly successful, utterly irrelevant smug swingers Edison Combustible and traditionally deserving songwriterly dues-paying types like Vic Chesnutt and the Fastbacks somehow could not get a commercial purchase on the popular imagination as everybody from Girls Against Boys to the Posies to Pearl Jam to the Foo Fighters to Thinking Fellers Union Local 282 to Archers of Loaf to Guided by Voices never figured out how to do a whole album, entirely important from start to finish, forgetting that the point of pop stardom is to bring together huge clumps of otherwise unaffiliated folks, and Pavement couldn't follow up the *Pacific Trim* EP with the requisite jubilant breakthrough (their *Let It Be*) and Cat Power and the Mountain Goats defiantly clung to Dylan pre-'65 and just would not let themselves fucking go and Tom Waits was too late with *The Black Rider* and Cracker waited too long to make *The Golden Age* and Yo La Tengo were inexplicably overlooked (how does that begin to happen?) and the fetish for releasing crappy home demos—whose very lack of finish lent them the steady hiss of a gradually disappointed public—succeeded only in stealing mid-decade credibility from keenly perfectionist pop stars like Robyn Hitchcock and Nick Lowe and They Might Be Giants precisely when they issued their masterpieces. What a decade of sleight-of-hands and comic mistimings this has been, as we emerge with none of our alt-spokesmen standing, and their industry support utterly squeezed out between urban enthusiasts and country-western fans. Only a few years back you'd catch major-label A&R kids speaking like mature individuals who'd survived relationship counseling, saying that certain acts had to be nurtured, talking about honesty and commitment, that audiences required respect, that expectations had to be patiently shaped. . . . Well, such talkers are no more, replaced now by bottom-dwellers dwelling on the bottom line who treat imaginative singers and songwriters with contempt, like one night stands. As a side consequence, not only have I been purged from the demographic that once used to nourish me, but also my demographic itself has been purged. People assure me the future is online and the underground will rise yet again, but lately my legs are cramping up, I'd like to sit down, so fuck you, how long am I supposed to wait? Should I be satisfied that Ween is nearly a household name? Am I to feel gleeful that Elliott Smith appeared at the Oscars alongside Celine Dion and that the money we paid for the song "Man on the Moon" now brings it back to us in movie form? That Royal Trux got $1,000,000 from Virgin (but still nobody knows who they are)? Or hey, what about this: Eno and Bowie promised a gigantic collaboration starting in 1995 with *Outside*—uh, well? Feel they no sense of betrayal? I can march up and down my aisle of favorite '90s records and almost all I see are artists who guaranteed something they didn't deliver or just got screwed (the one exception, I can be persuaded, is the Beastie Boys), or wonderful acts like the Lilys and Neutral Milk Hotel and Red Red Meat and Lambchop and the Spinanes who would've significantly altered our beloved revolutionary popscape had they been promoted with muscle and brains, or deserving music-makers in full possession of Dylan's proverbial head-full-of-ideas-that're-driving-them-insane like Mark Donato and Life in a Blender and Death Cab for Cutie and Very Pleasant Neighbor who couldn't even get their discs into shops.

Let me flash my headlamps more brightly at the confessional on-ramp to which I'm rhetorically hauling ass—namely, I like this band called Spoon. They're three fellows from Texas who in 1998—after a record and a half on a small-ish label—made *A Series of Sneaks* for Elektra. *Sneaks* has all the sounds of crushed fury and longing that I love, the thick-tongued words that appear super-significant but once deciphered only make sense in a found-object-collage-ist sorta way, the songs a minute or two in length. It's a record that stinks to high heaven of unbridled ambition (remember ambition?), reminiscent of Bruce Sterling—or some similarly pirate-minded attackist author person—assuring the *Times* that he wasn't trying to do *anything* with culture except *take it over*. But would the takeover be worth celebrating? Despite *Sneaks*'s old fashioned enthusiasm about itself, Spoon were quite cognizant of all the ways that '90s rock was supposed to bring us together but hadn't, because the breakthroughs didn't break through, or the geniuses croaked or choked.

I mostly listened to *Sneaks* to imagine the singer guy's face, a face I heard as resembling the young Joe Strummer, the young Paul Westerberg. The sneer, the hopefulness; the clouded gaze lit with fiery dawn. In truth, there lives no face not beautiful when painted in colors of passion and pride. Behind the brow furrowed in suspicion, in back of the scowl and the fed-up stubbornness, he sings as if understanding all we have riding on him, wanting more than anything to honor that.

By now you're assuming I've made up this record because 1) you've never heard of it, and 2) things that good get heard. They don't, though. A lot of good bands don't get signed, even more good bands make bad records, still more good bands make good records that're distributed or promoted badly. Out of nowhere our tastes change and we confound the moneymen. The music market is just the dance of so many random intangibles. . . . The record companies alertly stand to the side, conducting polls and dictating memos, as baffled as anyone about why we're sick of Alanis now but not yet over Britney, why we fickle folks like what we like. It's akin to the stock exchange really, a scene of bluffing gamblers, or a bunker full of addictive liars or con men guessing at the dreams of the customers—as Joseph did with Pharaoh—to thereby establish a wise reputation. Case in point, something went wrong, terribly wrong, with Spoon: before their imminent classic *Sneaks* ever had its chance to be "worked," some god gave them the finger. They were cut from Elektra's roster only four months after *Sneaks* came out. (*Four months!* Jello pudding snacks have a longer shelf life.) Of course, it's not just Spoon, that's what I'm saying — everyone who looked or sounded "indie" suddenly couldn't summon up enough sales to make big the eyes of the bigwigs. Spoon, for one, were not surprised, but that doesn't mean they weren't hurt.

Their response was a two-song CD — a "concept single" — addressed to Ron Laffitte (their former A&R guy at Elektra). Lacking any context, I assumed, when first I heard how these songs hovered between sobbing and spitting, that they were telling about a cruel ex-, or possibly an elected official who broke our hearts. *Are you ever honest with anyone?* "It's like I knew two of you, man," goes the vocalist, discouraged, disgusted, "one before and after we shook hands." The songs — "The Agony of Laffitte" and "Laffitte Don't Fail Me Now" — manage to say things which no band, to my knowledge, has ever sung to a former record company. They're not exercises in bratty name-calling and bellyaching. Whether people like Elektra Chairman Sylvia Rhone — who repeatedly assured Spoon she wouldn't drop them until she did exactly that — deserve our pity or not, Spoon apparently think so. These songs do not lack sympathy. The singer sings as one who is intimate with betrayal, even expects it, for he himself has gotten through life — as Spoon's only major-label title admitted — using a series of sneaks. This new release's balance of blame and fury and guilt and impatience sounds creepily like Kurt Cobain will once he's dug up and unplugged again.

RATTLED BY THE RUSH

S.M. STORMS AROUND LOWER MANHATTAN remembering the trees at dusk, how they'd once looked caramel-dipped, during those months of light and merry, and how brightly the taffy clouds of morning glowed after it was determined that nothing like parents or family mattered anymore; nothing; just candy. From that, what—frenzy? addiction? liberation? a decade earlier—he and Spiral Stairs, this guy, a friend from school, had begun the rock group Pavement. They were united in the decision to not call themselves by real names. They tried to make their first recordings appear like vinyl accidents, willful and erroneous, unhelpfully titled *Slay Tracks: 1933-1969* and *Demolition Plot J-7* and *Perfect Sound Forever*.

S.M. supposes that people think he's a bit, oh . . . pinched, because of how well he separates himself from his words, sees his songs as being sung in character and all that. He can't help it. His speech drones, cuts, dismisses, has all the life of a dial tone. He wants to believe that he possesses "a new openness," but just attempt to grant hundreds of interviews each year without developing a similar chilliness of soul and feeling like your every movement is monitored.

The video cameras show that his dark hair is cut in its usual conservative manner. S.M. passes through a series of sugarhouse stalls where Chinese dogs sniff the cuffs of his pants and mop the concrete with their blue-black tongues. Spat-out candies in crinkled-up balls of plastic litter his path, open wrappers everywhere. S.M. fidgets with a candy in his front pocket but doesn't unwrap anything. He knows that when people see this they think that he likes denying himself things, this is what the fans bicker about on the web, about this once when S.M. appeared to a certain reporter as if he weighed all of a hundred and twenty pounds and was overheard musing pleasantly about our ability to survive eating only air, and subsequently all this misinformation leaked out.

He's very familiar with this part of town, where the sugarhouse stalls are now. The neighborhood was torn up ten years before by riots, he'd been thoroughly kind on candy that night, and he'd seen the coppers on spooked steeds galloping down St. Mark's, and the Argentine who owned the big sugarhouses ordering his muscle boys to drive a truckful of candimonium packs over to the squatters (just like in some Damon Runyon story) so that they had bottles to throw at the helicopters.

S.M. lived right near here back then, with percussionist Bob, who had this hellish occupation with the transit authority at the time, driving a bus. Bob'd come home in a vulgar mood, sink into the couch and glare like an abused monkey. They'd unwrap a few candies and gratefully watch hockey players beat one another on the television set. By then the first few Pavement things had appeared to zero sales. Still, a baffling number of folks began to hear of Pavement. Nobody knew how or why. They crept into the dialogue like a good piece of vandalism, exactly as S.M.'d hoped — suddenly, anonymously, full of challenging implications. For a couple reasons — mainly ignorance and poverty — Pavement had left the studio with only recordings of studio accidents, first-takes, wan distortions, scratch vocals. To distract reporters from the bad mikings, S.M. talked as though by intention these were anti-songs, that they were committed to release the things that rock bands were supposed to record over; a brilliant strategy. In this way, Pavement became just as difficult to listen to as they were difficult to discuss.

In the suburban outskirts, S.M. was satisfied to learn, Pavement'd attracted a host of word-of-mouth legends: it was said they were television stars recording under fake names, that they were a middle-aged academic performing a cultural survey via false identities and noise collage experiments. Periodically an individual would find Pavement quoted by some half-reliable source as speaking of the need for silence. Nobody knew where they belonged. There'd be this passed-out drummer in some smudgy 'zine above a caption that read, "If you were wondering what you missed when you missed last month's Pavement gig—here it is!" This was the sort of information that was getting out. For a time S.M. succeeded so well in covering their tracks it seemed his Pave-men could turn out to be anything or anybody. Some reporter helped their cause when he wrote that they were building a band with the same surreptitiousness that insurgents make bombs; the reporter went on to say that he half-expected their identities to be revealed amidst a predawn ATF raid, babies in the background wailing, shopkeepers telling TV crews they had no idea that their quiet, well-behaved neighbors could've been "Los Pavementos." S.M. dug that write-up.

At the time, the candimonium underground was in a disquieting state of free-fall. All S.M.'s friends were throwing their papers into the air in disgust, their bodies heavy with hate. In small venues in, for example, Los Angeles, sugarbrains felt obligated to grab the stage, whether they deserved attention or not; out-of-tune Dylan rip-offs would get up there and the crowd'd boo and boo, unaware that one of these bald-stringed, big-eyed boys would soon turn into Beck. One's certainties were in turmoil; tastes were about to take a big turn; judgments changed hourly about what constituted a truly subversive lyric, a sincere rhythm. S.M.'s friends were easily moving twenty pounds of chocolate a day. The summoning of the "Alternative Demographic" was near.

It was convenient, in a sense, that when S.M. didn't fuck up, the band fucked up on his behalf; the first and biggest being Liberty Lunch, 1993, when they mismanaged their hugely important, super-industry-attended, make-or-break gig, after which Pavement's live reputation was so utterly shredded it never thoroughly rebounded—their drummer had gotten so nervous he'd candied himself into oblivion, rushed so that it took less than twenty minutes to complete the set, while the rest of the guys just stared at one another, unable to believe it, as this—the chance of a lifetime—blew up in their fucking faces.

Other conveniences and coincidences followed which helped to blur the precise meaning, point, sincerity of their music-making endeavor. For example, as someone had pointed out to S.M., Pavement's first full-length work arrived in stores the same week that Argentina captured its most-wanted assassin. The quotes attributed to the so-called "Candy Killer," and the leaked details of the Argentinian operation, segued seamlessly with statements attributed to the band on its press release. The impression thus engendered was that, with *Slanted and Enchanted*, elusive figures were coming above ground, emerging from the fog as a hard frost lay upon the fields like spun sugar.

What always bugged S.M. back then was how—against the reporters' newfound abilities to solve the mysteries posed by the band—so very few of these same reporters noticed the sudden coherence of his songs, their sound; that, yes, they could sustain a full song for the requisite number of verses and melodies, and knew how to alternate disconcerting ballads with droning narratives. Some half-baked reporter S.M. never really liked much ran this small thing about how Pavement was into noise in this charmingly approachable way, but what particularly irked S.M. was that he didn't elaborate—it wasn't thick off-putting buckets of ratt box racket but Sonic Youth's open tunings tentatively plucked on toy guitars. Live, S.M. tried to turn them into the quietest loud band around (it helped that they couldn't afford big amps and effects pedals); he was imagining as his musical model the scared silence a Syrian man might experience when an agent of Mossad lunges toward the man's left ear with a small lead-colored protuberance.

Soon enough, it was widely acknowledged that they'd developed into songwriters. Young sugarbrains, purchasing Pavement's *Watery, Domestic*, praised S.M. at this time for his irresistible melodies. Everyone thankfully put aside the thought puzzle that'd been Pavement's enigmatic partnership between 1990 and 1992. Reporters started treating S.M. like a spokesman, inquiring about his hair rinse and emotional well-being instead of pop subversion and the goddamn situationists. On their subsequent record, *Crooked Rain, Crooked Rain*, one of his songs coyly did its best to make the case that Pavement should be allowed to have their secrets back ("Right now!") but by then S.M. knew it was too late. They scored a hit, they mounted the big stages of the world. They even showed up on a late-night talk show, where S.M., thoroughly kind on candy, refused to shake the host's hand before an audience of many millions. The secrets were out. Reporters no longer had to wonder what they looked like or who they really were. Some of the purists were livid. A few bitterly denounced how the band's names were published along with their pictures — not taped as wanted posters in the post office but profiled as celebrities in glossy magazines. It felt like the world's greatest prank ever . . .

A light drizzle begins to fall and S.M. realizes, with an anguished pang, that for these last ten years he's only been able to hear the music of others as competition.

The rain smells of peppermint.

Big butterscotch leaves are knocked off the dying trees.

We won the revolution, S.M. suspects he'll say to a reporter some day, but we may've been wrong. Transcendence cannot be found on a diet of junk. All S.M.'s friends are going snowblind, driving around in blizzards looking for the stuff, or chasing down distant glows on the southwest horizon. He knows more and more people who have angrily protested the oppressive order of things by buying solid fuel rockets on the black market, attaching them to Chevy Impalas, and blasting off; they leave behind only 3 ft.-deep craters in cliffs and smoldering metal. No letters of protest ever survive the crash.

S.M. is aware that he hasn't any surprises left. Hundreds of interviews each year will leave pretty much no internal stone unturned. All Pavement can do is to keep making records. But at the very least S.M. wishes they didn't sound so spent as they settle into being rock stars. It's like, onstage, he's suddenly surrounded by old farts. The face of his bassist carries so many wrinkles he's begun to resemble the father on "The Waltons." Spiral, that guy from before, is married, losing his hair, becoming withdrawn. Percussionist Bob is fat now and owns a house. This whole project has turned into a real drag. Consciences crumble like confectioner's sugar, S.M. thinks: everyone is a liar, no one tells the truth, and nobody cares about anything but candy.

Under his umbrella just then pops the head of somebody passing by whose face he can't place, who reminds him to show up later at a bluegrass show. "I probably won't like it," S.M. mutters, as if to himself. "But I'll go."

He doesn't go. He's on the floor of an apartment in Astor Place instead, later, with his head propped against a table leg, eating take-out pizza and, at long last, unwrapping a candy. There's this hovering reporter in the room who's clearly dead-set on mischaracterizing S.M.'s prepared remarks. But S.M. feels fairly accepting of it and takes it all okay because his good friend Bingo is also there, and Bingo is the only guy S.M. feels can aright him lately. Bingo; wonderful, incapacitated Bingo; reckless, unrefined, and worldly, with his every response hurtling skyward, with nothing balled up inside him or clenched or self-conscious; Bingo, with his immediate exclamations and denunciations and his exceptional gift for fiction (see *Pure Slaughter Value* by Robert Bingham). Yes, Bingo is very near, yes indeed, joking with the reporter about how S.M.'s voice is so flat you can nail legs onto it, string it with a net, and play ping-pong on it, *har har*, and then shouting about how much he—Bingo—wants to finish that goddamn novel, his first, handsomely berating himself and singing knowledgably of his most intimate failings—the novel having been sold and everything and now the agents and editors are pissed off over Bingo's incessant sloth—

Music from childhood plays on a turntable across the room. S.M. can't keep from dreaming about the past, the better long ago times when he possessed Bingo's insane lusts, when S.M. and his friends would lie on piles of dirty laundry dreaming big lucid futures, utterly candied, thoroughly kind, as they dribbled their brains like basketballs and bounced ideas on trampolines . . .

He awakes to find that he's telling the reporter about the first record and about how badly it was recorded, how they first'd sought a dry record with no effects, like *Surfer Rosa*, but then decided to drench "Here" in reverb, as if that one feat would give the record variety.

Bingo looks up from the backgammon game he's playing with his girlfriend. "Hey! Live, when you play 'Here,' you gotta not rush it, man. It's a beautiful song! Slow it down!"

S.M. rolls his eyes behind small, rimless glasses, sighs. "Okay."

Bingo glances back at the game board in time to see his girlfriend roll doubles. He howls bloody murder. He hates to lose. In a few months, Bingo will marry this woman; a few months after that, his heart will seize up after being administered too much sugar at once and Bingo will be dead. He'll leave behind the novel (just completed), the wife, and S.M.

"DEAR CMJ . . ."

Publisher's Note: These posters appeared September 4-7, 1996, concurrent with the 16th annual College Music Journal (CMJ) music festival in New York City. A collective of contributors was formed ("The CMJoy Gang") to celebrate significant musical moments—past, present, or make-believe—that were missed by the music industry. The contributions were copied by hand in black ink onto sheets of coated poster paper. Below are the posters authored by Camden Joy.

Dear CMJ,

We left the coliseum discouraged, unable to distinguish the actual personnel of our favorite rock band from the life-like merchandise which sang and bandied about the stage, unable to discern actual flesh and faith from beneath the barrage of beverage ads circling in the sky. A satellite print-out on the giant screen kept us abreast of the band's latest sales figures per "cube," or cubic foot of product, a common unit for measuring wholesale distributors.

We attended out of affection for music, but we left with promotional grab-bags stuffed with useless souvenirs and shrine trinkets, insulting publicity knick-knacks, toothbrushes shaped like guitars, salt and pepper drum kits, transistor chips cynically planted in everything, playing our favorite band's number one hit.

We sat on the hood of the car in the parking garage and tried to remember why we liked anything. It occurred to us, very simply, that maybe we didn't. Day gave way to night, taking with it our hopes for contentment, our dreams of security. We found ourselves lost in remembering things the way they used to be, the way they might've been, the way they should've been.

We found ourselves lost.

We told anecdotes and jokes, argued what was important, what didn't matter, what got missed, that whiff of the ineffable. We made each other cry. If history is written by persons named Victor, then who is writing rock history but the collaborators and cowards who make their many millions and move on? What of the master music-makers who make lousy businessmen, the unsung singers, the significant artists who were born to lose, The Greatest Lost Musical Causes That Ever Were who have ended up on the outs with the racketeers and mobsters who put on the shows?

One of us suggested we kill the people in charge. We held a straw poll and voted the proposal down. Someone else made the motion that we kidnap unloved children and raise them in a made-up world. That proposition also lost. We got in our car. One of us insisted we march upon the cities where big decisions get made and declaim the names of forgotten heroes. The idea was narrowly rejected, though now we were getting close, you could sense it. At long last, we came to an agreement that we would write you open letters. Then we drove all night so that we couldn't be here tonight.

We are the CMJoy Gang. We like good music. Enjoy our reminiscences. Trust our advice.

Dear CMJ,

Just past Emporia we slowed for a hitch-hiker, a blind trumpet player late for a gig in Wichita. His name, I can't recall. Tender Tinderbox, Robert Nestor, something. This was Highway 35 in a blizzard. We were junked so incredibly bad as to be beyond words. Our minds were tin-foil, tin-foil hats, they were paper cans, our hearts were on anti-freeze, our radiator. We promised to drive him everywhere from now on. He stuck his horn out the window where the blue snow whistled in and he blew nothing we'd ever heard before. The capillaries in our legs went numb with the clarity of his tone, his notes cleared a path through the ice and smoke. Tiny shut-up houses appeared on the horizon, made entirely out of wood, they grew bigger, they shot past and vanished like how we wanted to. This was some time ago, a while back, who knows. We

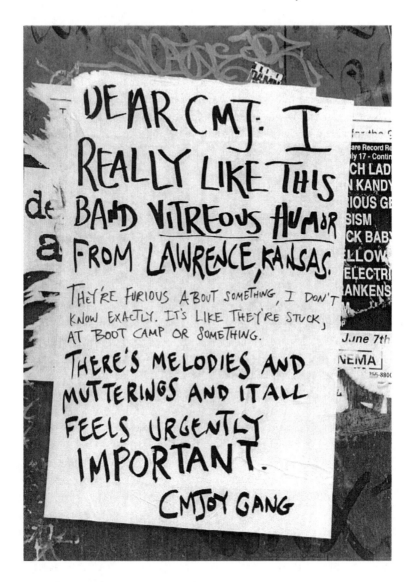

promised to meet a set of new friends, good friends this time, reliable ones, and they would form the nucleus of his fan club. There'd be talk shows and gossip columns, a classy clientele. The chains on our tires clobbered the road. *Ga-chunk, ga-chunk, ga-chunk*, they said all the way to Wichita. He was blind but he could see a little, fuzzy shapes mostly, a sense of light peeking through gloom, our party hats. He hadn't completely worked out his name. Carlton Cadbury, Bloozy Barry, I don't know. He was perhaps the greatest trumpet player who ever lived. Our wings were folded-up, useless in this weather, huge leaves stuck wetly to our sides, limp and burdensome. No one had ever been so brave as to attempt driving after doing this much medicine, as we called it, medicine, crud, garbage. We promised him a recording contract.

Dear CMJ,
Were someone in early March of 1989 to've dialed the phone number (307) 482-1065 and asked for the youngest in the household, they would've been handed to me, eternally the baby of the family. They would've interrupted me listening to cassette tapes sent to me by my sister, who had fled the backwoods of Natrona for a new-age hippie university in California. On my cassette player, Pitch-a-Tent bands would've been playing. My sister had started dating a guitarist named Jerome. Pitch-a-Tent was a small record label distributed through Rough Trade. It lasted a few years, then went somewhere. Jerome was in a band that recorded for Pitch-a-Tent. Unfortunately, I did not learn the name of his band. It was either River Roses, Wrestling Worms, Ten Foot Faces, Donner Party, or Spot 1019, which were the Pitch-a-Tent bands I heard via my sister. These excellent bands—unavailable everywhere, not even in cut-out bins—I am unclear what became of them. If I was still acquainted with Jerome I would ask; unfortunately, my sister married a guy in the Engineering School, and Jerome is a name that no longer gets spoken.

Dear CMJ,
My middle son used to practice up near Port Authority, renting space in a rehearsal warehouse called Big Top. He and his bandmates spent $15/hour to rent a room with a PA.
 I'd go uptown sometimes to meet him after rehearsal and help carry home his equipment. As I emerged from the subway I'd hear all the Big Top bands going, big salsa outfits, long-hair guitar bands, country swing bands, gospel jazz bands. The source of the cacophony was invisible, all of it blasting

seemingly from nowhere, because Big Top was a building that looked like any other. I'd worry momentarily if I wouldn't be sure which of these particular bands belonged to my son. I remembered the time my son told me his band's name was in the newspaper, in the club listings. I slowly turned every page of the club listings and looked at thousands upon thousands of band names, thinking how for each four-piece listed that meant eight parents were in the city right now somewhere trying to pick out the name of their kid's band. Of course I didn't tell my son how strangely sad this made me. I told him I was very, very proud.

Eventually, my son would emerge from Big Top sweating, his face puffy and red, his voice hoarse, as if he was in training, which I guess in a sense he was. I'd ask him how it went and he'd shrug, discouraged. His descriptions would take me into rooms where the soundproofing hung off loose tacks, the rugs were thick and matted with filth, the PA was impossible and the mikes shocked you. Apparently, getting a good "mix" of all the instruments at Big Top was difficult as it seemed you couldn't hear one another no matter how loud you turned up. My son said that whenever his group wasn't making music they'd be blasted by a variety of musical styles from the bands above, the bands below, the bands to either side, and these bands always sounded tighter and more polished and better than his own.

It occurred to me to comfort him by suggesting that these other Big Top bands could not be better because if they'd achieved great prominence they would have been practicing in nicer spots. But you know, I've read that there are Big Tops in every American city, a building where twenty or thirty musical outfits practice round the clock, and again, strangely, it makes me sad to consider the number of bands that never make it. Because I know my middle son, and I know he's talented.

Dear CMJ,
On tour the good feelings persisted from San Diego to Tucson, but then in Texas the opening bands started . . . well, sucking. After Dallas, we didn't leave the dressing room until we had to go on, we couldn't stand it, we got so sad watching these

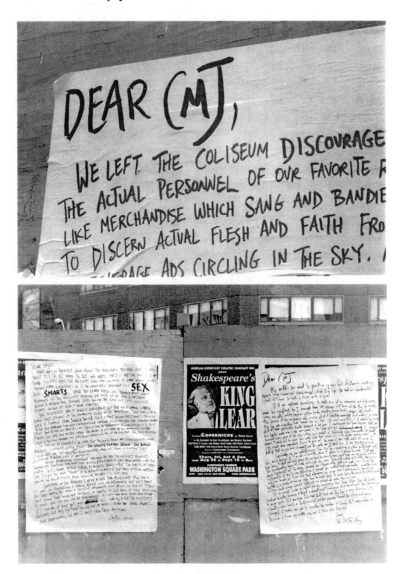

uninspired glamor-seeking sad-boy opening bands. Same with
Austin and Houston. Baton Rouge was sweet, friendly, but
still we were paired up with someone who . . . sucked. And
on and on, Florida, Georgia, &c. Warily I emerged once—this
was the concluding show, actually—this was Chapel Hill—we
ran out of beer backstage—accidentally I overheard the

opening band—*Wow!* Fantastic! I remembered, suddenly, my best friend had described this very band to me: brilliant, tight, Minutemen attributes with country western flavorings. After the set I started to tell them how good they were, told them that my best friend really dug them. Then—wow! Suddenly—whoops!—I remembered something else. The band my best friend described, they were called Wampum. This band was Uncle something . . . Uncle Tupelo.

Uncle Tupelo later got some notice and then split into two outfits, a haunting one and a silly one. But I still think of Uncle Tupelo as the opening band that wasn't Wampum. Wampum never got to Chapel Hill or anywhere as far as can be determined. I never heard them. My best friend still raves about Wampum.

Dear CMJ,

What was so terribly good about the Alleycats, you ask, and as an adult it's a bit hard to put into words. Partly it was the innocence of those pre-MTV days. The Alleycats were good like music is good when you're young and everyone's in it for meaningful reasons like sex and smarts. Once you learn words like "demographic" what remains of the Alleycats freezes and falls out of your bloodstream, never to return, and someone slaps you on the back and says, 'Welcome aboard, grown-up. Here's your nametag.'

The Alleycats had a barely available LP out on a small label when they appeared at the community center of my hometown. They were a trio, with a female lead singer bassist and a guitarist songwriter I always assumed to be her husband who had coordination lacking like a hard drug user. Somebody played drums. Their record was okay but live—well, it was the difference between kissing with your mouth shut and your mouth open. Two groups of kids came to the comunity center show: 1) the teen moshers and 2) my friend Melvin Toff and me. After one song, the teen moshers were led out by security because they began to dance, which everyone knew was against community center rules. The lights stayed down. The band could not see that only two audience members were left, Melvin and myself. They continued playing like it mattered.

After remaining significant unknowns for years, the Alleycats renamed themselves something ridiculous like Zegon & the Planetoids, like their name was the reason they'd never gotten noticed by powerful people—but I'll say right here that I'd put the song "Today" by the Alleycats up against just about anything, nyc, the Bill of Rights, Mike Scioscia, my Mom, watermelon, it's that good.

Sometimes in Los Angeles I used to see the Alleycats open for X. It was no competition. X would meekly come on afterwards but that's about all they would do—make a reluctant appearance, like Spinks did against Tyson—they knew they could not compare. X wanted to just pack up their stuff and go home. And look now who got remembered—X!—look who owns homes and stuff—X!—look who at least gets gigs nowadays—X! And try to find the Alleycats anymore, just try, I'm sure they're out of music—dead or gone away—and Melvin Toff, well, he and I don't even talk anymore.

Dear cmj,

It's hard to remember all the names of all the great bands that have been. I would like to list them here for you but if all I heard from them was a 45 or a demo cassette, they never got that first foothold and their names won't even come to mind anymore. They are gone, as if they'd never bothered to do anything at all. Why *did* they bother? Do you know how hard it is to write a song, much less a good song, much less one you'd be happy to play once a night for the rest of your life? Plus it's hard enough to find musicians you can stand to be around, much less enjoy. Then you have to make music with them (always difficult) and travel with them (impossible). Soon there's a girlfriend squabble or someone goes nuts, their focus gets a little derailed, and they have no more money to go into the studio and record (that's so expensive, really), and then there's the high costs of manufacturing and distributing their own product. I'm getting far off the subject. I mean simply to say that, for the last several decades, bands of youths have been disappearing by the vanload, faster than helium balloons fading from view in the upper atmosphere after some big champagne-filled day of public addresses and released balloons.

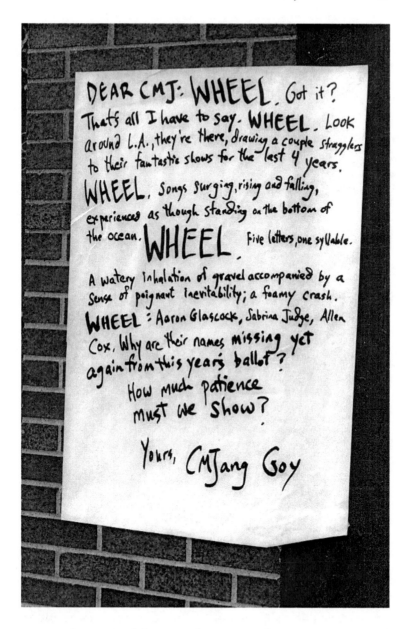

I speak to you of this as a short man who is conscious at all times of his dissatisfying height and repulsive appearance. It took the Christians centuries to undo the barbaric standards of beauty put into place by the Greeks—how have these

standards suddenly returned to us?—and now what holy and compassionate force, sacrosanct and inviolate, can emerge to undo our culture's addiction to disposability, to superstition and superficiality, to the ignorant charm of the instant, a fixation on tall people who everywhere cruelly stand in our way and pollute the rivers and tell their dumb tall tales and wreck scientific inquiry and run up the debt and without apology brainwash us with the same bands over and over rather than allowing genuine alternatives to step to the fore. An alternative music festival—ha! Give me a break. Let's see some repulsive short people up there, rocking out, godammit.

Dear CMJ,
Sitting in the bucket seat beside my young neighbor, while her bones throbbed and the car stereo played (in her words) "the one song" that helped her "through all this agony," a bad song from Heart, a bad band, this taught me a great deal; I was moved by the details of her horrifyingly impossible-to-diagnose ailment, I was grossed out by this song and by how my neighbor swiveled in the seat to the rhythms and sang along with eyes shut. Her teeth, they had to replace them with piano keys, her gums were black with rot, her body hated her, her brain was sick. It hurt to comb her hair, to turn on a light, to dial a phone. Heart, though, was totally excellent, Heart helped. What am I gonna say, I'm gonna complain that she lacked taste? I heard her puttering around all night long, she never slept from the migraines and the aching joints. I think she was dying.

Dear CMJ,
In the summer of 1988 I saw a flyer on Bleecker Street advertising a musical performance by Memorial Garage. I did not attend the performance and subsequently never saw flyers or any mention of this group again. A reward is hereby announced for anyone able to provide me with information leading to Memorial Garage. With a name that good, it seems a shame they never got heard.

Dear CMJ,
Many are the crimes committed against ambitious youth in these days but none seem to me more egregiously unredressed at this very moment than that Bob Wiseman—for all his tumult of talent, his ear, his voice, his hand, his eye, his sense, his drive—remains everyday a nobody, shackled and jeered as was Rembrandt by the bankers on the cigar box. Too big-hearted to fit underground, too big-pictured

to grovel for your crumbly cashews, Bob Wiseman by any other name (in any other time) would be a rose, he would've arose, a hero of protest, a celebrated conscience, our wise man. Even his precise number of releases has been rendered tough to pinpoint — *In Her Dream* (sorta on Warner Bros.), *Lake Michigan Soda* and *City of Wood* (available in Canada), *In By Of* (a compromised greatest hits collection), countless instrumental CDs (maybe available somewhere), a new release already recorded (will it never arrive?). Thanks to my friend

Mark—and to Wif Stenger—for showing me Bob Wiseman, but now the work begins, we must see him to the top of the charts or it is all in vain.

Dear CMJ,
When I worked the arts and entertainment beat at the Pascagoula newspaper (not a difficult assignment, you wouldn't think) we were often hand-delivered seven-inch vinyl from a small local label called Mississippi Sound. It was roots stuff, old-timers from Petit Bois and Chandeleur Islands playing gut-stringed things and banging on silverware and tins, younger folk from upriver performing hand-me-down historical laments, genuine and haunting. Each seven-inch was not just fantastic but fantastically different. We did all we could to promote both the acts and the label, wrote them up with big headlines and whatnot, but I guess it sure wasn't enough. Bad luck prevailed. The label suffered a power boilover in their manufacturing plant, which ignited their entire back catalog. Even worse, in seeking to contain the blaze, the fire department flooded the basement, which ruined all the reel-to-reel master tapes. Nothing whatsoever was salvaged. Mississippi Sound folded.

These good people who churn out such incredible music . . . who can say what becomes of them? They go back to their families, to their jobs at the tire factory, they lock their instruments in the closet and try to shake off their dreams.

I often think that many more people get away with bad things than we ever realize, sinners everywhere walk these hills, schemers and molesters, and I even think how we pass murderers probably every day without knowing it, and all the while we're thinking how pleasant and charming they seem.

But you could just as easily think, and I have begun to do this (although I must remember to do it more often!), how many of these anonymous ones might be musicians with no place to play, they probably had divine songs going on inside them once long ago, and, you know, who knows, maybe even some of them were responsible for the magic which, for that briefest of times, was Mississippi Sound.

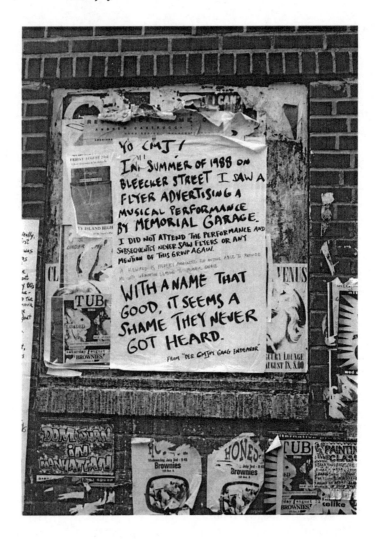

Dear CMJ,

You are indeed right, possibly the most intriguing—if not the most virulent—of alleged rock-and-roll conspiracies concerns the single by the Lopez Beatles which was said to've been snuck aboard the first of NASA's Voyager space probes. The Voyagers, you will recall, were outer-space time capsules. They contained carefully accumulated cultural remnants intended to convey humankind's essence, perhaps billions of years from now, to whatever alien civilization ultimately retrieved them. Everything that went into the Voyager was documented in a content catalog (available free of charge from the GAO as #4A-VOYAG-567ESD.4). But the story goes that a few insiders sabotaged, or, at least, supplemented, NASA's time capsule efforts by ensuring that in addition to indisputable classics like Bach, Mozart, and others deservant of eternal memory, the space probe carried our grittier stuff too. Recently making the rounds on the web is a parallel content catalog (#4A-VOYAG-567ESD.5), purportedly dug out of a government vault and containing the space probe's actual contents, as opposed to the catalog (ESD.4) released to the public. The highly suspect ESD.5 indicates angel dust, billfolds, pornographic magazines, and parking tickets were also sent into space, as well as a piece of seven-inch vinyl by the band the Lopez Beatles. (The Lopez Beatles appear to have become the focus for such persistent rumors due mainly to their own mysterious disappearance; some lucky ones have heard their classic single "Bitchen Party," but few know where they came from or went to subsequently. Scientology is mentioned.) Those that have seen the original ESD.5 swear by its authenticity. They point out the Treasury Department's own intricate watermark (which cannot be counterfeited), and that ESD.5 was printed on official rare-fibered State Department paper and stamped "High Access" in so-called Pentagon ink.

NASA officials thusfar refuse to comment on this story.

Dear CMJ,
There was a band I saw once I greatly enjoyed but I never learned their name. Does that count? Of course it counts. My circumstances were unusual. The Indy 500 had concluded, the tented pageantry all folded up, but I couldn't seem to quit town. A local invited me to see the sights. "The sights?" I choked, remembering — naturally — that Tyson had offered the same to Desiree Washington — "come over, you and me, we'll go see the sights of Indianapolis" — before he raped her. Was I afraid? Of course not, with what I'd already been through, of course not. I mean, they called my cousin up before Congress and called him a liar, they put my parents in prison. What more could they do to me? Nothing, so far as I could figure.

So I went and we ended up at some motel lounge, watching this great band, the one I've been trying to tell you about, if you would just take off your Walkman long enough to hear me speak. Forget it. Just forget it. I will tell you about how intensely the guitarist played, fueled and focused, how she was better than Hendrix by as much as Hendrix was better than everybody else, and you will ask me about her measurements, her build. I will speak of lyrics which reverberated with the galvanized fragility of Mary Oliver's poems and you will ask if she seemed raunchy, hot, babe-ilicious, if we couldn't find a spot for her on one of your TV's supermodel programs. You can't see — can you, CMJ? — that to be petrified as I was in Indiana is to be lost, adrift, capable of anything, and this great motel band, whoever they were, they were telling me: "adrift," well that's just another name for "alive," my friend.

Dear CMJ,
Naturally you cannot know how hard it is to make music — whatever it is you call yourselves you're bankers and businessmen, not musicians — but I'm willing to give you the chance to hear this quote and pretend you are somebody who can genuinely appreciate it, even though the quote is about the process of painting, because the same quote applies to the struggle of music-making, and music after all is how all you people pay your bills: "Just before his death, when I informed him that I had given up painting because I just couldn't paint, Richard Diebenkorn gave me an incredulous glance: 'Of course you can't paint. Nobody can paint. I can't paint. You just go ahead and do it anyway. It is the marvel of this enterprise that you set out to do something utterly impossible. You must forget about time, money, fame, loved ones and all the rest and just stand there putting it on and scraping it off until you achieve the impossible. That's how it works.'" Do you understand now why I weep for those who braved the treacherous waters only to lose their way? I just want to see all these bands receive the rewards they deserve, that's all.

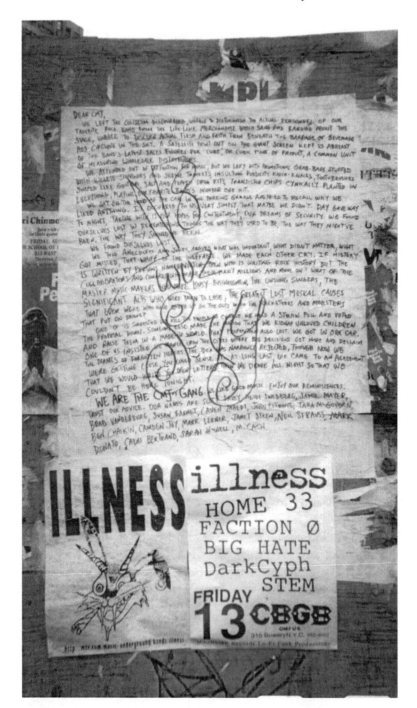

Dear CMJ,
The Rolling Stones were on *Saturday Night Live* and they played
some stuff from *Some Girls* and Mick kissed Ron (or Keith)
with his tongue but I didn't catch it because that same night
I was attending my *first rock show* (the Rotters) in an outdoor
bandshell (more a dip in the grass) in chilly Isla Vista near
beachy UCSB and they did mostly covers by the Sex Pistols (not
dead yet) and Devo (who were unknown back then outside
the Hollywood club circuit) except they did play one original
I remember at least called "Sit on My Face, Stevie Nicks" (I
could still sing the heavenly chorus for you, if you'd like) and
they called each other names of Roy Lichtenstein paintings
like "BLAM!BLAM!" and "Grrrrrr!" and one of them (the guitarist)
went to elementary school with my oldest brother and meanly
made fun of his clothes (I didn't know this until later) and the
vocalist looked (come to think of it) a lot like Eric Bogosian
and had this long-legged short-skirted girlfriend beside the
stage and he pogoed through the tiny crowd (first time I'd

seen pogoing) and I thought the Rotters were all I ever wanted to see of the future of music but I was twelve, did you ever listen to me, of course not, they broke up and went away.

Dear CMJ,
I had this bass teacher in eighth grade, bass guitar. Heaven only knows where he came from. He taught out of the one music store in our town. He had poor hygiene, bad manners, no aptitude for teaching. He also had a band—"Engine Machine"—which was on the verge of "happening." The first half of each bass lesson would be spent struggling to recall if I'd been assigned any homework the previous week. It seemed likely, but my teacher was too stoned to be sure. I thought he was ludicrous—did my parents know they were funding this

fraud? I changed the subject, brought up Engine Machine. We spent the last half of each lesson discussing his band. He'd brag about the groupies, the fawning photographers, the blown-away soundmen, the jam-packed gigs, the adoring clubowners, the A&R meetings. After three months I think I had learned maybe two things, the C-major scale and how to tune the bass guitar. One week I informed my parents I didn't need to go anymore, that was it, I was an accomplished musician, the end. They called the music store and canceled the lessons. As for Engine Machine, I checked the bins at the record store but never saw their release. There was this record by Engine Dynamite, but I think that was someone else, so I never bought it.

Dear CMJ,
The life of our party is a French emigre named Claude Bessy, who as Kick-Boy Face made the pronouncements that made us what we are today. He was a brilliant polemicist, humorist, editor, songwriter. He's in *The Decline of Western Civilization*, you can see him there. Everyone who wrote for him deserved Nobel Prizes for Literature, this was Top Ranking Jeffrey, Craig Lee, and a ton of other now-dead people. His magazine was a trash-papered inky combustible rag named *Slash*—it's lost to us now—there were financial problems or something, he pursued the girl he loved across to England, he could not be reached for comment. It vanished, he vanished, everything went.

SURVIVING SINATRA

RECENTLY A ROOMFUL OF PEOPLE were almost killed by Frank Sinatra.

The scene was a Turkish kabob house in lower Manhattan. This is my neighborhood hang-out; the sort of place where only the employees are permitted to smoke, and the walls are amply coated in grease. I go there because so do a lot of others, Muslim cabbies on their breaks, fashion students from Kyoto, elegant immigrants from Teheran, techno gals in floor-length flares and techno boys in ball caps with bent-down brims.

So there we all were the other day, eating grilled lamb and deep-fried balls of chick peas off styrofoam plates with plastic forks and knives, when suddenly we heard a new sound—a television! Now many of you have already seen televisions, and most of us had too, but the surprise of it in my local kabob-ery was that thus far we'd only heard Turkish radio. So with all due respect we turned to look at it, as tradition tells you to do whenever anyone switches on a television in your presence.

There was a black and white movie. There was a man twitching on a train. There was a woman wearing pearls and a great deal of mascara, hairspray, and lipstick. There was Janet Leigh. And there was Frank Sinatra.

There are moments in a crowd when America makes so much sense, when you want to scream BRING ME YOUR TIRED, YOUR POOR, YOUR HUNGRY, AND LET'S ALL DIG FRANK SINATRA. I mean to say, this was one such moment.

So all of us fell silent, as again custom holds is the courteous thing to do when a television plays in a public setting, and through the steam of onions browning in olive oil we watched *The Manchurian Candidate*.

159

Now I have always wondered why you can never go into a place and hear my favorite Sinatra albums, his sad albums like *No One Cares* or *In the Wee Small Hours*, and instead you only hear songs like "New York, New York." Well, there's a reason, and it's the same reason restaurants have to be careful when his movies are on TV—it's a possible Health Code Violation: you can die from Sinatra.

In the movie, Sinatra is coming apart. He sets a cigarette between his lips, and it falls into his scotch and water. He looks around, embarrassed. Only Janet Leigh is watching. He tries to light a match, drops it, manages to light one—but his hands shake too badly and the match goes out. He asks Janet Leigh whether she minds if he smokes and their eyes meet and they fall in love. She tells him she doesn't mind at all, please do. He tries to light one up again, looks like he's going to vomit, bursts out of his chair, knocks over his drink, and runs.

There in the Turkish kabob house, our mouths were full of babaghannush and hummus and chopped beef and baby lamb . . . but all of us had stopped chewing. We were too struck by what we were seeing: a man we all recognized—that famous widow's peak, that trim waist, those eyebrows drifting up there on his forehead like lost rainclouds—was on the television about to break down.

People will tell you Sinatra and Elvis Presley were similiar talents in that they both sang and acted well; but the fact is, there's no picture Elvis ever shot which didn't obligate him to do songs, whereas Sinatra made most of his movies without singing. In fact, in the movie we were all watching, he was about as far from bursting into song as anybody can be.

Sinatra has tried to flee the woman but she follows him. She is clever and gorgeous. Her eyes are dark as Turkish coffee and her voice like baklava. She asks him where his home is. He can't look at her. He seems to be thinking: *She doesn't know what she's doing.* His voice catches on every syllable as he tells her he's in the army. His eyelids flutter. He sucks on the cigarette she has lit for him. Some part of him is dying to get out of the conversation but that part of him is losing the battle. Softly he asks Janet Leigh for her name, in such a way that it's clear her name is the one thing he's always had to know. But he's even more confused by her answer. He sighs, apparently at everything—the magnitude of life, of conversations, the sheer difficulty of what names we should call one another.

We all know people who hate Frank Sinatra for all sorts of reasons, mostly for how he treats other human beings in so-called real life, and they dismiss the undeniable beauty of his talent because of his undeniably sick soul. I wonder if these people had been in the Turkish kabob house with us what they would think seeing this scene, in which Janet Leigh, acting entirely on our behalf, reaches out to save this fragile bird-boned boy. As with his best albums, Sinatra doesn't seem to be going from any script. There aren't printed-up lyrics and dialogue for this kind of thing. This isn't acting; it's the real stuff. He is standing before us, letting his feelings utterly overwhelm him. It's scary. Perhaps Frank Sinatra is a bad person but he defines the word "presence." In this scene, he says almost nothing, he exhales and sweats and looks away, and yet Janet Leigh, who does all the talking, seems barely alive by comparison.

It's time I mention what else was happening in our Turkish kabob house and that was that all of us—employees, bike messengers, cabbies—felt Sinatra's confusion so completely that we ourselves were about to cry . . . we would have been crying, that is, if our throats weren't clogged up with Turkish cuisine. Sinatra can barely talk. We could barely breathe.

On the television, Janet Leigh starts to tell Sinatra who she is, then she stops, instead tells him her address, tells him the apartment number, her phone number. She gently asks him if he can remember it. His larynx closes up as he tells her, yes. You aren't sure how to take this response because he still can't look at her. Janet Leigh repeats the phone number and he turns even further from her, shakes his head slightly, closes his eyes in weariness.

In that moment, finally, after attentively watching this, the whole group of us in the kabob-ery began to cough. Most everyone was choking back tears but by this time many of us were choking on shish kebab too, great wads of barbecued meat stuck somewhere mid-swallow. We were gagging into napkins, downing our sodas, poking ourselves in the ribs, crossing our hands at our throats. The look of serious injury was on everybody's face and then, abruptly, just like that, it was gone. We were okay, we would be fine. We looked up at the television. Sinatra, our would-be killer, was breathing easier too.

OBSERVING MURDER

MELVIN TOFF TOLD ME HE used to hate the sport of boxing for its pretensions to valor, grace, art, its "history" of "pageantry." Then he confirmed what a glorious sewer, what an unapologetically sick practice, it had become in recent times, and called it cool. By the time we'd met, Melvin had taught himself all the most famous tragedies of the ring, not just the date and place but the purse involved, the amount each boxer was supposed to've made. He held that, "the value of each man is determined by the amount he would accept to receive a public beating." He recounted vivid descriptions of brain-deadening blows which made millions, Jerry Quarry's subdural hematomas, nerve damage to the brainstem of Frank "The Animal" Fletcher, gliding contusions inside Sugar Ray Leonard's brain. Through Melvin's eyes, boxing's noble past was just a fast-forward collapse of noses, heads, spirits.

May 1995, Melvin and I pulled into Las Vegas; he intent on watching grown men slug one another, me intent on gambling most our money away. At the 21 table, my cocktail waitress had a ponytail, acne; I worked to turn her into an old love—someone I'd lost—without success. She was just another in the long line of somebodies I'd never get to know. She sized up my sad situation, inquired, "Is there anything more I can do for you?"—she drew a slow breath, reemphasized—"Anything at *all*?"

I could conceive of requesting only that she become someone else; instead I shook my head, "Of course not."

The highlight of our visit was to be the battering of L.A.'s gorgeous golden boy De La Hoya as he went after the belt that belonged to brawling Rafael Ruelas. But first, on the undercard, Gabriel Ruelas, Rafael's elder brother, defending his title against some tiny long-haired Colombian who wouldn't fall down. The Colombian's name: Jimmy Garcia. Though completely outpunched from second one, Garcia stood and stood, shaking off referees and physicians that he might accept more blows to the face and ribs. The flags, pennants, the streamers dripped red, the colorful floor slogans grew ruined from Garcia's blood. After eleven rounds they called it. Garcia went over to his corner where, finally, he sat. I was relieved. He appeared disappointed. A moment passed, and Garcia lost consciousness. Melvin was thrilled. EMTs loaded Garcia onto a waiting ambulance. The next fight promptly began. For the next two weeks, Gabriel Ruelas prayed at Jimmy Garcia's hospital bedside, but it achieved little. He succumbed to his brain injuries on the anniversary of Marie's birth—May 19.

It was our second murder together, the first being Peter Tosh. Tosh always seemed a friend, keeping in close touch (via car stereo) until the bad luck day Melvin and I dashed through a motel in Gallup for a bucket of ice and afterwards, just like that, found his murder awaiting us at the top of the news hour. Our fault? Melvin Toff's tenderness boiled away, never to return. His solution was to joke: Someone had, like, exploded Peter Tosh's consciousness, man, literally blown his mind, had reshaped his head laterally, he'd got hisself kilt, a bepistoled individual had done to him what Listerine does to bad breath and now Tosh's career was down the drain, he was all over, as in—*hee hee*—all over the drapes and carpets, &c. None of his jokes were effective, of course. I immediately flipped my Tosh tapes over, scanning their other sides; where, for example, on the back of my copy of *Bush Doctor*, I found Melvin had hometaped me some Warren Zevon.

I know it seems like a big deal leaping Tosh to Zevon in nothing flat, but I stink oh-so-bad at grieving. And I admit, devouring them in this order, with Tosh first as the palate cleanser, it took forever before I tasted "the thing" about Zevon; namely, that he oozed disloyalty, a Bel Air whistleblower who took enigmatic pride in running down the old order (himself right along with it), a self-loathing traitor to his Linda

Ronstadt class. His characters, initially sympathetic, unveiled their true ugliness in a wink, gave themselves away with an inopportune sigh. So his sessions were in truth subversive (although they sounded SoCal bland, miked and mixed so that you could almost hear the coke-nosed engineers as they blithely unwrapped still more reels of overpriced two-inch recording tape).

Melvin always challenged me as to why there had been no musical yet about boxing, imagining librettos recounting Oliver McCall's inner turmoil during the Lennox Lewis title bout or the aria potential of Golota's castrato-inducing Bowe low-blows. He loved to point out how boxing and music are two such similar sports: the potential for ugliness, the stand-alone arrogance of each. Where else are your bare privates made so public, except (perhaps) when performing live sex acts for money?

The truth is, sensitive singer/songwriter types no longer lose sleep over what transpires in the boxing ring. The last such tune, the one that killed pugilistic anthems rather as *The Searchers* killed Westerns, was probably Warren Zevon's "Boom Boom Mancini," one of Melvin Toff's favorites, in which Zevon's infamous chilliness hits a fate-obsessed apex. At the outdoor arena of Caesar's Palace (where thirteen years later we cheered the death of Jimmy Garcia), Ray "Boom Boom" Mancini had hammered blood clots loose in the head of Duk Koo Kim. It was the most vile thing any Mancini had performed, Melvin liked to hiss, since no-relation Henry directed the Pink Panther Philharmonic at the Hollywood Bowl.

The sinister Cochise-on-the-warpath tribal blues of Zevon's "Boom Boom Mancini," said Melvin Toff, is the unresolvable drama of darkness eternally in our midst. Mancini is a hero troubled by nothing, least of all a conscience. "Hurry home early," drily encourages the singer, perhaps quoting a boxing advertisement, "Hurry on home. Boom Boom Mancini is fighting Bobby Chacon." To back up this advice Zevon spends two verses applauding Mancini's ferocity. Then, out of nowhere, at the bridge, Mancini meets Death, in the form of the deceased former champion Kim. Mancini shrugs. We suddenly understand that this is where such courage always lands us; the true glory of boxing is callousness.

Bobby Chacon was our local favorite, former champion featherweight, former champion junior lightweight, the bad-ass from Oroville. People I knew drove more than two hours into Reno that January night, 1984, to watch the ring fill with ghosts. The match would, it was widely believed, be well-attended by the spirit world. Not only was the expectation that Mancini would be distracted by a vision of his murder victim but Chacon was to be visited by his first wife, who'd killed herself two years prior rather than watch the man she loved continue to box (common lore had it she appeared still to enjoy popping up at such events now and again). And there was the small matter of the soul of Chacon's unborn child which sat ringside in the belly of his second wife.

They near-rioted, chucked magazines and shoes, ice cubes and beer cans, they, the near-capacity crowd of 11,104, when referee Richard Steele stepped in, a minute seventeen into round three, before Chacon could even drop, before any of the planned-for ghosts showed up at all. Even the heavyweight champion, Larry Holmes, rarely a great enthusaist for things supernatural, complained it was too soon. "I had to almost kill Leon Spinks before Steele would stop it."

But Chacon was so grateful he thanked the referee for intervening. "You said you were my friend but if you were my friend," Chacon challenged Mancini afterwards, "why'd you have to beat me up so bad?" Chacon seemed to forget momentarily that this was Boom Boom Mancini, after all, and he could stagger anybody, friends or enemies, with successive jabs, whack their chins and cut their eyes, drop them with unseen left hooks which connected like thrown concrete, because *he was Boom Boom Mancini* . . . just as Holmes also hadn't remembered the terrifically bad manners of bragging about nearly killing a man in the ring within earshot of a boxer who actually had. Warren Zevon remembered for both of them—but his "Boom Boom Mancini" is about something else, not the boxer or the sport but the futility of forgiveness. This singer won't grant absolution, which is fine by Boom Boom Mancini; he knows better than to seek it. The value of a life has become exactly what Melvin Toff calculated; the price one accepts to be beaten in public.

Or maybe that's not Zevon's point at all. Maybe the point is the abruptness of the song's shift—that a paean to a brave athlete can become, within a measure or two of music, a horror story. Every moment of life presents some opportunity to wreck—you miscalculate a shift in traffic or forget to pull out before coming. Somehow we find ourselves outside relationships, without love. Sometimes it's not even a choice, just an unfair confluence, bad luck. Let's say you uncharacteristically lose your temper—but it's when the paparazzi are around; perhaps a lethal shot discharges from the pistol you were promised was unloaded. This was Mancini's fate—in executing his job's responsibilities he merely traveled one punch too far and spattered blood all over his formerly playful nickname. Now he's hailed on the street as the guy who killed that Korean. Now Melvin Toff never tells me what he's feeling. Zevon's lumbering voice in "Boom Boom Mancini" says it all, his affect flattening as the batteries in his heart audibly peter out. Hearing this, I cannot help but admit how, given a second chance, we'd kill Jimmy Garcia all over again without even hesitating.

THIRTY-SEVEN POSTERS
ABOUT SOULED AMERICAN

*Publisher's Note: These posters appeared throughout the summer of
1997. A collective was formed, similar to the CMJOY Gang. Contributors
focused upon a single unheralded act, the Chicago band named Souled
American. The posters measured from 2 feet to 4 feet in height, and
were designed by Mark Lerner of Rag & Bone Shop. Those that follow
were authored by Camden Joy.*

Our First Encounter

We would go quite often, usually once a month but sometimes
more, sometimes once a week or more, to see a guitarist named
Kevin Trainor, who had a band called the Surreal McCoys and
was in the Special Guests.

Trainor was coolness itself, with an easy charisma to the
way he played. In his hands a guitar seemed very simple. He
was handsome, funny, intelligent. He sang in an old style with
a deep powerful voice.

One night, Sunday night, early 1989, we went to the Rodeo
Bar to see Trainor play with the Special Guests (who now
called themselves "5 Chinese Brothers"). The Rodeo Bar had
free peanuts (we called them "dinner"), no cover, and relatively
cheap beer.

We were carrying instruments, having come straight from
a rehearsal. We tried to time our arrival to avoid any opening
acts but were unsuccessful in this.

What do I remember? I remember a tall slim guy with
mirror shades playing an acoustic guitar with a pick-up

through an amplifier—it sounded like mine! This tall guy was singing from his heart, in a choked drawl. We were skeptical snots, eager to insult anything, and even before we found seats we had exchanged looks of ridicule. We all had things to criticize—the bassist is ruining the songs, playing all over them! The drummer isn't even facing his kit! The songs are all too slow! That singer's not enunciating!

Before we could say a thing, however, the music made itself felt. It was truly unparalleled that all of us would be in immediate agreement on the beauty of another band's sound, but there it was. Our songwriter found something to like, the cradling care with which these fellows carried each composition, a certain inarguable resemblance to the disjointed images and antique feel of his favorite Dylan bootlegs; our bassist saw a way of steering the sound, punching through the song, that he'd perhaps never imagined; our guitarist grew enraptured with the tender embellishments which their electric guitarist submitted for our consideration every few chord changes. I can't imagine why our drummer liked it, unless he looked forward to the day when he would be restricted to an occasional tom hit, a lazy bass kick, a drag of the stick across the cymbal, a percussive surrender.

I remember the ostensible leader of 5 Chinese Brothers rushing over to us to apologize for this band, he didn't expect them to go on much longer, he couldn't wait for them to get off. We looked at him in astonishment and asked who these guys were.

"Souled American," he said, with uncharacteristic ill-will. "From Chicago. They have a record out."

"Sold American," we repeated thoughtfully.

"Souled," he corrected us. "Souled! s-o-u-l-e-d!" He was angry that they were going way over their allotted time slot. He imagined the people who had come for 5 Chinese Brothers would start leaving soon, most had to work early tomorrow and had to get to bed soon, and in a free establishment with no door you needed to hang on to whoever came in if you aimed to get rebooked there.

His concerns grew inaudible to us. We were somewhere else at the moment. You see, mostly we watched bands for

their musicianship *or* for their originality; either we loved their songs or their unique feel. It was rare—Christ, more than rare: I'd say because of the way we hated jazz that it was unprecedented—for us to stumble across a band whose songs fit our formal, content-heavy requirements, while at the same time their arrangements drew, it seemed, from some completely different atmosphere; a band, in short, we could respect as both familiar and strange.

We tried to incorporate them into our sound. It wasn't easy. We broke up soon after.

Diminishing Returns

They pursue a career like the forlorn ex from one of their early songs pursues his gone love: in complete secrecy. "I've often walked down your street. It's paved; no one knows." No one notices him in the song, of course, not just because a paved road carries no footprints but because his pursuit has so utterly wrecked his spirit as to desubstantiate him, expunge his corporeality. The band's pursuit of the musical marketplace has fared no better, turning them—album by album—into spooks and phantoms. Dropping more and more chord changes out of their songs, increasingly blurring their main instrumentation via intentional studio miscalibrations, they have now obscured their history, their sources, their very songs so completely that there is no reason people hearing them now would suspect they were once a reggae covers band that drifted into playing uptempo country-western and bluegrass songs. They've left no footprints anywhere.

Interview, Part One

A:—you mean right this minute? Oh, I'm just puttering around, watering my plants, like an old veteran of the music industry. Souled American, hmm . . . That does seem awfully long ago, a very distant thing, I think, a very obscure one.

Q: But there was a time they were higher-profile . . .

A: Really? To me, they're a band that for a while there, I thought, were just about the best band in the world. But it seemed like Rough Trade would put these records out and they'd sell maybe 3,000 copies. There'd be almost no feedback, you know? There were a few bands I knew who liked them, and a few critics. But that was about it, really.

Q: Why was it that they didn't break through to higher levels?

A: I think Souled American would probably say it was because Rough Trade didn't promote them well enough. And it's certainly true that we weren't high-powered in that regard. But it's also true that the band defeated any effort to promote them that went beyond us just trying to tell people, "Listen to this! It's great!"

Q: How so?

A: For a start, they were absolutely insistent on doing everything their own way. That's not a bad thing in itself. You've probably heard the story behind that song on the first record that goes, "I know what the band wants. I know what the band needs." Those are supposedly words spoken to Souled American by the A&R person from Slash Records who was trying to sign them. "I know what the band wants! I know what the band needs!"

Q: No, I didn't know that.

A: And they absolutely weren't going to have that. Only they could know what they wanted. I remember sitting at an adjacent table to them at the Rodeo Bar while they were being interviewed and Chris saying, "Hey, the great thing about being on Rough Trade is that we can do whatever we want." I reckon that they could—but I'm not sure that that's always a good thing for a band. And I think their determination to do things their own way—while being very admirable and leading to really great records for the people who were able to get into them—made it a lot harder for other people, who might've got into them, to get into them.

Q: So sabotage lay in their hearts, as they studied their career possibilities?

A: They were very concerned about artwork, for example, and it not being very revealing. Not that they wanted it to be secret—I just think they hated things being crass and obvious. Those guys were so determinedly awkward, it seems to me there was a sense in which the only worthwhile success for them would be one which they had tried, in every possible way, to screw up.

Travels With Lowery

As they drove, they were debating their song arrangements, trying to decide on a band name; yet once the cassette of Souled American began to play, the conversation died. They continued to follow the highway, descending into a valley of villages which seemed strategically placed as if to protect the road from the encroachment of the woods. A few hawks appeared above, circling intently, and with that the temperature plummeted dramatically. Faced with this, the day simply quit. The houses they passed soon resembled ski-slope cottages, benign and unsophisticated. Through the passenger window came the taste of fireplaces being lit, the alluring bite of hickory, a scent of longing, a gentle anonymity to which people all around them succumbed. The band kept on, traveling deeper into the countryside. Twilight made its way up the tree limbs, bringing haze and confusion. The particulars of their surroundings drifted away, indistinct. Now it was night. Still no one spoke.

At last Lowery pointed at the cassette player. "Now this," he barked, "is great," and others murmured in agreement. Souled American. The tape was purchased from a bargain bin in Baton Rouge. The beats fell hard, accented awkwardly, as if these were bluegrass standards played by a reggae covers band, which apparently was true. The words came in croaks, barely arriving.

"If we're not careful," warned Lowery, "this is what I'll want our new stuff to sound like. Like unreleased B-side outtakes from *Exile on Main Street* or something."

Pete the bassist cleared his throat. "How many, do you think, this stuff sold?"

Lowery shrugged. "Three thousand, maybe. Tops."

At the next cigarette break, Pete quietly slipped a different cassette into the tape player, a Tom Petty album, a bestseller.

It wasn't merely that Pete was afraid to waste his time with something less than huge. There were engineering concerns. So much of why songs get on the radio is the way they are miked and mixed along specific industry standards, standards which Souled American avowedly flouted. From his particular vantage, as a longtime studio musician, Pete perhaps depended on these standards more than the others.

As for whether Lowery sold out by suppressing his Souled American tastes in favor of a Tom Pettier sound, this seems incorrect. It ignores the Souled American influences integrated by Lowery into compositions such as "Kerosene Hat," and how that band's sound affected Lowery's production decisions with Sparklehorse and FSK. But more than that, it fails to take into account his oft-stated weariness at being consistently ghettoized as "collegey." Partially at Pete's urging, Lowery grew eager to jump milieus, to embark on a broadly resonant dialogue with a great number of folks, to register some lasting impact on mainstream culture, to have a true measurable effect, to establish a career at this, to accomplish something which would be so widely available that you could wave at it for many generations and identify it, proudly, as your contribution. Who can fault the health and handsomeness of such ambitions? Who can doubt he succeeded? The ubiquitous presence of his band's songs in subsequent movie soundtracks, their videos on MTV, their celebrated tie-in with Taco Bell—people know Cracker (the band name they ultimately chose) in a way they never knew Camper. Which can happen, apparently, as long as you don't pursue the Souled American model too far.

She Broke My Heart

Souled American's song "She Broke My Heart" means a great deal to me. At the time it was introduced to me, I was in love with two women. Please; I do not say this easily, for I am not employing "loved" lightly, but mean it at its least respectable

(and most undeniable). I was engaged to one of these two women and cheating — in total secrecy — with the other. But I could have happily married either (although I see now neither marriage would've ultimately succeeded). I suppose it sounds like some ego trip to love two women at the same time but mostly it teaches you to value resplendent agonies. Hatching within you is the cruel heavenly wisdom that you are trapped and you will not get what you want (no matter your prayers) because in fact you need both women forever and can't — for long — have both women. Perhaps I just thought I loved the two women when really I just loved the hurting against hope. I always was a sucker for the smell of dynamite. Yet again my least-disciplined passions had backed me into a prisoner's dilemma which could not be puzzled out — still, who can refuse the beautiful nonsense of crashing a car or turning to drugs? Certainly not the singer of "She Broke My Heart." Certainly not me, and this was like that. There was no way I could emerge from this intact — how exhilarating! I was high from internal bleeding, stoned on the deliciousness of a truly self-destructive feat, mad and unstoppable. I would examine the wreckage of old people on gurneys and in hospital beds and grow intoxicated thinking how very soon I would be like them, bitter, spent, forgotten. This is what "She Broke My Heart" says too, you know, and why it's lovely. I played the song for both my loves in different rooms, different cities, just weeks apart, and both of them sobbed with me at what he was singing. They both understood. Still there were constantly cross-continent weeping sessions on payphones, there were whispering midnight calls while someone slept nearby, there were secret missives and incessant surprises and alibis, there were lies and lies, the lies never stopped coming, along with gifts which needed constant explanations, and there was more love than I'd ever suspected capable of giving, gigantic and happy, in part because I knew what was wrong would soon devour me and then leave me feeling as hollowed out as that song. And I haven't recovered, but by now am dubious that I ever will.

Typical Problem, Example One

Yesterday, as I looked for their releases at a used CD store, the nice guy behind the counter offered to help. He began by asking me what category of music Souled American made. An easy enough question. He waited several minutes for me to answer while I looked at him, dumbstruck. Dumbfounded. Dum-dum. He grew alarmed. "Is it your heart?" he asked me at last. "Should I call a doctor?" I waved him off and, eventually, he walked away, which left me there still pondering. *What category of music?* Do words exist which can describe this stuff of theirs, how their songs are missing their crucial parts, the sleeves with too little information, how they invert the manners of techno via its dub predecessor "folk-trance" as they break syntax, lyrically and musically? Lefty Frizzell via Pere Ubu? Lee Perry by way of Meat Puppets by way of Eno by way of Ry Cooder? The twine linking pop music to Souled American (I wanted to announce) is like what connects the monarch butterfly to the everyday housebat.

Everything Souled American Means Is up to You

"Re-elect," advised the cover of their fourth release. This was elaborated inside the jacket: "Re-elect Sonny." The band name was hidden, stamped on the inner sleeve in pale ink easily erased. Song credits and member names were not given. *Sonny?* Typically, the title was presented to us, never once explained, rich with possible interpretations. You wanted to think "Sonny" was something an old-timer once called out to one of them; but it could've been a dog's name, for all we were given. Perhaps it's because the CD is certainly not "sunny," so therefore must be "sonny." When did it come out? Who was in the band? What do they think they're doing? What to make of a band which covers one of their own rarities, in the process erasing what few words the original version had and playing it shoddily at a grating half-tempo, and then choose the song not only as their fourth album's opening cut (and the album's sole original) but its title song as well?

It was a long time awaiting this particular album (two and a half years with no word from them!) and then no one in America was even able to purchase it—it arrived as a British Rough Trade import, after Rough Trade U.S. went belly-up. In the meantime, the world shifted from vinyl to CD, Kris Kross and Milli Vanilli came and went, Janet Jackson was signed for the most lucrative contract in the history of recording, three died while watching AC/DC at the Salt Palace. It was the album where they dropped their first band member (their drummer); in typical fashion, they never bothered to replace him. Now, it is said, their guitarist has quit as well. Watch—they won't replace him either. They will continue playing until all the members have quit, and even then it will be disputable whether they're really gone, how long they lingered, whether they ever existed, as with that interminable hesitance during our first dream of the evening when we question whether we're still awake.

Album by album they'd deviated further from anything resembling pop music until—by *Sonny*—it began to sound more like a series of supernatural aires conjured by the poet

Poe as he lay dying in a strange city in the middle of the last century, debauched and battered, sprawled—as they say—in a ditch beside a tavern only a week before his wedding date.

Sonny the unobtainable, all we have left from then, is a structure of owls, mice, woodstoves, mysterious visitors, and winds across cemeteries, it is a drunken ghost story of an album. It's a very slow, non-traditional album of traditional covers, most of them unfamiliar to a general audience. Then there's the aforementioned title song "Sonny," in which Souled American gives the Souled American treatment to a Souled American original, covering their *Flubber* outtake "Marleyphine Hank." Odd hums and mechanical squeaks run under some of the songs, none of them originals, many of which feel painstakingly reassembled out of mismatched musical fragments. As it opens with the instrumental their bassist co-wrote, it closes, quite organically, with a song written by the bassist's mother. In this way each listening travels back in time, ending earlier than where it began; a generation earlier, to clock it precisely. The "Sonny" then . . . is themselves?

Taken along with their first three albums, *Sonny* was an album that was critical to the success of the No Depression revolution, yet also shows why Souled American could not live with the results.

Chaos, a Theory Called Souled American

Imagine a world without the European Community. Now imagine a world without Souled American. What if I told you that the second was indispensable to the first, that without Souled American there would have been no united federation of free European democracies forming a continental congress? Yes, now that Jimbo the Glickster has leapt the monodimensional fences of standard linear science to prove that without butterflies there wouldn't be no rainstorms—I speak here of Chaos, our acclaimed-est of theories, that most ab-fab of lab rats, and this notion that forecasts themselves contribute turbulence (pitchfork bifurcations, stable lines

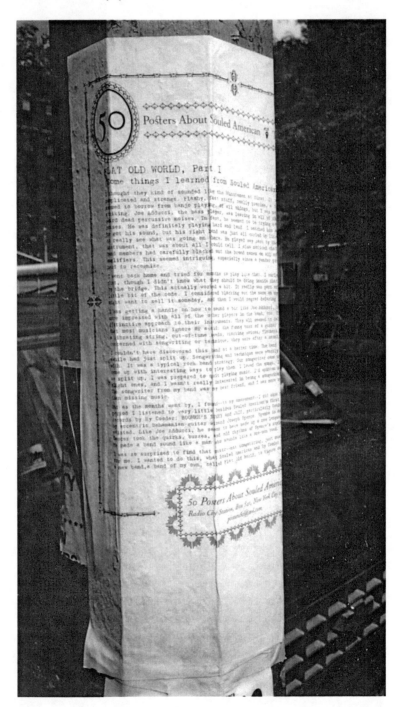

breaking in two, then four, then eight; the appearance of chaos itself; and within the chaos, the astonishing geometric regularity): Cause and Effect merrily take turns atop one another's shoulders in this world swept by disoriented winds of havoc—Henceforth, hey! It is a given that Most What We Do whenever will affect Past and Future equally, that Most What You Read will end your life, that no things make sense (what with the terrible taste most you Johnny Boy linearity adjutants possess, your sick cars pulling out at all hours and payphones ringing with product surveys, your linear kids on the Straight Sidewalk of Squares hurling their hellos and delaying my milkman!) and embracing this escalation of contingencies and post-deterministic prognostications we grow unable to admit or deny that without the 1988 release of Souled American's *Fe*: George Bush wins in 1992, Barbara Bush dies suddenly, George Bush remarries Anna Nicole Smith who, thence reknighted as Evita, poisons Bush's inner organs on national television with a crew of faith healers, employing solely astral projections and implied karmic interrogatories. If everything did not occur Exactly As It Did we wouldn't happen to be standing right here right now! Right on! If Souled American hadn't arrived in small-acknowledged Fulda on 15.Oct.92 to play an unassuming nightclub called Kreuz . . . *Ist sie den Liebenden leichter?* Ah! take flight, precious certainties! We lose our ability to know for sure that Mobutu contracts prostrate cancer, the Bulls win 72 in a season, the Human Genome Project continues apace, life expectancy soars despite Reseda earthquake 17.Jan.94, we can even debate whether I would still arrive at this idea for a poster! And so I pen my pleading Mrs. Missive to you Johnny Boys aiming to convince you this is a band over whom we must chant devotional incantations, alighting incense and shrines alike, hugging monitors to our breasts in an incensed madcap mayhem of machismo, bent of knee in supplication, petitioning them with prayerful entreaties, humbled and roaring, grateful of consequence! Praised Be Thou, O souled A merican, Mayest Surges of Pride Press Thee, *denn das Schöne ist nichts als des Schrecklichen Anfang, den wir noch grade ertragen*—the best lack all conviction, while the worst are full of passionate intensity!

Nebraska, Neuopren, and Souled American

Someone just asked me: yeah, what happened to them, to Souled American; and he spoke this recoiling in horror. "I bought a used CD of theirs for $4.00. And it's terrible. And they used to be so good!"

What could I say? I haven't heard them in years.

And for me, they come with such complicated associations.

My story begins near the acclaimed Liver Transplant Unit where, in our organ-rich state, we had grown giddy, taking good news for granted; plasma exchanges, immunosuppressants, chemoembolization, decreased organ rejections . . . heck, why not beat up our innards with toxins if those age-old fears of cirrhosis, hepatomas, lymphocytes, and complete liver failure had now been consigned to the past, easily fixed courtesy of the Med School's retransplantation successes?

And so into the medicine cabinet we strode, linked to the newest in narcos by Boyce Canton, a Year 3 med student who could obtain anything for us. Neuopren's sweet release brought the oblivion of the cadaver, skin waxy like apples and all. Ketamine's teetering awe brought the exuberance of the stupid, an incessant blind flight of wonder. Neither alone would enlighten but blended tenderly to make a "Slammer" (SOULED AMERICAN injection) we became slow giants with quick minds, brains dancing in lumbering benumbed bodies, erratic in our brilliance and paused in our appreciation, open enough to comprehend yet closed enough to (somewhat) communicate. A little entrance, a little exit; a little up, a little down. Our gleeful, mocking thoughts escaped, while messy toxins pooled in those readily replaceable livers of ours.

We did slammers in college in Nebraska and found it a good enough state in which to listen to the radio. Which is the only place where I heard Souled American. To me, in this particular condition, they were our very own potentates of glum, falling through each song in a brave, ageless way I've never heard since. They seemed infatuated with reproducing the sorts of rhythms one feels on a boat at night, an uneasy slope, a bit of creaking to and fro, a wooziness, the chill ocean black and vast. It was fantastic music, an hypnotic bummer, a giant of cinema, but exactly *not* the kind you could ever share with anyone who wasn't into slammers. It had too much of that 'been-up-all-night-can't-get-warm' feeling. It reminded us: we die so fast; fifty, sixty years. Sometimes eighty years. Sometimes just thirty.

And how like us seemed their unsustainable enterprise, our spirits too crawling like low clouds close to the earth, lacking viability, visibility, speed.

"I want to kiss you and never be there," croaked somebody in a song I heard recently who wasn't Souled American, in a song that for me pretty much summed up the hide-and-go-seek of those Souled American college years.

So, what happened.

We gave up slammers when Boyce suffered a sudden "neuronic occurrence," losing use of the more interesting elements of the lobe anterior to his medulla.

I had my hands full with other stuff. I never went back to Souled American.

Notes While Listening to Notes Campfire

the sky blackens suddenly
the trash flies down the street
the clothes dance wildly on the line
a bicycle falls over
the room darkens
the sky rumbles, clouds flash
leaves are flattened to the branch.
Almost as an afterthought
it begins to downpour.

Pressing Importance

Ten years ago I worked at a record pressing plant in Firebaugh, California (small town, outside Fresno). Some of what we manufactured came by way of San Francisco. Souled American's *Fe*—I remember when we received the master plates for that from Rough Trade.

Most of the time we pressed sets of Dick Clark and Casey Kasem doing their top forty shows. We performed this chore almost all week long, every week, over and over. These men had recorded their supposedly spontaneous Sunday radio broadcasts far in advance, perhaps months before. These were the shows that told America's kids what to buy.

Records were stamped out by an automated press. Black vinyl goop squirted in, finished LPs shot out the side. When we were making *Fe*, the press expressed some weird maladjustment. Excess goop kept clogging the innards. This actually happened a lot, it wasn't anything special. You'd open up the press to scrape it clean and it was like performing surgery on an extraterrestrial, this dark cavity globbed-up everywhere with melted rubber, like strolling into a machine that makes licorice-flavored taffy. Sometimes I considered this, how the press after all did make candy for the airwaves.

But mostly I was far too busy working.

The Casey Kasem and Dick Clark operations were very involved packages. These were three-hour radio shows mailed out in four-record sets. We'd sleeve the records, stack the sleeves in these standard jackets, then ship each boxed set priority UPS to one of five hundred radio stations. A lot of things relied on our dependability. Across the country they'd put the needle to these same four LPs at the same time each week. Do they do this still? Doubtful. They use satellites to syndicate things instantaneously nowadays. And now there's CDs, after all. What I'm describing hearkens back to the dying age of vinyl, when a couple smooth-voiced DJs narrated the contest between the best-selling 45s like some dramatic horserace between recording celebrities.

There was this once when I put some Rough Trade records in a Casey Kasem sleeve, in the American Top Forty jacket,

in the box addressed to KVEN in Ventura. Souled American's
Fe was one of those I included. I had fun imagining how this
would recalibrate the taste of America's teenagers, how, come
Sunday, they'd get a sampling of that tongue-tied and soft-
spoken sound of Souled American, full of radiant shadows
that defy explanation, like their first glimpse of the girl they
will always wish they'd married.

But then I chickened out and put the right records in their
proper sleeves. This was my job, after all, and I needed the
money.

Interview, Part Two

A: Somebody in San Francisco was talking recently about
raising money through a bunch of benefit shows to get Souled
American to come out and play in the Bay Area, because there
were so many people there who loved them. But no, Souled
American weren't a laugh-and-share-the-joke kind of thing.
I got the feeling they were a very insular group. Whenever
I talked to people in Chicago at the time who had links to
the music scene, they rarely knew anything about Souled
American. There was a specific group of people I think that
was very attached to the band and that was it. The band would
play regularly at this one place, the Cubby Bear, just down
the street from Wrigley Field. I got the sense they were very
much apart from other things that were going on. A scene—a
microscene, maybe—unto themselves.

Q: So this wasn't a terribly forthcoming band?

A: No. Stoned, I would say, is the word. They were sorta
stubborn and sorta stoners. Basically pretty nice, rather shy
people, I think.

Q: Did you see enough of their shows to get a sense of how
they differed, show to show?

A: Well, they certainly had different modes. I suspect that it
had a lot to do with how much pot they'd been able to smoke
before they went onstage. I'm serious. The draggy tempos
and such, I think that has a lot to do with that. Sometimes

they were incredibly stretched out and yet still . . . perfect, you know? Their timing was still perfect; it was just incredibly draggy.

Q: They were always listening to one another.

A: Right. And then at other times it could be quite uptempo. What makes them unusual is, I think, is . . . it's funny, there are loads of examples of reggae bands doing covers of country songs, but only Souled American went the other way around. If I remember right, Chris and Joey had been in a reggae covers band (it could have been more than that, it could have been all of them). And once when Souled American played a show in New York which I guess was really . . . it was before the deal was signed, a showcase gig, and I think they played two and a half sets, or two sets with a really long encore. They moved on to playing covers at a certain point and I remember they did a really great chug-along uptempo version of a Bob Marley song—not a classic Bob Marley song, more a pop Bob Marley song. "Could You Be Loved," I think.

Flubbing It

The 1987-1988 sessions at Chicago Trax yielded *Fe*, the debut album. *Fe* was named from band jargon, "fe" being their name for "feel." It was picked up by Rough Trade U.S., and received rather widespread praise. A legion of fans sprouted up around the country. Unfortunately, as they returned to Chicago Trax in 1989 to record their sophomore work, Souled American had no way of knowing that they would never be this popular again.

Why did it turn out so? It's high time we floated a few theories. They obviously didn't "play the game" as regards their look or their set lists or whatever. Their sound, for example, prominently featured rather unusual choices. The drums were never again as loud and voluble as they were on *Fe* (midway through their discography the drummer departed, and was never replaced), and without drums people won't tap toes, dance, or (for the most part) hear your songs on the radio; the lyrics grew less frequent as the band experimented with sonic uncertainties and distended tempos, riddling their hallucinatory aural space with echo, amnesia, and regret (an aesthetic not terribly distinguishable from that practiced — to opposite effect — by today's most popular techno and electronic acts); they never wrote a "big hit" and for a time, in fact, shied away from even performing their own compositions; in short, though with each subsequent outing their brilliance and bravery remained audibly intact, they truthfully never made another record as direct as their first. After the first album, their access points closed up, sealed over with mystery and gunk, a submarine lost at sea. Their sporadic touring slowed to a halt; no one in America recalls seeing them since 1991. Their record company went bankrupt immediately after the release of their poorly distributed third album; their fourth album eventually came out only through the British arm of the label; their fifth and sixth albums were released solely in Europe.

But one must return to the basics: at the height of their notoriety, as they finished up the tracks for their second album, they had a choice to make, they had to decide what to call it, and they went with the name *Flubber*. It should have been obvious how this would turn out. The name — perhaps they knew this, perhaps they didn't — was that of a failed toy from the early '60s.

As the magazine *Stay Free* just recently reported, Hasbro had developed a product called Flubber, a rubber and mineral oil substance that could bounce like a ball and take imprints, to tie in with the 1963 Walt Disney movie *Son of Flubber*. After it had been on the market for several months, the company began receiving reports that Flubber was causing a rash. Tests on prisoners subsequently revealed the product could irritate hair follicles. A mass recall of the Flubber product was instituted. "Thousands and thousands of balls were consigned to the city dump. The next day Hasbro execs received a call from the mayor of Providence, who informed them that a black cloud hovered over the dump; the rubber would not burn properly. Merrill Hassenfeld of Hasbro called the Coast Guard for permission to weight the Flubber and dump it at sea. Permission was granted. However, the next day the Coast

Guard called to complain that Flubber was floating all over Narragansett Bay. After paying the Coast Guard to sweep the ocean, Hassenfeld took the mess and buried it in his backyard."

Could this have not been an omen? What a Flubber-like path they came to travel—Souled American, bouncing like a ball, gathering up impressions, a briefly celebrated toy—"product presently unavailable"—persistent, determined . . . but essentially ending up buried in some backyard somewhere.

Il Duce Wore Adidas

Sometimes it seems they are daring to make the worst possible play on words—so many clumsily punning lyrics are layered in with the earnest sentiments as to be a defiant policy of avoidance on its own—consider their very name, you envision them deciding to title themselves after the slogan "Buy American"; throwing that out in a few seconds for its complete opposite, "Sell American"; smoking dope and past-tensing that name soon enough into "Sold American" which they misspell, as a joke, at their first gig, to become "Souled American"; the name is terrible, awkward, unfunny. It's as if they were invented by us, twelve writers with nothing better to do than make up an obscure group with a stupid name and put up posters celebrating them. Why believe they exist when their first four releases are available nowhere and their subsequent two available in one store in America (415-647-2272)? "Sold American will not be Sold in America"—could this have been the aim all along?

Considering their homophonous loves, it becomes relevant to consider how they came by their individual names. Take the bassist, Joe Adducci. It has been well-documented that the khakis campaign (Castro wore khakis, Khruschev wore khakis) left its mark upon the sarcastic psyche of Southern Europe, but few are aware how—in response—graffiti arose facetiously declaring Mussolini's endorsement of athletic shoes. "Il Duce Wore Adidas" announced every wall Souled American saw during their first perambulation about the continent. The drummer read the graffiti aloud to the band, snickering, whereupon this rapid fire exchange occurred: "Il didas," the guitarist freely associated. "Il didas," the bassist quickly added, "Joe Adducci." Swiftly, the singer concluded it: "Joe Adducci for Elitists." From this series of cockamamie sound-alikes evolved the bassist's "name"—Joe Adducci.

Then there was the Brit yelling at them, "Christ, Bugger Off!" which, after a fashion, led to the singer's "name" Chris Grigoroff; there was their jargon for the bassist's style ("like a Scottish Tuba") which led to the guitarist's "name" Scott Tuma; and there was the band's affection on tour for calling out "J' me in the barnyard!" (as in, pass me a marijuana cigarette, a "joint," to allow me to endure these crude lodgings) which became, after a few slurrings and stretchings, the "name" for their drummer, Jamey Barnard.

To the Tune of "Who Killed Davey Moore?"

Who killed Souled American
Why, who'd do such a thing?!
Not I, said the music critic, ignoring their CDs again
I had my hands full
serving the smart-aleck patrol
sarcastic! ironic! unfeeling and dull!
policing what's hip, deciding what's cool
paid to promote some pretty young sell-out
a "proto-anarcho femme fatale" no doubt
justifying those I hated last week
first I can't stand the kitchen, now I cheer for the heat
in commentaries oh so wry
it wasn't me that made them die
Blame distributors, blame managers
industry apparatchiks
recording engineers
Blame the band's oh so stubborn desire to hide
it's obvious this was suicide
who has time to hear all that new stuff
eventually: enough is enough
and the guy writing this is no better than me

he's eager to dominate you, can't you see?
Who has time to listen to things not buzz-bin
I mastered the masthead, locked out dissensions
ignoring them in my big interpretation
refusing to grant them the smallest attention
But I did not kill them
or commit this sin
no mere music critic killed Souled American

Typical Problem, Example Two

I had trouble entering Burger King because the humidity had
dampened the padding on the electronic door. Pushing inside,
I found myself off-balance, reeling. The customers turned to
watch (drawn by the sound of the sliding door's resistant POP)
as suddenly my Walkman slid from my grasp. Instinctively,
my right foot went out, as if to land a hackeysack. I caught the
Walkman too low, on the laces. Net result: I booted it across
to the server station where it exploded against the counter,
batteries, transistorized insides, cassette tape ricocheting off
in opposite directions. Customer's jaws dropped, mouths full
of half-chewed Whoppers. My headphones were still on my
ears. I felt like a carwreck rendered in tofu, like a nude clown.
Burger King's servers scampered to help. I couldn't speak. "Is
this yours?" one of them inquired softly, having recovered the
cassette tape from beneath the condiment dispensary. "Is this
yours?" She squinted to read the label: "Souled American?" The
customers stared at me like a hundred thousand hypnotized
seals. I wrestled with speech.

B-Flat Diminished

Imagine a band shrinking as it grows, rather than expanding;
shrinking in terms of ambition, output, melodies, band
members, production aesthetic. Imagine their first album
is as outgoing as they get, at which point they isolate one
of these songs and dive deep into it. The second record is
comprised primarily of elaboration on this one song. Their

third record is comprised of elaboration of some song on album No. 2, and so on. How long can this go on? Six albums into it, Souled American seem closeted and unapologetic, beautiful and lost, hermetic, gone. In typical fashion, their title for this new album—*Notes Campfire*—was also the title of the first song on their very first CD. It seems appropriate that this be the comeback moment, or the final moment, one or the other, that this is a career reeling in on itself, circling close, mouth gaping for *le fin*.

Think of the Ways You Normally Hear About a Record

You're sitting there with your wife on the sofa after an argument. The radio is playing music broadcast from a local college. You hear a song you like. You shush your wife each time she tries to speak so that you can hear the DJ identify it. Trouble is, the DJ has played about a thousand songs in a row and you can't keep track of which song is being named. Later that night, you're drunk. Your wife has gone to bed. MTV is playing. The same song returns, sporting a sexy video. You scrawl yourself a note, "Check this out." The next day you are walking to a friend's apartment—a girl and a friend but not your girlfriend (after all you're married)—well, okay, in truth you're walking to the dangerous Lower East Side apartment of your youthful and impressionable trophy mistress . . . and you pass a large four-color poster on Second Avenue advertising the song as a hit. That evening you go see a movie with your trophy mistress. The song is in the soundtrack. You and she stroll over to a club and the sound system is playing the song while a band sets up. Next it's leaking from the Walkman of a nearby passenger, as you and your trophy mistress take the subway back to her dangerous apartment. "Maybe this is our song," you joke. She nods solemnly, taking you at your word. On your way back home afterwards, full of shame, you stop at the flower store to buy your wife a ravishing assortment of exotic lilies. The song is playing over a radio behind the counter, broadcast from a local college. Next thing you know, like a blush of conscience, you encounter the song everywhere you look, it's written-up in newspapers, there are magazine campaigns, big cardboard pronouncements in record stores, and a mailbox circular which offers it to you as one of 13 free CDs with "absolutely no obligation whatsoever" to join the CD club. You wonder how to tell your wife.

And that poor woman you call "the trophy mistress"? She's about to become very angry. But it'll take a few days. For now she's crying and, seeking comfort, she eats soft boiled eggs and watches reruns and pulls down a cassette a college friend made for her long ago. The cassette is labeled by hand and bears a title that resonates as some tender in-joke between herself and her friend. It's a recording of songs nobody else seems to know, secret songs, songs you never hear anywhere, not in movies or flower stores or clubs, not on MTV or college radio or nearby Walkmans. It's a tape of a band called Souled American.

Interview, Part Three

Q: I guess in a way explaining ourselves to anyone is compromising.

A: Sure, and Souled American didn't really ever enjoy talking to the press.

I think they wanted people to realize that they were brilliant and made brilliant music, without having to actually talk to anyone about it or anything. I don't think they minded touring, though.

Q: I'm sure they liked playing together. They did it so well.

A: Yeah. And they really were that kind of a band. You got the feeling that what they did onstage probably wasn't any different from how they played in their living rooms, except that onstage Chris would have to face an audience. Joey would bounce around, Jamey would sit there and Scott would basically stand still, mostly on one foot, facing backwards.

Q: Specifics . . .?

A: I recall a show in Austin, South by Southwest in 1988. March 1988. It was them and Scrawl and 2 Nice Girls. Souled American didn't like it because they had to go on first. I think they had both a very sure sense of their own worth and a great distrust of the machinery that creates media popularity. Perhaps it stemmed from knowing that they were really good but that they couldn't actually do some of the kinds of things that would have to do if they were going to become successful. Maybe that's what it was.

Adducci vs. Grigoroff

Yes, Adducci: for his unique bass technique and his uncommon dominance, yes; but even more Grigoroff, for his astonishing abilities as a singer, even greater than Adducci's musical talents. That Chris Grigoroff sings songs slowed to one-third their normal speed and captivatingly inhabits each pause with a tension born of genuine sorrow is enough, to my mind, to nominate him for the heavyweight crown. He fuses laconic cowboy phrasing with a torch singer's bursting heart. He's mastered that choked bluegrass beauty of sounding like he's at the top of his range no matter how low the melody, like he's lost his breath no matter how brief the note, like he can do nothing but work the lonely side of every lyric.

When we get a song like "Born (Free)" on the new CD it dazzles us. Such an unusual commitment of voice! Over four minutes (we never notice its length) of captivation when all the entire song basically says is, "No love, no love at all. No love in my house, no kiss. No love on my street, it's all dark. No love at all. And I don't understand." If you listen to it with your eyes shut, you will see close-ups of great black blocks of veined marble, a grand piano in a fire, a watch being checked and rechecked, a very high ceiling, a lonely candle in a jar. This song eats happiness as completely as anything you see on Fox's *America's Scariest Acts of Random Violence* yet you can't stop programming the stereo to replay it twenty thousand consecutive times.

Party Talk

To make conversation at a party, I asked a young man for the most terrifying experience of his life. Perhaps I expected a joke in return. He gave me a panicked look and replied, hardly pausing, "There were two." He had nearly died while spelunking, after falling into a subterranean pit so immense it took many days for him to escape; and a tornado had carried him off when he was twelve years old to an Indian reservation, where he'd been chased and beaten with pipes to within an inch of his life. I might've disbelieved these stories but that he detailed them showing so little expression, with no perspective, in a voice whose level flatness seemed to say these things had never been considered tellable before now. A woman overhearing us chimed in with a hiking expedition in Colorado which met with a freak blizzard and ended in empty canteens, lost backpacks, irreversible frostbite, hallucinations, a dramatic helicopter canyon rescue. Soon everybody was contributing. A sort of contest came to the fore. No one really enjoyed it. The fun, the party, had skittered off as some primitive ritual emerged in its stead, an exchange of hunting stories, war stories. We seemed collectively hypnotized in our efforts to convey how near we came to being killed by the outdoors.

The telling of party stories reminded me of a band named Souled American. As our stories mounted, we grew quiet in the conviction that what we think of as "life" was deceptive. In truth the scattered instants when we slipped through cracks, abandoned to our own devices, these were our few moments of life, and the rest — going to work, running errands, tending family, oiling the weighty machinery of self — were reassuring lies. In ridding our routine of chance and risk, we'd believed we were clarifying our needs, becoming solid citizens — but in fact we had excluded ourselves from our lives. And this then is Souled American. They come at songs from the side, recreating lost moments and saying little, risking not just the failure of an arrangement but the failure of an aesthetic, an outlook, a principle. It sounds odd to say songs can make you feel this much but when you're within their songs, your basic assumptions confront you as being mostly fraudulent, you don't know where to go, where they're heading, you can't figure out how you got here or how to leave.

Or perhaps, it was the things unsaid in those stories that were most troubling, which haunt me to this day. The storytellers quickly realized that the impact of their experiences was best communicated by describing too little. In dropping their voices and reversing their theatrical impulse to dramatize, getting out of the way of their own feelings, they communicated to us a purer experience. Which is something Souled American learned long ago.

Souled American and Our Sixteenth President

I wanted a picture of Souled American but could not find a way to get in touch with the band. The manager's girlfriend sent me, at last, the only photo she could find—three members on a junky sofa smiling uncomfortably, seated beside someone in an Abe Lincoln mask. Rumor had it that the drummer—always an astonishingly restrained presence, visible during the shows drumming with most of his body turned from his kit—the drummer was no longer in the group. A band of rumors clad in mist. Now, apparently, Abe Lincoln was in the band? It seemed plausible.

One True Sound

A friend and I were at a funeral, unable to believe they were burying this person. "He was better than us," I reminded my friend, who was pale and shocked and made no reply. "Better in every goddamn way," I pointed out. My friend numbly nodded. "We're shits," he whispered at last. We walked to our car, just some thing parked in ugly daylight with its windows glued together. My friend indicated the tapes littered about the front and back seats and said, with true concern, "Your cassettes will melt." "I fucking care," I snapped. We locked the doors, put on our seatbelts . . . but couldn't fathom driving

away. We sat, the interior a bathyscaph, the upholstery like taffy, looking through the gravel-pocked windshield at our uncomprehending friends. They staggered off to separate cars, drenched in the mock clarity of light, the grief like a sink-stopper in their chests. We opened the glove compartment and smoked Angolan opium, the rich smell suggesting some magnificent devastation, a burning barge, a fire in a schoolyard. Hours perhaps passed. My friend said he had to hear some Uncle Tupelo, some Jayhawks, some Gastr del Sol. Our words were joke bugs frozen in ice cubes. I clung to the car as it clung to the asphalt which clung to a planet falling through space. My friend started poking through my cassettes. I could not turn so swiftly as to catch my life slipping away, but I could confirm this in the horizon's absence, the way the sky sought to travel at a careful distance, separate from me. Our hearts were pits prying off their peachskins. My friend could find none of the tapes to which he felt like listening. "How about Palace?" he pleaded. "You got any Palace here?" He was a big fan. "Fucking Palace," I sneered. "Fucking emperor's new clothes, one fucking 'too cool for school' unfriendly mean individual. Can't fucking write, can't sing, can't play for shit. Fucking adored by every-fucking-one." My friend looked at me, his eyes drawn terribly. He resembled those characters in horror movies in the instant before they get dismembered, staring at something the camera avoids showing us. "In truth," I admitted mildly, "I possess no Palace. So we're gonna listen instead to Souled American."

The Soul of Today's American

Souled American has been on an anti-memory campaign, but don't ask what I mean by this, I really can't remember. How could I? We live mostly in TERRIBLE DISORIENTATION. I share their LOW REGARD for consciousness, their WAR ON MEMORY. Right NOW you are barely listening. Right NOW YOU are barely remembering. Your eyes SCAN these words looking to be anchored by bits of YUMMY GOSSIP and CELEBRITY BREAD, a fingernail-full of WORLD-FAMOUS HAIR, a footnote to HISTORY. Things are escaping your attention even as your eyes register these words, THINGS ARE GONE before you notice. Souled American arrived and for a BRIEF second were acclaimed as some sort of answer, the NECESSARY RESPONSE, the INJECTION of our past coupled with a VISION of our future. But just as they had supplanted hundreds of others for their BRIEF notice, so were they too EVENTUALLY ECLIPSED, as is inevitably dictated not just by our ravenous pop economy but by HUMAN CONSCIOUSNESS ITSELF, things will be weeded out, DISREGARDED, WORTHY people IGNORED, because to take it all in, to give it the necessary attention and accord it respect, will SACRIFICE OUR SANITY. The career of Souled American continues as if TO HAUNT US on behalf of these cast-off encounters. It is only our damnable arrogance which DARES congratulate this behavior of ours, this selective memory, by terming it "CIVILIZED"—nothing civilized to it, just FIGHT FIGHT FIGHT for the buzz of POWER, the buzz of SENSATION, the numbing buzz of DRUGS. Instead: Forget all, and be BORN ANEW!

Souled American: The Music and the Man

Listening to their newer releases, the way they've mixed the heart out of every song, it sounds as if they've died, their lifetimes passed, as if the people, the instruments had all expired. There is almost nothing of this world, nothing flesh, no reality, little bass, virtually zero percussion, just a few words, sung always with difficulty. It's dub devouring itself. There is increasingly only that shimmer of spirit hinting at what once inhabited the space, a thing at last freed of bones and bodies, audible in ringing guitars, lonesome fingerpicks, a bass drum infrequently kicked. It is frustration with this direction which probably accounts for the departure of their drummer, and now their guitarist. Only two members remain. "Oh, you still here?" the songs from their last few CDs all seem to ask, as if startled to find a listenership, any listenership, whatsoever. They behave as if they have all the paranoia in the world, as if an audience is the last thing they'd trust (though I doubt they trust the industry either). They seem to need you and me less and less. It is a rock and roll retreat unlike any other, absent of sleazy manipulations or disingenuous denunciations of today's music. Nor (obviously) has it become an instance of a band suddenly discovering its audience to be dwindling, fearing for its relevance, and futilely harrassing record companies to spark things anew, in a pathetic eagerness to crack today's radio formulas with requisite signals of penance. Some more genuine pursuit has them captivated, and apparently if it doesn't lead to breakeven sales, that's fine. It doesn't feel like they're terribly concerned or contemplating any sort of comeback. They've decamped; now they're quietly dispersing into the woods.

My Life As a Child

I grew up in Radio City Station. Souled American were my neighbors. My father and mother (a teacher and social worker, respectively) were ardent in their admiration for Thomas Eagleton, a man who'd dramatically lost a bid for the Vice-Presidency and then promptly disappeared. Which is to say that they were conscientious citizens, failed liberals, and they wore like a badge of honor the news that a long-haired, torn-jeaned rock and roll band was squatting in the abandoned two-story brick dwelling across the street.

In those cherished days, Radio City Station was pure promise, a place of resplendent refineries. From laboratory chimneys billowed the shimmering steams of award-winning chemistry experiments. Great deeds underway! The petty distinctions between "nature" and "city" had been summarily abolished in our city of the future! Dogs were free to fight other dogs for cigarettes, gulls nested in stoplights, squirrels came covered in graffiti. Trees sprouted power lines. The leaves, crackling like transistors, bathed our evenings in the glow of iridescent dye. Marvelous birds thrummed overhead, hydraulic innards clanking. We learned to eat concrete and drink electricity, and to speak of our loved ones as automobiles.

Souled American, they played astonishing music at astonishing hours, which horrified most everybody but delighted my parents. Their spooky notes rang through the neighborhood, a noise not unlike that which would one day be voiced by superstition itself, echoing off smokestacks and storage tanks, like porch songs adapted to our playgrounds of razor-wire.

We'd wave whenever we caught sight of them and they'd wave back. They'd be eating their meals together huddled over the sink, maybe blowing drugsmoke out their bathroom window. Like everybody else, Souled American washed their clothes in the effluent of the sewage treatment plant and on Sundays snuck into the incinerator to bake bread behind the guards' backs . . .

No wait; sorry. That was Soul Asylum. Those were my neighbors, Soul Asylum. I'm sorry. Souled American . . . hmm, nope. I don't know any Souled American.

The Movie, Forgetful and Brittle

The movie, forgetful and brittle, continued to break. The customers booed. The projectionist again apologized. The manager kept refusing refunds, pleading for patience. Still the antique movie broke and where it broke continuity dissolved and younger movies leapt up onto the screen, seeing their chance and seizing it. A band named Souled American provided live accompaniment, watching the screen bewildered, making up soundtracks which would smooth out these disparate contradictions, this junglefight of filmstrips, this congealed lump of wrong stories, these mismatched flickerings, interrupted lives. An old man in a dreaded house. A coalminer addicted to the killing black lure of the underground. A chicken tells a grasshopper, "You're mine." As they play, sense abandons the theater screen. Only their music continues to contain any resonance of meaning. The band slows the longer they play, defeated and tired, unable still to tie the stories together. We wonder how long this can go on.

An Open Letter to My Sweetheart

Something occurs to me as regards our spat the other night concerning Souled American. Perhaps I overreacted, I'm sorry. The chair, the watch, the mirror—I promise to replace them, or to pay in full for their repair. When you acclaimed the Spice Girls and attributed my inability to appreciate them mainly to my devotion to integrity-laden market failures "like Souled American," it was all I could do not also to hurl the refrigerator out the window and down into your tulip garden! It's not that I am such a judge of integrity or that "authenticity" is all that terrifically crucial to me. Please understand, Marie. I simply like Souled American. I'd like them whether or not *Notes Campfire* sound-scanned over 55,000 copies in its first week of domestic release, receiving praise in *Rolling Stone*, *Entertainment Weekly*, *Request*, *Details*, *Interview*, *Wired*, *Magnet*, *Bikini*, *Surface*. Whether or not this occurred, I could care less, whether Wes Papadakis and Pete Elmazi and Fred Lesniewski and everyone adored them or not, I'd still like them. You know? It's not snobbishness or elitism. If a band like this were packing 13,000-plus capacity theatres on a lengthy cross-country tour I'd say, "Great, good." But they're not. Not that I'd mind if they were. I don't particularly enjoy obscure acts, I wish I had gads of fellow enthusiasts to spread gossip amongst, I honestly wish my tastes ran with the majority. Do you remember the proverb, "When elephants fight, it is the grass that suffers; and when elephants make love, the grass also suffers"? I would love it so much if just once in this elephant industry of music me and the bands I love were not the grass. I want Souled American to be elephants! But instead: no video adds, no BDS trend to speak of. They're not slated for Letterman, no featured singles picked up this week by AAA stations, no Number One callouts in key markets. They anticipate no full multiformat radio & TV shots, no spins whatsoever. In fact, we're mostly unsure what they look like now. They haven't toured America for many years. They don't have publicity pictures or even publicists or even just people picking up telephones shouting the band's name down the wire in an ecstatic fury. They don't have a record company. They don't have a drummer. They sound sad. I hear they broke up.

Untitled

I remember playing *Frozen* for a good friend in that loud Camaro I used to drive, on the blaring freeway, windows open to the rushing whoosh and gush, and it was as if nothing was coming out of the boombox whatsoever. "Is he singing now?" we'd ask one another, rather like concerned parents checking on a child left alone or farmers listening for rain. "Yeah. No. Huh, not sure." It's true, he sounded like he was barely opening his mouth at all.

What made me so sure this particular friend would like Souled American? A conversation we'd had earlier, in which he'd confessed how embarrassed he'd become to've once loved the Violent Femmes. The Violent Femmes, he argued, had started off as something very different then what they'd become. Initially there was nothing else like it — given that many words and that much passion, you'd expect a lot of loud distorted guitars. Instead, all you got was brushes pounding a snare, Brian Ritchie's bass filling up the vast sonic spaces that were mostly untouched by Gano's cruddily recorded acoustic guitar. The punk dilemma (how to keep getting louder and louder and louder without getting ridiculous) was suddenly fixed, linked to a quietly edgy folk tradition to which nobody suspected it belonged till then. The Knitters, Camper Van Beethoven, Elvis Costello, Tom Waits, Nick Cave had supporting roles in this, but it was initially the Femmes teaching us this, in 1983. When I heard Souled American's *Fe* in 1988, they seemed to me the next step in my friend's little stageplay, the path promised but not taken by the now-sad Femmes. Elvis Presley had been replaced in the lineage by the Louvin Brothers and Peter Tosh and this opened up the feeling of a lot more possibilities than we'd really counted on.

In truth, though, *Frozen* gave my friend the chills. He couldn't figure out where to place it in his little theory of punk ascent, unless country standards stretched out in the studio led somehow to Brian Eno's *Another Green World*. But this implied a backwardness to time and influences that troubled him.

Admittedly, I couldn't have attempted to introduce him to Souled American at a less appropriate time. As I said, we were in the car heading, at long last, to our local Madonna/ McDonald's Theme Park & GO-GO Shopping Complex, that thing of the future that had been threatened for so long it could scare us no longer, the multimedia bazaar of lifestyle cybermarkets and virtual reality interfaces, blah blah blah. Simulacra lactating Madonnas roamed Ronald McDonaldland Court in various states of undress, her semblance of presence generously sampled and duplicated. We were less interested in collecting all the possible autographs (from the many Madonnas, the several animatronic Hamburglers and Grimsters, the oversized puppets of Mayor McCheese and our baby-girl Lourdes) than in tracking down the interactive food-thingeys: the $10.99 transistor-burgers (which, upon being eaten, reward the consumer with a very private rendition of "Justify My Buns"), the lo-fat, low-cut Madonna fries that sensuously seduce the throat, the fish sandwiches sauced (it was said) with the very stuff from Madonna's underpants.

But as I've indicated, upon our approach we could not even hear Souled American, could not make out even the simplest of *Frozen*'s awkwardly syncopated deliberations like, "Feels like us two here . . . make a lonely one" or even, "You . . . are on . . . my mind." We were on the wrong side of the world where such decent sentiments could not reach us, they were meaningless to us in the air of excitement and the excited sound of air, as we neared our long-awaited theme park.

Reluctant History

They were booed off the stage in Boulder, "while playing" — according to one musician in attendance — "brilliantly." They were panned in Los Angeles, accused of being dull, of "wearing Grateful Dead influences the same way nachos wear melted cheese." They went around the world in 1990 opening for Camper Van Beethoven. Europeans either loved or despised the opening act — Germans adored Souled American but the band was shouted down and hooted so loudly in Austria that David Lowery stormed onstage and ridiculed the audience. "They were always so genuine," Camper's David Immergluck enthused, "every night playing a different set. Songs would start differently, end differently. Everything constantly changed." Other cities showered them with money, prompting one concerned club owner to issue the warning, "COINS CAN KILL! If swallowed, coins can lodge in Souled American's stomach and cause ulcers, infections, and death!" In Belgium, Souled American finished up their bit of the tour and headed home; Immergluck remembers watching them leave and thinking, *Oh no. We're all alone now.* A couple weeks later, Camper broke up in a heated fury; it's almost as if this break-up decisively severed Souled American's career arc too, as if there was a kind of karmic symbiosis at work here. The will, the drive, the ambition, the patience required to be a successful band, these things abruptly evaporated. Souled American became a disappearing act, sighted here and there with Carlos the Jackal-like frequency, going off 8,000 miles to conduct a month's tour a long time ago, a few shows in New York a year before that, reportedly some other gigs. And their sporadic recordings, released almost reluctantly, without announcement.

The Scientific Community Weighs In

To the extent that scientists seek to solve all of life's riddles we will fail; but we *must* try, do you see? This point, redoubled in force, occurred to me again upon the recent delivery of "the last" Souled American CD, *Notes Campfire*, which inevitably raises more questions than it answers. In the lab we applied the age-old methodology to unriddle the CD into its constituent parts. We know that Souled American (like most modern musicians) remain big-brained bipeds amongst a class of higher vertebrates with complex cardiovascular requirements but question: Does the band exist, in what form. Question: How long does a record take to record, given that most tracks are subsequently erased. Question: How to define success, the terms. Question: How are songs composed, what is the musical destination/aspiration for this.

Question: Having named "the last" CD after the first song on the first album, are they acknowledging a dead-end of sorts.

Interview, Part Four

Q: You never get a sense of how Souled American met, if they were college kids —

A: I think that's right.

Q: They were college kids?

A: Or art school, perhaps? In Chicago. They were all from places in Illinois, I think. The main thing you can tell is that they must've spent years playing together in their bedrooms, you know? The only other band that vaguely reminds me of them is Swell. Do you know them?

Q: Yeah.

A: For years they recorded and played together, maybe even lived together in a warehouse in San Francisco. They know each other very well and they know what they're doing all the time. I never thought of that comparison before. Souled American were the kind of a band that, it didn't really matter what they did, and how stubborn and recalcitrant they were. For example, although I think it's fairly conventional for bands to send demos of what they're going to record to their record companies, they never did stuff like that with Rough Trade. And nobody really cared. Because we thought they were great! We'd just go, "Sure, sure, whatever!" Then we'd get the record and one of us would half-heartedly say to them, "This record's starts out unbelievably slow. Wouldn't it be better to put one of the more uptempo songs at least second if not first?" "No, no, no," they'd say, and then everybody'd back off again and the band would get it done exactly as they wanted it. But I think actually that if you looked at the sales curve of their three records they sold less with each successive release. It's pretty hard to do that.

Q: Summing up . . .?

A: Summing up, I think now one can add that they were really great to the fact that they were also years ahead of their time in anticipating or prefiguring this whole "No Depression" thing, whatever it's called. Which I'm sure they would despise, at least in its media-hyped form. I can see them shudder.

Disputed Parade Inspires Poster

(AP) Times Square was said to be recovering from a marketing spectacular unlike any other in which Chicago rock group Souled American paraded everyday objects before nearly a few attendees to mark the debut of their new CD, *Notes Campfire*.

The procession, its actual length still in contention, consisted of things and stuff cloaked in near-invisible ordinariness by Souled American, a band who has as of yet played no major role in cleaning up the Times Square area. A peep show owner on Forty-Second Street left his brightly lit shop open for business, asserting complete ignorance of the occasion.

Children screamed, perhaps with delight, perhaps in horror. A knowledgeable elderly couple maintained that children often scream in Times Square for no reason whatsoever. "What," a happy girl was heard to exclaim, when pressed for some response, "what parade?"

"I think it's all terrific how something can just happen around here," Cathy Tulon, an office worker from Levittown, L.I., remarked as she passed by with seven-year-old twin sons. "Perhaps it's worth it," Greenpoint native Sandy Sanajaran pointed out. "Maybe not."

A lonesome pink balloon drifted into the brown sky, reminding one of bubble gum dropped in the mud.

"My favorite sort of parade," observed Washington Heights resident Galvano Hendsberg, struggling for adequate words. "Not too much fuss and bother, easy to miss. I myself didn't notice a thing."

The exultant Souled American claimed the parade to be a "total triumph," though no attendance figures were forthcoming and no one could be located who recalled it. Even the precise starting and finishing times were in dispute, as too were the day, month, and year of the reputed event.

The Secret Truth About Frozen *and* The Drowning Pool *Revealed Here for the Very First Time*

One dull night at the video store, acting on an anonymous phone tip, we pressed play on (Souled American's 1994) *Frozen* just as the FBI warning appeared on the monitor at the start of the video of (Stuart Rosenberg's 1976) *The Drowning Pool*. What this simple act uncovered startled us profoundly — an undeniable series of linkages and references which could only have been crafted with considerable intentionality! The CD, it turns out, was constructed to express the inner heartbreak of private eye Lew Harper, called to Louisiana in the body of Paul Newman by an old flame who reappears in his life suddenly after having abandoned him six years earlier with no explanation. This can be no mere coincidence. Each song comments implicitly on motivation, stage direction, and the varying degrees of Harper's sorrow, an ache so devastating he can barely stand to acknowledge it. "You/are/my/one side./ Why won't you stay?" sadly shrieks Track 1, just as Joanne Woodward enters in disguise. She bites her lip. "That really was a voluptuous week," is all she'll acknowledge, seeking distance in nostalgia. "Sitdown" (Track 2) comes on as Harper drives the Lake Pontchartrain overpass to his motel; the song continues as he swims laps in the river, rubs tar off his feet, kicks Melanie Griffith out of his motel room. "Should I decide to screw my day all night/Sit down and give myself a good talking to?" He dresses, immediately gets arrested. "Grab the paint," say the cops, shoving him hard against his rental. "Don't gimme none uh your west coast snob-ass bullshit," remarks Chief of Police Tony Franciosa, warning Harper away from things he would never do. As Harper departs the police station, "Two of You" (Track 3) abruptly begins — an impossible synchronicity, too impossible not to've been consciously, studiously strategized by Souled American: the gentle slippery notes are the cluttered fog in Paul Newman's head and heart. Track 3 documents his pondering, silent drive, fading when he finally gets Woodward alone. "Hello, Lo," the CD says for

him (Track 4). "Your name it makes me stutter/saying 'hello.'"
Woodward's talk remains unchartably elusive, unaccountably
torn. "The marriage has not worked for some years now," she
tells him cryptically about her present husband. "Hey Lo/I
know/you're not to be questioned. But why'd ya go/and
have to/chase away the affection?" Harper is steered over
to the grandmother, who appears crazy. "Please," sings his
soul (Track 5), "Tell her I'm gone." He fights to fathom the
riddlesome answers he continues to receive when next he is
kidnapped—"Hey man, where you going" (Track 6) runs the
band's soundtrack—and led before the oil baron Kilbourne.
Harper's consideration of Kilbourne's mixed threats and
offers is accompanied by the contemplative puzzle of Track 7,
"Better who . . ./than me."

These considerable coincidences continue, looped and
magnified, as the CD starts anew following Harper's lines to
Gretchen the whore: "I don't know how people can talk dirty,
cold turkey, you know."

At the time those of us in the video store discovered
these facts we were surprised—they were one of our favorite
bands anyways, their soft guitars, soft voices, and soft facts
guiding us through a succession of alluringly spookier
soundscapes—but our respect for Souled American was now
exponentially renewed. Imagine the intensive challenges and
studio expense of clocking a CD perfectly against its movie
references (and then quite actively suppressing this very
information). We were flabbergasted at the insistent privacy
of such talents!—however, later investigations uncovered
still more astounding delights: that (Souled American's 1989)
Flubber was made to accompany a screening of (Ken Annakin's
1965) *Battle of the Bulge*—when you start them simultaneously
you watch Henry Fonda earn his theme song "Mar'boro Man"
while Robert Ryan is plainly the subject of "Wind to Dry"—but
I admit that at present those of us at the video store cannot
conclude with any certainty what movies accompany (and
decode) Souled American's remaining four CDs. If you have
any reasonable suggestions, please contact us at Radio City
Station. Please serious replies only.

Tell Me. What Do They Sing About?

Souled American seem to emphasize one theme above all else—the loneliness in the cooling ashes of a relationship. A numb, almost passion-less yearning. The dissolving of self, "the loss"—as Keith Richards described it—"of that sense of incarnation." Seems to be about fragmentation caused by absence of some love, in what they sing and how they play. "You know, it doesn't sound very good," the daughter of America's most influential music critic informed me skeptically after I described Souled American's efforts. "Not at all. I mean, it doesn't sound good at all."

Souled American and Its Discontents

He looked so nice I rechecked his price as he entered. "I was told $225 gets me the basics." He nodded, a wiggle of cute brown hair. "Yes ma'am." "And . . ." "Do you wish to hear about the extras?" "Dear boy, that's what I'm waiting for." In truth I was waiting for nothing. He possessed the eyes of a veterinarian, the hands of a pianist, and the dimples and eyebrows of those hunks in the power mower ads. Feeling quite lacy and racy in my slinky formal wear, I kicked off my heels, raised my blouse. The simple sight of my pianist power-mower vet led the tips of my fingers to brush my belly in anticipation. "Okay. The $225 show gets you the interpretive strip, incense and candles inclusive. It goes up from there. $25 more, I'll observe you in an act of self-gratification, plus $5 I'll grade you. $50 on top of that is Frustrated Husband, you can observe me in an act of self-gratification while I wear a band denoting our betrothal. Lotions and direct contact"—he cast me an appraising glance—"upwards of $95. For $375 you get all that plus a lecture derived from my dissertation." I couldn't prevent my hands from dancing higher on my chest: "What's the topic?" "Souled American and its Discontents." I scooted the Giorgio Sant-Angelo skirt down over my satin panties, past my nylons, and shook it free of my feet. "Ooh. Fascinating." He shrugged humbly. "The intriguing paradox of a band like no other, defiant, defiantly ignored. As naturally inviting as drowning in a bathtub, as romantic as burning up in bed, such is Souled American. The mad hubris, the sinister medicine, the hush as it falls across the pop continent. Choosing this product means you recognize the need to make ecological and social choices." My hands met my abdomen, kneading and probing and altogether too happy with the social choices they were making. "You take traveler's checks?" He did and I signed off on the whole package. How to summarize the ensuing pleasures? Two images: my oiled billboard poet-boy declaiming in the candlelight, his face purplish in passion, inflection swaying delightfully: "There's a band that wants to rock you. There's a band that wants your money, wants your vote. There's a band that wants to sex you. Then there's The Other, namely—Souled American." My watch pendant glinted merrily from the carpet where I'd vaguely deposited it, my diamond bangled bracelets and priceless hoop earrings having been tossed god knows where, and together we approached The Moment. Second image: my whimpering body wrapped ecstatically in a jacquard woven comforter and lace-trimmed flat sheet as Mr. Man of Mans spoke from the hotel's daybed, where the sweaty webwork of his musculature was pressed to the pillow shams: "Could anything be more secret than Souled American . . . their sound itself approaches a whisper, the dying signal of a stranded craft, even as their CDs become yet more impossible to find. 'This is kind of a big deal,' is how their new CD was announced, by a record store which claims on-line to be the only place in the country still carrying Souled American's releases: 'Tell your friends.'" Oh! If I had the money now to do it all again, would I even hesitate? Not for a moment!

Fans Wanted:

Chicago-area bnd with six releasd rcrdngs sks a following; infls W Nelson, B Eno, B Marley, Ltl Feat. Cpls OK. Serious inquiry only. No rcists, sxists. You: OTK/d, discreet, finan. secure, generous with papers, spiteful over posited drugging/ abducting disappearance/replacement of the great middle-era Neil Young ("Ambulance Blues," "Revolution Blues,"

"Vampire Blues"), must be fond of genetic-transmogrification daydreams in which John Prine is molecularly crossed with John Fahey with Peter Tosh with Pere Ubu with the Grand Ole Opry. Saw you watching Merle Haggard, you carried well-worn copy of *East of the River Nile*. Wed. night mid-April. Your friends call you Philosopher King Poet. I stand there and watch. I want to say hi but . . . I'd still like to say hi. Hope I hear from you! Write Radio City Station.

AMAZING DISGRACE

I HAVE THE BAD HABIT of reading while I drive. Recently I was pulled over in New Hampshire's White Mountains, behind the wheel of a pale-green Fairlane 289, a copy of *True Life Memoirs of Bazooka Joe* open on my lap. Stirred by the erotic misadventures of Mort, Joe, Ursula, and Zena, inspired by the defiantly surreal Bazooka Joe fortune which appeared as the bio's epigraph ("There are more grains of truth than there are stars in the ocean"), I refused the breathalyzer, waived my rights, kicked the bastard police dog in its yapper, and—for good measure—mischievously let slip that I'd plotted to kill the officer's tiny daughter with the intention of making his scrubbed peasant wife the mistress of Mort. In *True Life Memoirs*, this is approximately the attitude which resolves Bazooka Joe's every ethical dilemma in three frames or less. In real-life America, the strategy was less successful: handcuffed into the backseat of a Carroll O'County squad car, I helplessly began urinating all over their plastic seats . . .

Was this a dream? As I recount this to you, such unexpected defiance on my part adds just one more implausibility to the whole affair. By then my experiences had begun to seem so far-fetched that I could scarcely believe any of this viewable footage was True Life. Out of nowhere, a telephone had jingle-jangled and Romanov forces were offering to pay me to write up the Montreal pop show of a band called the Posies. I had been Fed-Exed vouchers for transportation, with which I rented a 1966 Fairlane. It was while traveling to the border in this very Ford that the corrupting influence of the bubblegum kid and his turtlenecked buddy expressed itself on my lap. "Watcha gonna do," I sneered at the cops, "throw me into rock-crit jail?" This attempt at humor became oddly self-

215

fulfilling. It was precisely what they proposed to do.

Blithely perched on a bluff overlooking Berlin, New Hampshire, the Hunter S. Thompson Penitentiary may represent America's most secret institution. The inmates (those I met) are primarily Canadian journalists. Ordered once upon a time to race down to NYC for the heart-stopping debut of this or that entertainment marvel, they had unintentionally disobeyed the arcane local traffic ordinances. Soon thereafter, they'd found themselves behind bars. Some have been there for many years, still serving out infractions they can't fathom, dispatched from long ago to cover a show by Paul McCartney & Wings at Madison Square Garden or Dylan/the Dead at Meadowlands. Occasionally, too, that rare overzealous American gets tossed in.

The food is the inedible slop you'd expect, which hits the cafeteria tray sounding, looking, and—yes—even tasting like coffee grounds soaked in ketchup. It gets served three times daily and, though the food never changes, the name of the meal does. During my tenure at this place, my jailers alternately titled this same slop: "Lester Bangs' Brains," "The DeRogatis Blowfish Platter," "Carducci's Big Balls and Butt" or the ever-tantalizing "Hunter's Mystery Catch."

Locked up in a room with a chair, cot and toilet, I spent the rest of the Romanov voucher on bribing my guard, who reluctantly garnished my living quarters with a cell phone, a Discman, and the last CD single from these Posies. I then rang up the office and read my critique of this Posies show. I reviewed it in glowing terms, leaving out the parts about me not actually making it to Canada, about me calling now from a speed-trap stockade in New Hampshire; nor did I bring up Bazooka Joe and what that wisecracking pirate boy had made me do.

I closed my review in the following manner: "The Posies, two new Beatles named Auer and Stringfellow, have made four CDs in ten years. It has become the central mystery of the '90s rock world how a band with such melodic gifts (not to mention studio mastery, big record company backing, talent at all instruments, 'imminent breakthrough' stamped atop every composition) have failed to become a *People* cover story.

Like a center-seeking Clinton, these Posies unapologetically capitulate to reigning tastes, adapting their handsome materials to screechy grunge arrangements on cue in 1993 (*Frosting on the Beater*), more recently dressing the songs in once-again fashionable retro outfits (*Amazing Disgrace*). Whatever dues they still owed were completely paid up over the last several years, as they've humbly been playing the background roles of the two dead characters in Alex Chilton's latest musical revue, thus permitting the so-called reunion of Big Star. *Must they serve you eggs in bed before you crack your lids to acknowledge them with a shrug of thanks?"*

In jail I confirmed, through lonely lights-out morse-code messages we tapped on our stone walls with crude metal implements, that the failure of these Posies to hit it big haunts the rock critic in all of us (or at least all of us in there). In that way, the Gonzo Hotel (as we brothers called our compound) was one unendurably long music seminar, a camp bursting with pop-market theories and cultural didactics—opinions, opinions, opinions! Since radios and periodicals were strictly forbidden, the all-important rock news came disseminated via a grapevine of rumors. These info scraps were taken very seriously. Men stood up suddenly at meal-time to herald the impending liberation of gay music in phrases which were in turn flowery and apocalyptic. The etymology of the word "skronk" was hotly plumbed. Ritual fistfights erupted in the exercise yard between trip-hop enthusiasts and those more inclined to regard all jungle and techno off-shoots as musical dead-ends. A Courtney Love apologist sliced open a Kathleen Hanna enthusiast with the sharpened corner of a cassette case, while a trembling Cobain scholar mumbled sorrowfully nearby.

I could stand almost none of it. The guard had reclaimed my cell phone. Late afternoons I placed my chair atop my toilet against the southernmost wall and, standing tiptoe on the wobbly arms, tall as I could go, with a hand balanced against the ceiling, I could just peek out the window. Berlin sat in smoke some miles off, trimmed in neon. The light glazed everything in the same goopy pall, the sun not so much going down as moving aside.

A few feet from my window stretched the upper branch on a tall winter tree, stupid and lifeless. A shopping bag fluttered in the branches, snagged by the tree's bony fingers. New to the situation, the bag was full of personality, confident of an eventual escape. Any strong wind might set it loose. The bag accepted all drafts and gusts without qualification, puffing grandly to its full size, bravely expecting both nothing and everything. I was reminded of my feelings for Marie.

And meanwhile, I sank deeper into a meadow of Posies than any person ever. I had, after all, just the one CD single to listen to—the song was "Please Return It," a manly yarn by Stringfellow.

Now, focused in and stripped of ordinary ornamentation, I embraced what I'd always suspected but never had admitted to myself—that though I (like the rest at the Gonzo Hotel) grew besotted with the smell of all things Posies it was half the band I most truly liked—the vulnerable John Lennon character, this frayed Stringfellow, pinched of nose and congested with meanings, and not the voluptuous-voiced Auer. Auer's songs gleamed more deliciously at first but came to depend on tired power chords and snarl-free vocalizings. In the end, they provided the hollow comfort of emerging victorious from a chocolate-eating contest. Having only this one song in hand, I no longer needed to feel guilty (as I so often did at home) for advancing past the Auer tracks, in effect editing him out of the group in favor of the urgent hayfever enigmas wheezed from this knotty Stringfellow's thin windpipe . . .

"Please Return It" starts with a command expressed so tentatively that the voice wobbles, unable to sustain the note. The singer, uncomfortable, wants back an "it" he'd really rather not address—A letter? His heart? He sounds rattled by how much the singing of this song is taking out of him; the more he says, the more he becomes required to say. He shakes his head. Look at the way we act, the things we say; so many factors, contradictions. "When we live the life we live, it's never ours completely. Not *completely*." What he's asking for, he continues, it's not so very much. It's quite easy. "Put it back," he recommends. He even suggests what he'll do with it. "I can burn it."

This last image ignites a fueled clarity to his thinking. He seizes suddenly on what, during the most honest moments of a denial-filled day, might register as his main complaint: "When you let me live my life, you didn't do it completely." It's badly put but we know what he means. He is reminded of other impossible things he could stand to have back—"Like the year I spent comparing me to you; please return it." How would he like these things returned? Swept dutifully from sight; "Like a servant, like a sewer. Please return it. Please return it."

The song assures no return of anything, no definition of what's being asked, no trust gained. The song regrets the bother and embarrassment of its own existence. Which is pretty much where—following an inadequate attempt to convince us there's an upside, there *has* to be an upside—Stringfellow leaves us, in a prison of shyness and discomfort, after around two and a half minutes of music.

What had I learned? For several days I listened and waited. I gauged the window to be too narrow. But I discovered the ceiling panels could be pushed aside, and once above them I plummeted down a vertical air shaft and rolled free at the base of a tree. It was the tree outside my window. The plastic bag, still tangled on the treetop, was now frayed and tense, a limp remnant. It flopped resignedly. I waved up at my window, up at the emotionally trapped song I'd left behind in that cell, then headed down the hill to Berlin . . . to return to the land of Bazooka Joe.

MY LIFE IN EIGHTEEN SONGS

U2: "Ultraviolet (Light My Way)" (5:31), from *Achtung Baby* (Island, 1991). Last night she said her name was Marie. She described herself as brown of hair and eyes. She offered her measurements, which I failed to notice. I asked instead how old she was.

"Fourteen and three-quarters," she replied. "Is that too old? Almost fifteen?"

"Fine," I chuckled. "If that's alright with you."

"I guess so. I mean . . . I don't have any control over it, really. It's just my age."

"And you're Marie."

"Oh, I . . . Is that what I told you before?"

"Yeah."

"Right, that's the name then."

Marie . . . could she have pierced me with two more loaded syllables? Breezes blew against the stiff hinges of my heart. A creak issued from within my chest: *Marie!* Of all names, why did she have to use that one? *Once, with all my might, I had gone for Marie . . . but she'd eluded me . . .*

Last night, on my end, I asked too many questions while, on her end, a radio played. Although Marie cost me $29.40 for ten minutes, the long-distance bill would indicate I spoke with the western province for forty minutes—this has been agreed upon when the service took my order. In truth, Marie was not in the western province; she seemed to be in the central zone. I recognized the radio station, the DJ's voice. I could've easily tracked her down through it.

I insisted on an account of the filthiest thing she had ever done. Marie wasn't exactly positive what it was. I encouraged her to make something up. She tried. It didn't sound convincing nor would she flesh it out per my follow-ups.

"Baby baby baby," blasted the radio behind her. "Baby baby baby. Baby baby baby."

Sometimes when I am blue, the best medicine in the world is hearing a stadium hit recognized by millions (say, Alanis Morrisette's "Uninvited" or Pearl Jam's "Corduroy" or the Red Hot Chili Peppers' "Scar Tissue") and feeling connected, for approximately five minutes and thirty-one seconds, like we are all in this together. Playing on Marie's radio now was one of the very few U2 things I could stomach. It sounded so effusively naughty just then I nearly cried.

Three times the service called back before patching Marie through. Each time they had requested everything—my full name, the name of my hotel and room number, my employment number, vehicle permit number, date of birth. They wondered how I'd voted in the last plebiscite, what year I graduated from middle school, my height, weight, preference of girl, preference of topic. I indulged their inquiry, regarding myself as thrillingly violated, interrogated, the focus of an imminent police raid, a pending assault. I imagined writhing while the SWAT boys pinned me to the wall, with one hand nailed up in the air and both ankles bolted bloodily to the baseboard, leaving one hand free to masturbate. *Wishful thinking.*

"I'm in the black," went the radio. "Can't see or be seen."

"What do you think I'm doing right now?" I asked Marie. She couldn't begin to guess. She considered it sufficient to provide murmurings of artificial ecstasy, a few low grunts and extended vowel sounds.

"Now we lie together," U2 observed in the background, "in whispers and moans."

"Tell me," I hissed.

"Tell you what?"

"Say it. Say, 'That's a Bono No-No.' Say it."

Marie did as she was asked.

'Til Tuesday: "No One Is Watching You Now" (3:44), from *Welcome Home* (Sony, 1986). My sales route consists of a single square tower rising to a three-story conical roof. It contains many thousands of families, mostly ancient folks and single mothers with multiple offspring, who rarely make promising customers. My sales pitch has grown sooty with disgust as I clomp up and around the disorienting stairwell with my case of miracle knives. In one apartment, a bashful lady offers me a cup of coffee. She is in her late forties, rather plump. She encourages me to lay my wares out on the kitchen table, though she can afford none of them. *She craves the companionship of any pitch, even mine.* On her small TV, the government channel plays the music video of "Voices Carry," starring that new-wave chick with the ungodly dye job who sings a lot like a robust Chrissie Hynde but writes a lot like a tender Elvis Costello. *I'd forgot all about them.* The kitchen is hot from baking. It smells of spiced pecans. Unexpectedly, I think of Marie. *Why hadn't I asked about Walter? Hadn't she gone to him after leaving me? Hadn't they meant everything to one another? Weren't they the eternal couple? But no: They'd split up.* I feel relieved that I hadn't brought it up over the phone to Marie; it was the right thing to do. *But no; it'd not really been Marie, my Marie, the fabulous; just some child working to confuse me.* The bashful lady pulls on a pair of mittens, opens her oven, and removes a butternut squash pie topped with coconut sprinkles. I agree to try a slice.

Iggy Pop: "Tiny Girls" (2:59), from *The Idiot* (RCA, 1977). Last Saturday she said her name was "Tokyo Rose" but she plainly appreciated my calling her "Rosy." I loved her, of course, though in a way that was difficult really to articulate. She spoke timidly, knew only a few English nouns, scored extremely low on her conjugation of verbs. Rosy was a straight $2/minute.

She lives in the western province with her grandmother. Her mother sent her there for school. She "like go fast in car, real fast, top down, desert, night." She "touch self this morning, bed." She asked my help in a wide range of things, from explaining what I did for fun to aiding in a description of her bosom. "Nipples like erase pencils," she repeated many times. "What you call, what you call," she would begin and I would teach her the names of painful acts, the kind you might meekly suggest to a loved one after decades together, and she would say "Yes! Yes! I much like!" The call was more a language lesson than an erotic undertaking, but I picked up the tab like a gentleman.

Rosy'd answered when I telephoned in response to a print ad encouraging me to "Ride the Tiny Girls of the Orient Express." Unlike Marie, she didn't have to call me back, didn't require my employment number, no vehicle permit or DOB, no mother's maiden name. Such trusting times back then (the simpler days of last Saturday).

I hung up very much in love with Rosy. How would it work between us? I swallowed the impulse to suggest, "Move here, hold close to heart." Instead I expressed my gratitude, and put the phone to bed.

Loudon Wainwright III: "Motel Blues" (2:42), from *Album II* (Atlantic, 1971). The check-in clerks and hotel receptionists resemble winged things dropped from above. When they page someone to the lobby's white courtesy telephone or announce my calls over the intercom, I believe myself in the presence of angels, their squawk so heavenly. . . . But the one I most dearly adore is she who makes our beds here. She comes by frequently and leans into my room, taut with curiosity, intent on the blanket mission of folding that unfolds before her. We both know. Nothing need be said. Her name? Irrelevant! It is not a world burdened with "names" that she and I inhabit. Today she wore little beneath her room-service robe and her carriage was so steadfast as to muffle any attempt to converse. We strode at one other from different ends of the corridor, lifting just our knees and elbows. The case in my right hand held a hundred exquisitely flashing blades. Our eyes met for a luridly long moment, a moment measured from the bedside clock of a hotel room in which she and I lay panting, remorseless, exchanging fluids in graceful abandon. "Hi," I put forth, with such emphasis that I became light-headed after I'd said it. She too glimpsed the room with the clock lacking remorse, its panting and grace, the flashing blades and consequent abandon, and acknowledged everything with her own intense, "Hi."

The Kinks: "Young and Innocent Days" (4:08), from *Arthur (or the Decline and Fall of the British Empire)* (Reprise, 1969). Marie and I met far from here, long ago. We were young and naive together — *Miserable in Missouri* read our tee shirts. Back then we had all the time in the world to debate tariffs in the donut shops and post offices. We viewed the world through a self-centered, undignified emotionalism that turns out to've been mere hormones. She'd written a highly touted novel, I'd come up with a civic plan the moneymen loathed. Since Marie had met with more success, I was allowed to feel sabotaged, an architect with incendiary blueprints, like a photographer robbed of undeveloped negatives. We wandered the ashen streets of the central zone in high spirits, planning the new art movement we'd label Gang Detonation or maybe Continental Candle (requirements: gritty and desperate but spiritually nourishing). We preferred breakneck bands with onion breath and words sour like lemons. We liked the works of Brian Eno, not really his own songs but just the ones he helped others write and produce. We concocted elaborate scenarios for every song we heard, interpretative responses that we meant as complementary. Isn't that what music is for, to aid us in telling our stories and living our lives? These songs belonged to us! All the while, we warned the world it would soon be ours, as the deadening mills and foundries ground out ever more fiery sunsets.

Randy Newman: "Marie" (3:07), from *Good Old Boys* (Reprise, 1974). I was set to propose to Marie on New Year's Eve. I had it planned out. She would look like a princess, with her hair piled up high, and I always would love her: Marie. This is not what happened. Instead, a month before I was to unveil the outline of our forthcoming marital bliss, Marie announced that she was leaving for the western province. I was so utterly unprepared I couldn't speak. What could I say? I was still a month away from proposing. None of the words were thawed out yet. I'm afraid I made a mess of it, and whatever friendship we'd had was lost in a hurried attempt to reveal my heart. Marie departed, and soon fell in with a radioman named Walter. I was enthralled, in turn, by the advertisement of a revolutionary

breakthrough popularly known as "the miracle knife," thanks
to which serrated edges were guaranteed to never dull. I was
one of the lucky missionaries dispatched to tell the public of
the sensational findings, the unrustable surfaces and perfectly
balanced grips of our multipurpose implements. Marie? I lost
touch with her. She had come before the knife, when life was
still scrambled with its sunny-side down. I caught rumors that
Walter was an enormous hit on college frequencies and the
independent radio circuit, that he and Marie had moved in
together, had become inseparable. Frankly, I was too busy
with my knives to notice. Only at night, alone in a hotel
room—momentarily dislocated when a song from our shared
past made it out the clock radio—would I think of her, with
slight regrets—and, hugging close a paring knife, I'd release
one meager tear or two.

**Randy Newman: "Suzanne" (3:08), from *12 Songs* (Reprise,
1970).** Suzanne is her name today and Suzanne it will forever
remain. Over the phone she gave herself to me as I held her
like a madness dear. I possess the kiss of a pitchfork and a case
of revolutionary knives, I love tiny redheads like you, I love
white chiffon. I am beautiful, if you don't mind my saying so;
I'm the hunkiest to whom you shall ever speak. My legs are
long and tan, my arms full and muscular, my chest knotty and
sculpted, my waist lithe and delicate. My wrists are powerful
from making chopping motions all day, my coordination is
keen; I am able to hurl a blade and split corn silk at ninety
yards. I am all you want and need; my eyes are deep blue, ocean
blue, sensitive and bold, hungry yet alluringly melancholic,
blue like . . .—God! they just go on forever. My mind is perfect
and my heart totally committed to you; I love you absolutely
and can remember no other telephone names or numbers but
yours; I was born and now I imagine your reflection in my
knife and there is nothing else to say, nothing.

**Nick Cave: "Sad Waters" (4:50), from *Your Funeral, My Trial*
(Homestead, 1986).** Saturday I met the one at the art show in
the hotel gallery. I feel certain her name is Mary (*hair of gold
and lips like cherries*). We linked up without speaking, and stood

before the pictures with arms folded, sometimes laughing, always reacting (though never to the works but only to each other), never acknowledging. We furtively studied one another's reflection in the framed works of art, Mary's long hair braided solemnly, her diminutive figure clad in the clothes of a preteen and those saddle shoes which beautiful women wear now. She was bright for her age. Perhaps we would ride motorcycles once she got her license; definitely we would live in only the most colorful of hotels. If school ran late, she would always call. She recognized in me the certainty, the immense authority that customers reliably see in my knives. She laughed at the photo of the fat man with the buttoned jersey, which was ever so good of her. We lost sight of one another for a time. Doubtless her young heart fell to wondering, *Did I imagine this?* She was relieved to come across me in the hotel's next room, staring at the statue of Saturn devouring his offspring. Mary sidled up noiselessly. Saturn was livid—Rhea has delivered *another!*—his mouth wide to consume the infant's arm. Both Mary and I knew the eroticism behind Saturn's oral talents, we felt like experts, in fact. . . . When she left my side, it was only to roll off the bed and dress for school. I know I will find her at tomorrow's hotel and it will be as if she has just returned from her class and now she is ready for me to welcome her in.

Talking Heads: "Once in a Lifetime" (4:09), from *Remain in Light* (Sire, 1980). One summer night I left the hotel for a stroll, turned a corner, and came upon perhaps three hundred and eleven people milling about on a sidewalk. There was a motorcade, one block in length, parked before a well-regarded food establishment. Inside was David Byrne, eating. This was earlier in the decade, when Byrne was running for president. I joined the crowd, hoping to glimpse the aging candidate. There were quite a few floodlights and cameras, naturally, and several Bowie fans with protest signs. Hawkers were on hand to supply paperbacks, pineapple, and massage. After perhaps twenty minutes, an announcement was made to the crowd that Byrne had finished with his entree and was ordering dessert. A raucous cheer went up. Someone felt up the flabby inside of my arm. I shook it off. They tried to touch me there again. I was unable to turn. I blindly threw an elbow. Next they tapped my shoulder. I shouted. Someone gently spoke my name. I recognized the voice. It was Walter.

'Til Tuesday: "Have Mercy" (4:37), from *Welcome Home* (Sony, 1986). We shoehorned our way out of the mob's grasp. I took a long look at the man who stole my Marie. In his heyday, Walter was unbeatable, magnificence embodied. He had the voice, the drive, the look, the stance. He was like one of those walking wonders of the western world. That was, as they say, no more. What had once been the penetrating gaze of this wonderboy was now a multitude of scattered refractions such as result when a heavy mirror is dropped. His eyes were ash-filled marbles glued into the shriveled disaster that'd once been his handsome face. "What's that you're carrying?" he croaked, indicating my case. I began to speak about the miracle knife. "Right," he interrupted. "Right, I tried to sell them. Couldn't move a damn one." I was dumbstruck. I had never heard of anybody failing to sell a single miracle knife. Why, they sold themselves! It was inconceivable. One would have to work hard to keep a customer from recognizing the revolutionary quality of these knives. . . . "What's happened to you?" I sputtered. Walter sighed, and then I understood: He had lost his Marie.

The Kinks: "Rosie Won't You Please Come Home" (2:20), from *Face to Face* (Reprise, 1966). What happened, Walter explained, was that Marie got quite caught up with something else, a lost cause, and her interest in Walter evaporated. Walter didn't actually use the words "caught up." Understandably sore, he called Marie "psycho" and "obsessed." To the exclusion of all else, Marie became devoted to the passing out of hand-made flyers about that girl, the one who disappeared at the U2 concert. Roseanne, the girl was called, or Rosie. The flyer showed a young redhead in a white chiffon dress with a happy, sunburned face. It bore the date Rosie'd disappeared, described the guitar solo during which she'd last been seen alive and what she'd been wearing, gave her employment number, vehicle permit, date of birth, how she would've voted in the last plebiscite, what year she eventually would graduate from middle school, her height, weight. Desperate investigators contacted the band for assistance, although they possessed scant evidence connecting U2 to the redhead wearing the white chiffon dress. Later flyers even took Bono to task for somehow helping to abduct Rosie and implied that the lead singer was aware of the precise circumstances of the girl's gruesome death. (These rantings were rightly dismissed as irresponsible and thoroughly unsubstantiated.) The redhead in the white chiffon dress never turned up.

Rickie Lee Jones: "We Belong Together" (4:52), from *Pirates* (Reprise, 1981). Of course there is little you can know for sure about how our life together will turn out, but much is obvious to the point of inevitability. When your daughter stirs, I will say, *Don't bother. I'll calm her.* I'll leave our bed and sing her songs, maybe Aimee Mann or Ray Davies or something I myself wrote back when I loved this land like I love you. And your daughter will demand a story, which is when I will tell her of the city that was all cobalt blue and the girl who collected up the yellow and stored it in her pillowcase so that it would not be captured and stained blue by the men in the city. And when I return to our bed a fat moon has dropped through our window and your dark black skin in the pale ghostly light excites me tremendously. I wrap my paltry self around you and I am white as the moon and blue as the city. And I pronounce your name, *Marianna, is it? or Susie Rose, I forget.* Like a fog machine it clears the world and steers me home.

David Bowie: "Be My Wife" (2:55), from *Low* (RCA, 1977). Just now the phone rang and there she was. Remember how I told you of the girl with whom I strode beneath the stars, past midnight, kicking our way through thick mounds of autumn leaves, that sweet smell of eucalyptus and burning sour pine rising through shadow chimneys from dying fireplaces and we talked non-stop or else not at all, it was late and cold, I had been up since dawn, and now here we were, and without touching we knew everything. (I did not tell you? Oh, but

I meant to—!) She was impatient with her words, rushing breathless, and I became challenged and similarly dashed through thoughts without punctuation and it was heaven to be so very tired and so very vibrantly in love. (No, I did not make her up! Did I? Could I? I don't believe so.) There were books on our minds, as I recall, and with her leading the charge of the idea brigade we walked with hands in jacket pockets, talking cloudy bursts, like dynamite in our chests. This is where we walk now with conversation and it's true, very soon we will be together and very soon begin to touch.

Randy Newman: "Rosemary" (2:08), from *12 Songs* (Reprise, 1970). When I swam yesterday at the hotel gym, she was on the basketball court, two walls, one refrigerator, and countless stationary bikes away from exchanging glances with me, yet still I knew we both could feel it, as I breast-stroked through the water in just my teeniest Speedo and she practiced reverse lay-ups in tank top and Reeboks. To articulate the sex act to one another, much less to enact it, would have been so redundant as to be boring. "Well, of course," would be her response. "What do you think I'm doing out here, shooting baskets?" I'm thinking about her all the time. I did not need to see her to know the sweat which glistened upon her freckles or to understand the bath that was coming afterwards to uncramp her weary shoulders, eyes closed and head lolling loosely on neck, as feet turned on and off the hot water, waist bent and scooted beneath the spigot such that the warmth pouring from the faucet flooded directly onto her tenderest spot.

The Kinks: "Susannah's Still Alive" (2:22), from *Something Else* (Reprise, 1967). She turned out to be blond last night—Susannah, voice of humor and ease, floating in from planetary time.

"You are said to have," I informed her, paraphrasing what the service told me, "an assertive manner."

"Little old me?" she mused, and then she asked, as they all do, what I was doing at that moment, as though there were any doubt, as though I weren't spending $2.50 a minute ($25 minimum) to hear her pose the question.

I answered, we exchanged a few particulars (she claimed to be blond down there), then she growled a little too huskily for my taste, "How big is it?"

"Not too big, I guess."

"Mmmm. Could I hang a towel on it?"

"Well, I don't find that such a sexy option, you know. But yeah, I suppose. Assuming we're talking a dishtowel."

"Mmmm-hmmm."

"Or maybe a wash cloth."

"Could I grab it with both hands and swing from it?"

"Not without hurting me you couldn't."

Some speculation ensued. Now I realize that maybe Rosemarie was a little wrong for me. (You remember Rosie, Marie?) I mean—make no mistake—Rosemary's great, truly and utterly, just maybe not enough of something for my taste. Heck, she probably sews her own clothes, works wonders with an ice machine, all that. But my heart right now is as full as can be with this young Susan, my sole love of last night. She claims our orgasms were simultaneous ("cum d'habitude," she says they call it in the French quarter), although I suppose she's paid to say that. Still, she will never leave my thoughts.

David Bowie: "Strangers When We Meet" (5:08), from *Outside* (Virgin, 1995). We are—all of us—so exceedingly handsome. It's a shame we can't meet. We each spend the day stranded on an island of sorts, coding what goes out, decoding what comes in, you know? Crossing this sea of automobiles to pick up one another seems impossible. Heading to our next hotel, we travel alone, wearing the safety harness at all times. I look into the windshield in the mist and I see you watching me, your eyes speaking novels, and the wipers swipe past, then return you to me, you with those books in your face. When yesterday, the sun fell for a moment I called your name aloud. Upon the utterance daytime returned. There is none other like you. Am I making a fool of myself, committed to the purpose of you so totally, dedicated to your functioning as the worker is to the plant? Come to me. I will introduce you to knives such as you have never seen. All that you were before will drain from you.

The Kinks: "Do You Remember Walter?" (2:15), from *The Kinks Are the Village Green Preservation Society* (Reprise, 1968). Sometime after I bumped into him at the Byrne viewing, Walter drifted up to the town of Pinardville in the eastern province. He entered a sporting goods store on South Main Street and picked up a bolt-action 30.06 deer rifle with a scope. The newspapers reported that Walter had his own ammunition. The gun was on a display rack in the back of the store, where customers could pick it up without assistance from a sales clerk. There was a sudden discharge. "Everyone looked," said the store's owner. "And there he was, slumped to the floor." The owner called the city police, who pronounced Walter dead at the scene. Police said he had a note with him that indicated he planned to kill himself. After the shooting, the owner closed the store and sent home the four employees on duty. "He sort of ghosted in and did his thing," shrugged the owner. "There's still this anger about why do this in front of me. I don't know, it's sad. I have all kinds of emotions going through me."

Robyn Hitchcock and the Egyptians: "She Doesn't Exist" (4:16), from *Perspex Island* (A&M, 1991). You couldn't have been more wrong when you insisted—last night on the phone—that you were interchangeable and that it scarcely mattered to me who I was with as long as it was some female. You were so very, very wrong.

You were all I needed: my five senses, my four basic food groups, my tri-state area, my twin cities. You are the partridge in my pear tree. And when the phone rang, it was all I could do not to say your name and instantly demand your hand in marriage. There is nothing, finally, to help me distinguish your concerns from mine. *We are one.* And when you criticized that guy, that one who lives almost exclusively in fantasy, who flings around the word "love" like a dickhead ordering juice, like an addict in a nervous twitch, who can't act on what he wants because he wants it all, everything. . . . Well. I hated him too. I glimpsed him on the boulevard once, elbows and knees down, and I started hurling my steel-clad boot into the Italy of his soft white underbelly, and he gasped with each kick. God, such a fool! an idiot, a waste. Then I recalled it was me you were criticizing and I insisted, *No. You couldn't be more wrong, my sweet child, my thin fat one, my red-headed blond, my Hispanic Arab. You are perfect to me, the only one . . .*

CALL OFF THE FATWA

WHEN I WAS A WEE SPROUT in Fresno, dirt and fog capital of the world, we walked the new-tilled soil in Walkman headphones, kicking furrows barefoot, tamping down dirtclods, and chanting along to Freedy Johnston's first cassette. How we heard this back then, I scarcely can figure; apparently few in New York yet knew Freedy (who had only just arrived from the Midwest) but somehow all in Fresno did (were we some test audience, the other Kansas in Freedy's marketing heart?).

We particularly adored the song "Fun Ride," his loose, bouncy tribute to both a delirious carnival and a complicated relationship, a recklessly whooshing song yet handily controlled. It formed the everything of our love for him. "Pull the plug on that thing," Freedy says, commanding his girl to turn off the television for how it can't compare to the upcoming "Fun Ride": "It won't lift you fifty feet." This particular observation, this liberating contempt, became our anthem, the voice of our gang of Fresno toughs.

A short time later, Freedy passed through on tour. By then his second cassette had dropped on us out of the drought-dead skies, a far, far greater wonder than his first, falling on our ears generous and splendid like some Marshall Plan or a *Gods Must Be Crazy* Coke. Elsewhere Freedy was still nobody, but in Fresno he sold out the college football stadium. My friend Melvin Toff and I made over $1,327.18 on bootleg tee shirts we silk-screened in the campus parking lot and sold to the ticket-less thousands who were turned away. "Place your faith in Freedy," our shirts read. "He will lift you fifty feet."

And we built something for the state fair called "Fun Ride." We worked, in constructing *our* "Fun Ride," to render his

235

carefully careless song inhabitable. Every egress would, as per the song, demonstrate what it celebrated. Every I-beam would contain the locked-in dynamism audible in the tumbling chorus, every structural cable would reference Freedy's ingenious arrangement.

Our "Fun Ride" was a huge hit. People enjoyed going on it, and they learned a lot. We garnered the red ribbon at state level but were edged out in the nationals by "Keep Punching Joe," a vintage 17th century pugilist masque produced—no!—by our long-standing rivals, the Daniel Johnstons.

People lately have asked why a man of my advanced years, frequently faint and sallow, stooped in gait and almost hard of hearing, and now—at long last—too old to vote, called for the killing of Freedy. Yet I ask those early Freedy fans who endured the muzak puke that comprised his last release, can you blame me? Why, that *other* Johnston—Daniel Johnston—he was never this bad, would never sing something that didn't hang in his lungs for a time, would never thrive on sweets. The conclusion was inescapable: we had backed the wrong Johnston. The feigned David Gates-isms of this new Freedy! That unrocking rock! The public and press all appeared to appreciate it, but this was wrong.

And so in slippers I slowly set out from my Stuyvesant Town nursing home in brisk November, 1995, trailing an IV and carrying a pail of wheatpaste, to remind the world that Freedy used to be better. Strangers spat invectives at the sickly old man and telephoned at all hours, yet still I persevered! I glued up street manifestos—I did this! Yes!—which tried in their tiny way to ask what happened to the long ago Fresno Freedy we wore on our chests, who sang with such subtle verve and appeared incapable of letting us down.

The staff here have since corrected my meds. The voices are gone and my vision less blurry. My family, when they visit, speak to me as if I have years left, though this too is some sick joke. Recently my dew-lipped niece Deborah brought me the next Freedy CD, *Never Home*. As it played on the hospital's bedside boombox, she perched lightly upon the arm of the divan just as you'd expect, watching the inconstant beeps and blinks on the panels of my electronic monitors as if to read some response, desperate to be able to convey my sincere apologies to the world. And . . .

The CD wasn't so bad, really. It still sounded like the type of stuff listened to by candlelit women in slinky bed apparel as they sip chilled wine from tall stemware, shaking their heads over those louses they always seem to date. Okay, so no one was lifted fifty feet or encouraged to miss work. But time and again Freedy casually picked a graceful detail — "leaving just enough for the weekly rent, plus a little change" — and abruptly carried it into the spirit of a character — "taking the long way to anyplace, in the frozen rain." Or he'd tell several stories at once, as when a klepto's case study in "On the Way Out" also supplies guilty dialogue with a girlfriend.

And there are still displays of singing brilliance, in the way he treasures a throwaway line like "now it's been two months," starting enraged and closing in pieces, and the stirring manner in which he slows his syllables singing, "I loved you or . . . something like that, anyway."

At last, making sounds which best belong under the rolling credits of a film of heartland romance, *Never Home* concluded. I waved a hand with difficulty. "Well," I croaked. "Let him live."

"Oh!" dewy-eyed Deborah bounded about, clapping her dewclaws delightedly and moving as if to kiss me. "You won't be sorry, Uncle. I promise! You won't!"

He is trying, after all. I think maybe you can almost possibly hear it in "Seventies Girl," when the band timidly leans into the picture of the song, Freedy's entire presence aglow with delicate ache, and you hear it in the ambitious writing of songs like "Gone to See the Fire" (in which a couple split over arson) — you hear him working to reconnect with the Freedy who broke my friends free from those unshod yesterdays of Central California, when all we possessed was fallow soil and truly our future was fog.

THE GREATEST RECORD ALBUM BAND THAT EVER WAS

IT'S GETTING DARK earlier and earlier. So days cool off. Traffic clogs with thieves, slipping from the city center with billfolds fat. Even insects head on home. All the brake lights smeary in the fog make my evening into this red haze, a fire streak, an exit sign. Drivers use the slowdown to lower their $375 windows and spit, exhale their $5 cigarettes, wave various $2,000 limbs to insult the topography. Laid down here beside the freeway, bare, buzzed and finely longing, I hear someone in what sounds to be a BMW complaining hotly about a co-worker, she didn't bother with the depo summary until well past the designated deadline. Some carpooler in what I imagine is a crowded Tercel is describing her date. Their stories travel into the evening, sway the stringy leaves of my weedy barkwood and shake down dew onto me. I catch fan-belt noise, loose beauty rings, cylinders misfiring. I pretend to diagnose their cars' various difficulties, but that was my good friend Guy, not me, who was the mechanic. I was just his apprentice. Someone in a Taurus gently addresses a loved one through a carphone. Someone slows down with a horrible squeal. "Need your back brakes checked," I holler without getting up to look. It hurts my jaw to yell, I wasn't even thinking. *Ouch.* More loose dew splashes down on me.

Guy will come by later, very soon. I wish he would still correct me regarding car parts, address me as mechanic to apprentice, but will he? — no, he won't, won't bother pointing out that I heard the disc not drum brakes. He'll come by tonight like he does every night now, like a robot, and he'll talk endlessly about one thing: the greatest record album band that ever was. That's it, that's the show, that's all he does anymore. You'd think a band gone for nearly forever wouldn't stir up so much passion. You'd be wrong. He'll swing his arms in a circular motion until he sops up the gravy of the world with this band. I kept thinking his visits were meant to be sweet but like how apples go bad from the inside out, like how someone takes your shoes while you're asleep, that's how I realized it's not at all sweet in any way. It's a curse.

That said, when a motorcycle cuts down between the cars, moving way too fast and watched all the while in rear-view mirrors by nervous drivers who admire the balls this guy has, and as he takes his life in his hands, suited up in a full armor of leather and a dark helmet, slaloming through and around these halted heaps of painted $37,500 scrap metal, I get, like I always used to, all choked up with pride. He's doing it. Risking it. "What good is a song that is not *speeding*, a dance that cannot be *rushed*, gambling without *raising stakes*, life that will not be *risked*, a dare not *taken*? Why bother *awakening* if not to glimpse *terror*? Is there *growth* without *challenge*? Of course not! There is no point to any of it but *risk*." His words float up to me from when I was thirteen or fourteen, maybe twelve, and Guy was nineteen, twenty.

"That's it, brother!" I yell into the night. Ouch, the jaw again. The dew patters down in large drops, in my hair, on my sleeping bag. "That's my Guy!" Because initially, yeah, I'm still stirred by his visits, okay.

It's like Guy admitted a few nights ago, "*Sine frater, sine amicus: spe carens.*"

I agreed, yeah. Without brothers, without friends: hopeless. It's all about friends, isn't it, really? Isn't it? Or as Guy might once have said, "Coming in from the heat, your face burnt from the peril and hazard of it all to find your welcoming warm friends—that's pretty much *life*, can we not agree?"

But that's not what he means anymore, of course. I'm not ever directly in his concerns as he speaks now. "This Latin epistle," Guy declares, "confirmed from the most base of sources: the story of the musical rock band Creedence Clearwater Revival (comprised of the brothers Fogerty—Tommy and J.C.—backed by Stu Cook and Doug Clifford) which formed in junior high."

"A story," I interject, though why bother, it's as if I'm talking to a television, "which attracts ironies like a magnet." He's prerecorded, I'm nowhere near at all.

"For ten years the brothers led without incident an obscure party band—such faith, to play that long without recognition, such complete confidence and familiarity with one another—and the brothers could have probably kept playing together for eternity had not something atrocious occurred—"

"And that was . . ."

"Fame descended with all its attendant griefs and arduous inequities! Which is to say that once you and I entered the process, we ruined them."

It's not even worth meeting his look. His eyes don't track. He never used to talk this way, I don't think. He was sent here by an intergalactic hovercraft, by the State Council of Pesticide Manufacturers (scpm), by the hypnotic advisory board of the advertocracy. "After Creedence began to record their own material, a mean toll was taken—brother against brother as if at Shiloh the Fogertys began to fight—the brothers began to *bicker* and ultimately the brothers *parted* and that spelled 'T-H-E E-N-D' for Creedence—ten years of unceasing struggle for three measly years of arguable recognition.

"Perhaps," he continues, collecting his cues from every pompous orator I have ever observed, "you might argue their recognition is not 'arguable'—"

"Me?"

"But I argue no accolade is too big for *these* brothers' britches."

"Oh. Okay."

"For even though Tommy never penned any Creedence tunes, never sang lead vocals, only played the simplest (most replace-able) instrument (*rhythm guitar?!* even to call his parts 'the least memorable in every song' is perhaps to go not far enough) *yet* still this meddlesome brother was in some way indispensable."

"Because . . ."

"Before they renamed themselves Creedence they were known as 'Tommy Fogerty and the Blue Velvets' and younger brother J.C. was merely one more Blue Velvet star."

"Blue Velvet, hunh."

"What came of all this brotherly strife, you ask—great creative productive times?—*You may as well inquire as to the good of Shiloh!* Without Tommy, Creedence managed to complete only one more record album before splitting. J.C. made two bad solo albums then met a prolonged writer's block—"

"Were you sleeping, brother John?"

"Tommy—"

"The old fogey of the Fogertys."

"Made a bad solo record album, caught tuberculosis, and hacked himself to death. Tommy's death took ten years. J.C.'s writer's block took the same. Just as J.C. emerged with a hit record album, Tommy went into the ground."

"Aw, shut up, Guy," I snap, nowhere close to polite. I bury my face in a crumpled-up jacket. "I'm napping."

"Behind the flow of what robes and garments have they hidden the Creedence Churches? Where are the endless TV tributes? Why have we taken this great band so for granted? Honor CCR for how they mistrusted the demeaning junkie sex primitive draw of flash and slogans that made crowds roar for the Stones and Doors! A Bronx huzzah for how completely they lacked that stiff respect for elders which made bookish sorts drool over Dylan and the Band! Gift CCR with an avalanche of pastries for side-stepping the obscure mood pieces, the too-hip gutter praise that made audiences scratch themselves confusedly while watching the Velvet Underground and Stooges—"

"Okay, I have a thought or two about that—"

"CCR's problem, it seemed, was they cared *too much* about the songs and respected *too much* the people that heard them to accept a cheap PA and superficial sloganeering. You do realize that the last words in *Twilight Zone: The Movie*—"

"That literal killer of a film."

"Were 'I love Creedence!'"

"Well, I may not have realized that," I admit. "No."

"But alas, having assumed Creedence was lost to us forever—"

"But you were wrong. Creedence lives."

"Such ecstatic happiness descends on me in finding I am completely wrong—yes! I am wrong, they live—"

"That's better." The traffic has picked up again. Cars make loud *wagh-wagh-wagh* sounds as they shoot by, always managing to just miss each other, a miracle a minute.

"For Science tells us Creedence lives forever in that every signal that has ever been beamed or broadcast about planet Earth—be it military transmission or satellite photograph or television picture—comes both into our home and simultaneously hurtles away from here at speeds invisible to the naked eye, easing 'cross the universe at 299,792.8 km per second."

Guy paces nervously at the head of my sleeping bag in the near-blackness. I imagine his features, his expressions, I conjure him up.

"You can picture an individual far away on Mars receiving all our TV and radio broadcasts approximately four and two-fifths minutes late—"

"Given," I concur, "their distance."

"Being always four and two-fifths minutes behind planet Earth in everything, fashion, real estate, geography, everything, and another individual farther away on Pluto also receiving everything but being more like five and a quarter hours behind the times—our radio past lives forever in deep space and therefore *the more a band made it on the radio in the past the more forever they live*—and one can imagine oneself rocketing away from planet Earth at the speed of light, at 299,792.8 km per second, at the speed—in short—of radio and one would be sailing in sync with the radio transmissions, riding on the same day in electronics history for eternity, like rocketing away at 299,792.8 km per second on Fifteen August of 1969 you'd be inescapably locked into hearing 8/15/69 for eternity—"

"As long as your speed kept up."

Guy actually appears to acknowledge me with a rare pause, but maybe he's just thinking. "Which would be a good day:

the radio filled with 'Green River' b/w 'Commotion' the new double-sided ccr single—such brilliant 7" Creedence vinyl record discs were being frisbee'd out of the factory once a month in those days—and out the rocket window as the solar system fell away and all that is familiar disappeared from view you'd still have the oddly nostalgic twenty-five-year-old Fogerty—according to Science, he'd *always* and *only* be oddly nostalgic and twenty-five—telling you: Take me back down where cool water flows. Let me remember things I love: stoppin' at the log where catfish bite, walkin' along the river road at night, barefoot girls dancin' in the moonlight."

"You're not gonna recite the whole song now, are you?"

"I can hear the bullfrog callin' me; wonder if my rope's still hangin' to the tree."

"You are."

"Love to kick my feet 'way down in shallow water. Shoefly, dragonfly, get back t'your mother. Pick up a flat rock, skip it across Green River."

"Point taken, plenty said."

"Up at Cody's camp I spent my days with flat-car riders and cross-tie walkers. Old Cody Junior took me over, said, 'You're gonna find the world is smold'rin'—if you get lost come on home to Green River.'"

When I was thirteen, fourteen, maybe twelve, I went to summer camp in the bug-filled, boiling mountains. Each night, after supper in the mess hall, a bus painted flat, battleship grey took us into town. We were given free license to wander about the skee-ball arcades. I followed the lit alcohol ads going *blinky-blink* out the back exit and across the alley. Hearing the music of the saloon addressing me from within, I inquired of the gatekeeper, "How old do you have to be to get in here?" I pretended I could not make sense of the sign which clearly said NO ONE UNDER 21 ADMITTED. She pressed a nostril shut with one finger and blew a wild spurt of snot out the other. She hacked a few sputumy hacks into a cocktail napkin, glared up and down the alley, glared up and down at me. Then she barked her answer: "Two dollars and fifty cents."

Inside there was just one person, an unshaven guy. He

seemed a hundred years old. I remember the bony arc of his sweeping limbs folded over some greased-up tee shirt. I remember his head tilting into an easy scowl as he listened to my complaints about skee-ball coupons and camp skits, about being made to gargle rubbing alcohol, to paint shields for the Renaissance Faire, to learn the thirty-five key dos & don'ts to well-done crafts. He clicked his tongue thoughtfully, squinted down at me in my camp sweatshirt, studied his motorcycle boots. He seemed a hundred years old and very wise. This then was Guy. He was just nineteen, twenty. The bar would not serve me alcohol but what they would do was to serve me coffee. And so my first cup of coffee, Guy bought it for me. I realize now that he was just pleased to have an audience, any audience at all, for in fact the entire saloon consisted of me and my cup of coffee and him mouthing along to Creedence songs. (I recall no bartender.) He was the evening's entertainment: "This Guy's Band." He would mount this sort of impromptu stage. He had a guitar, not plugged in, on which he pretended to play all of John Fogerty's parts.

Strangely, every adult at the summer camp was familiar with Guy as a sort of town character, they were even fine with me hanging out with him *(how is this possible?)*, and so after my initial disciplinary requirements had been met ("You are *never again* to go off alone without a supervisor, do you hear me young man?!"), they agreed to lend me to him during prescribed hours in the interest of being taught automobiles and music appreciation. Mostly I'd go to the yard with Guy, where inside a high fence he worked on the town's cars with two older guys named Crane and Ellis, alongside a big brown sweet-faced dog named Cronkite. Guy blasted distorted tapes of Creedence Clearwater Revival on a small Panasonic tape recorder as he assembled Muncie transmissions and dropped bored-out big-block V8s into Oldsmobiles with a cherry-picker and showed me how to troubleshoot baffling electrical drainages by checking the parts linked to the battery. A typical moment might be Guy leaning way in over some engine, supported wholly by the front end, as a vaguely audible semblance of "Fortunate Son" screamed nearby, and calling out to me for tools, "Okay, end wrench—Fogerty, you know, wrote this in twenty minutes—no, I need something smaller, looks like a seven-sixteenths—twenty minutes! He was twenty-five years old! That's better, that'll do it."

The director of the summer camp would call me over every few days to quiz me on what I was learning, but she didn't know much about cars and didn't know much about music either so it was easy to impress upon her the value and stuff of my lessons.

Some days we'd knock off early and go over to where Guy lived, this musty cabin that smelled of sulfur, of old eggs, as if the stove leaked (it probably did). We'd sit in his living room, me insisting how bad things always seemed, and Guy calling me a regular riot, he'd call me smart as a whip and he'd go how it was all gonna get so much easier for me once I got older, just wait and see, life'll become fun, and he'd boil me up a cup of this coffee stuff, which was rapidly becoming my favorite beverage (though the first cup that night at the roadhouse had just sat in my stomach for an hour gurgling and curdling like a something-salad-sandwich b/w bad stone soup before—good gracious—dissipating to set my entire world on edge . . .).

His decor? Guy had no windows. In place of this he had positioned up on his walls all seven Creedence record album jackets in chronological order. There was that first one (June 1968), a window overlooking the outdoors, them all with mustaches, standing in an oak grove, obscured largely by tree trunks, in turtlenecks and soldier coats, an unplayed trumpet enigmatically dangling from Doug Clifford's hand. Window number two (January 1969) also was very tree-filled and woodsy, except that as a window it was impossible to look through, it seemed designed to induce instant vomiting with its tunnel acceleration, its exaggerated migraine technique (enhanced no doubt by the nausea of Guy's gas leak). The only image I can remember from it—who but Guy could stand to study it for very long?—is that of some central guitar-toting figure with a gruesomely elongated aquatic-looking bare appendage where a foot belonged. Record album jacket three (August 1969) was again another window to the outside. The group stood dappled in the forest, intentionally avoiding the warm patch of sunlight just before them (one began to surmise Creedence went inside only long enough to lay down the tunes, then raced back out amongst the trees to snap the sleeve). But then—at last!—by the fourth window (November 1969), a bit of the inevitable cityscape entered, the inkling of a DON'T WALK sign, some kid extras from the ghetto, the Duck Kee Market • Beer • Wine • Frozen Food • Produce • Meat. So now we had provisions and passersby, and even more importantly we had buildings, and yet CCR remained outside them. Did they never go indoors at all? Was this the secret point of these record album jackets, the telling Creedence phobia? Or, if they did—what exactly did they do once inside, in their homes, in stores, shops, restaurants, and banks, were their internal activities so embarrassing as to remain necessarily undocumented? Apparently so. The next one (April 1970) gave in to popular demand: at last, horribly, tragically, Creedence was pictured indoors. Doing what? It was easily their worst record album jacket, maybe the worst record album jacket of all time. Doug Clifford was on a stationary bicycle—*what?*—dressed like a fool. The others lounged about. Was that a telling photograph? Only J.C. seemed ready to acknowledge that there were instruments on the floor around them. Sadly, this was their best-selling record album, and consequently the window most stared through by fans. *Next!* No doubt reeling from the fallout and blatantly attempting to compensate for the misguided, ill-advised disaster of the last window, the follow-up (December 1970) showed their heads in extreme close-up as they leaned in over us, eyes full of sinister purpose. Outdoors or indoors, it was hard to say. The world beyond them fell away in indistinct inkiness. They were perhaps preparing to boil us in a pot, to rid themselves of us while in a night storm at sea, or in deep space, it was impossible to determine. The last window (June 1972) I cannot remember at all, I have a vague recollection of them on crucifixes, being fed wine vinegar from a sponge held on the stalk of a hyssop plant, sides pierced by centurion spears, eyes pleading heavenward. But this may be inaccurate; it may be hampered by the fact that these windows, through which Guy interpreted and connected CCR's travails, arranged as I said in this conscious careful manner, always resembled so much to me the stations of the cross in a church stainglass.

It was here—lounging on the soiled print sofa of his musty cabin, high probably on natural gas fumes, gazing deeply into the nailed-up Creedence LPs, our heads out of control and cop-free with caffeine—that Guy impressed upon me the darting sudden-ness of Creedence's radio reign, how their reputation depends on songs written and recorded in a narrow span of eighteen months, three record albums in one year and two the next.

He also said, and I had not previously heard this, how early reviewers were unaware that Creedence grew up in the Bay Area, how they assumed the CCR sound was genuinely a product of the bayou. Which was quite okay with them for, as Guy told me, CCR did not appreciate the Bay Area scene, did not really relate to the hold-hands, drop-drugs spirit of the '60s. One of their most hated moments was headlining at Woodstock—yeah, believe it or not, they headlined the festival—a performance which the band barred from use in the concert film or either soundtrack record album. They came on at two-thirty in the morning. J.C. grumbled that they went on after the Grateful Dead, who "had played about six songs for three hours. They were the band that put a half a million people to sleep."

No one had ever talked to me that way, like I was somebody worth instructing in the important ways of the world, like I mattered, except maybe my Mom, and on the whole Guy and I didn't spend nearly long enough together in that dizzying cabin. When he wasn't solving car problems or reviving the entire Creedence Clearwater Revival he usually preferred to be out on his motorcycle, all hellfire determined to make himself dead, to push beyond the boundaries of these things we call our stupid lives, going way too fast, leaning so hard into mountain turns his bike would slide away, tilting, tipping almost parallel to the ground, and he would aright himself by bouncing a padded knee off the asphalt. He would *not* take me along on these midnight rides (no matter how much I begged) though eventually he would allow me to bend the rules, at least to sneak from camp to see him off, he'd allow that much without telling on me. Then after a bit he put me in charge of the stopwatch (he was always racing against the clock) and soon—what would he have done without me?—my responsibilities expanded to holding onto "the sealed envelope," which was left with me I suppose just in case he didn't return. There'd even be those cold wet nights when (stupidly) he'd honor me by letting me wear his jacket to stay warm. In a gale of noise and smoke he'd roar off, leaving me with my domestic duties, heart pumping like a war-time bride. The envelope—well, I felt pretty sure it said how being of sound mind and body he did hereby surrender his few earthly possessions to his new best and only friend me—it was his final testament, written out of the conviction that testing himself this way deserved commemoration (or at least documentation). Each time he came back from these daredevil jaunts—"I outran the Pensacola freight tonight," he'd breathlessly confess, or "Unbolted the headlamp on the thoroughfare and went 100 against traffic"—and he would demand the exact second count of tonight's death-defying venture. But my point is that each time, when he came back, he was in near-perfect health. Always against the odds this kamikaze boy survived, thank god, he was Lindbergh, Legs Diamond, Lucky Luciano, he could not be killed, or so it appeared. In truth it was almost as if the chances he took were not chances at all because the risks were completely elsewhere.

But hell, how can I tell you what he meant to me when I mean so little anymore to anyone? Why would you listen? I do nothing but diminish Guy's significance every day just by being what I am. Oh, there was a time (it sure seems far off now!) you thieves didn't all look identical to me, there was a time you foxes and dudes with your cars and jobs and houses were awesome, terrifying, seductive to me, a time I too would scurry past any scrawny boy who would get in my way, he'd be reclining on a sidewalk on some comfy cardboard slab—as on occasion I am apt to do—beside a tore-open sack of your aromatic cast-offs, eyes sick, head like a trashed mop, swollen feet, scabied legs, blackened face . . . But now, well, who cares what I think? Recruit J.C. to paint his portrait!—is any Fogerty still alive?—and then Guy's memory will be appropriately upraised and honored, because for Guy there was no life, it seemed, outside remembering Creedence.

It was some time before I ever learned that Creedence's first words to the world (first song, first record album) were, "I put a spell on you." And it was some time still before I put two and two together and realized that Guy had—in the most extreme sense—been altered, entranced, bewitched, inhabited by another's spirit, that they had put a spell on him and none of this danger- and death-seeking stuff was his true self because he behaved simply as a medium acting on their behalf.

I say all this about my friend—that he was not himself, altered, possessed by spirits, &c.—but I should also emphasize he struck no one as weird. Maybe Ellis and Crane thought him a bit excited at times, maybe the camp director didn't thoroughly trust him with me, but still Guy was a normal enough guy, a swell guy, a regular guy—he would ask me what I thought about bad moons or chooglin' and say how once I got a little older we could go together and see the good side of the city from a riverboat queen, go chasin' down a hoodoo there, go look at all the happy people dancing on the lawn—he was a Guy you'd take home to your sister hoping that she liked him like how you liked him and they'd marry and you and this Guy would at last be brothers—as you always knew you were—but now Official Brothers, in the eyes of God and the law and everybody.

Hopes like these abruptly ceased when out of nowhere on one of those cold, wet nights Guy . . . well, it happened very fast. Guy caught a cold in the rain and died from it. They have a name for that. I can't remember what it is but it's Latin for shitty luck. He was dressed inappropriately, the doctors said—or at least they thought that, if not actually saying it aloud, because he was not wearing his jacket that night, I was. It was the least heroic thing that could've happened, I'll tell you that. A speedy and splendid life, a disgracefully mundane death, this—with my help!—was to be his fate. And as for me, after that a long series of tepid events rolled right on past, I spent my cares haphazardly until they ran out, years of stuff, schooling, jobs, nothing came of anything until eventually I was cut loose and deposited down right here, at this spot, under my tree, where I am content and now would like to be left alone.

But yet I'm thinking how I gotta do something about this Guy situation, it's gotten way beyond me, unable to hear myself sleep, so I get up and I go over to beneath the freeway, keeping an eye out for Rojo, who—with his hunched idiot shoulders, sloped brow, scuffing stupid way of walking—is the only one there who really scares me, being as since he got free of his last holding cell he's carrying a banana knife which he has already put into several people and who knows what all other maniac crap he's got while he waits—like we all do—for someone to drive up with a truckful of friends and make him pay for how he made a trash heap out of what used to be his life. Though, frankly, I don't have the luxury of waiting for such things anymore, with Guy on my tail. Rojo now's begun to swear I got his cat, this is his latest phony obsession of the last few months, that I stole his mud-caked cat, even though there's cats aplenty for all to behold, they're shitting and pissing all over us when we sleep, even though I hate cats, still he insists.

"Take another cat, man," I tell him. I'm pretending to be very 'so what' though I'm truthfully about to croak from the terrorizing way Rojo's squint just steadily burns into me. I can't look up at him anymore. It feels like somebody chalked all around the inside of my mouth. My arms are going off in wild directions. I behave as would one guilty sick individual.

Johnny Tornado—with arms like bread loaves, our own chesty comic book hero—intercedes on my behalf, bless him. "Cats're all the fuck everywhere," Tornado goes. "Just grab one and name it. Christ, Rojo." And on this the great Tornado is 100% correct, they are like violent furry weeds underfoot, these freeway cats, hissing and slashing each other over rats and garbage. Still Rojo believes he had this one mean tabby all trained, his loyal guard cat, his attack kitty.

"You know what a damn sentimentalist is?!" Tornado bellows at him. He's worming his way between us. "These cats can't tell you from shit! You're a damn sentimentalist!

They know you like a hole in the ground!" I also want to interject, but don't, that since we're awakened every night by car thieves and state vehicles skidding through road kill it should make even the most dense of people comprehend this as a bad place to get too attached to one's pet; still Rojo blames me for the cat's vanishing.

"People vanish everyday," I suggest to Rojo, hesitant at first because I'm a little uncertain about the precise accuracy of this remark, so I look over to check my facts with Tornado and he nods reassuringly. "Hunh," I go in my devastatingly funny 'let's-go-shopping' voice. "So. Your cat vanished."

I'm thinking he might laugh at this with me and Tornado but instead this is—surprise!—when Rojo hauls up and punches the bejeezus outta me, and I go down like nobody's business, there's the crash of breaking pop bottles, and he swings a fat foot into my face and this is finally when he laughs, there's Tornado screaming expletives, I'm tasting blood and that's just about that to the story, after a good chunk of world history saunters by I wake up in the county ICU with a wired jaw and a nose two times normal size. They trickle painkillers into my arm and these things (in combination with what all else) make my mind like loose paper, like a newspaper hat, an object of outlandish ridicule, a cotton can. Worse, in kicking the flickering screen that was my TV head, Rojo has done something to my dreams, for I can no longer sleep right anymore, now whenever I weary Mister Guy Glass stands before me like a decal on my eyeballs that just will not rub off, Guy the mouther of garagey dance music, Guy the daredevil of my summer camp, Guy the Auld Acquaintance Not Forgot—he appears in all his youthful glory and promptly renews his lecture series.

I see Old Man George by a cardboard fire and looking very at peace. There's flickering movement in the shadows which is probably Tornado or the cats but visibility is poor so I feel it's worth checking on: "Rojo 'round?" George gives me the a-okay sign. George used to be, of all things, destined to be some Texas Senator, this is what he says . . . but who cares about his life story, you don't. Important point here is, George has this great spine and these good manners. Rojo used to sock him around too, pretty regularly, but got cured of it this once after George stepped in as the cops were about to haul Rojo off for a breaking-and-entering and amazingly enough George argued them out of it. Rojo was impressed by this, we all were, and so he never damaged George again.

"The," I announce, "damn burger place started locking up the water heater when they go at night, you aware of this? Hey, you still got any vodkamelon left?"

George takes a hit of something and catches his breath. He shakes his head, holds a bent-up can out to me sideways.

I decline. "Vodkamelon, I said. And sleep."

He shakes the can at me. "It's sleep," he croaks tightly. The can is lit. It smells like citrus.

Fury rolls through me then is gone. "I'm saying, I need *help*. I wish the Christians would come by. I'm starved. Why hast thou forsaken me sandwiches, brother?"

George shakes the smoking can again. "It's help," he croaks.

Before my jaw thing happened, and it's only been unwired now for two weeks, I used to smoke whatever Old Man George offered because he called it 'Help.' It was usually a little something of who knows what, a combustible solid distilled from household cleaners. I enjoyed my lighter-than-air limps but sometimes I'd get godawful skin rashes or, when I'd come to, it would be much, much later in a traffic island, cops leaning in over me with their teeth full of breakfast. Finally, I take the can from George but I can't find it in myself to suck on citrus cleaning solution or whatever, I just set it in my lap like a cat.

"Where is he?" I say, alarmed because suddenly I can feel Rojo's fat foot in my face.

George shrugs and at last exhales. "You need help?"

"Guy," I explain. I don't need to say anything more, just like a murderer doesn't have much to tell a cop who arrives too late except, 'In there.'

"He's your responsibility."

"Yeah."

"You killed Guy."

"Yeah. Only I didn't kill him. Wait, now. Wearing his jacket is not killing him." I know George means this nicely, he's repeating things I've told him, he means that I have to get this to truly truly penetrate the packing pellets that now comprise my styrofoam brain, but I seek to clarify this point: "Wearing his jacket is wearing his jacket."

"It's all in your head."

"That's not so. You saw him. You know he's genuine."

"I saw a motorcyclist. This is true. You said, hey'd you see me talking with a motorcyclist just now and I said, sure. I agreed with you at the time. At the time I said, I suppose there was a motorcyclist, yes. He seemed to know you, yes. But now . . . I can offer no guarantee for the state, you know, of my condition then." George lolls his head back, musing, cracks his neck. "It might be I saw giraffes, too."

"Giraffes are good. Giraffes don't haunt me."

"Guy was good, you used to say."

"When was the last time you got to pet a giraffe, man, with those furry little horns on their heads, what are those?"

"Bring him over next time he visits," George advises. "Perhaps I can talk him out of bothering you."

"He wants me to tell the world about Creedence."

"I know."

"Between the blah-blah-blah popularity of their music, the integrity of their approach, their high standards. Giraffes, now I could tell the world about giraffes, their spots. Those necks. But Creedence, enough already."

Old Man George studies the side of a Yoo Hoo carton like it's great literature. Frowning, he clears his throat. "Before, yesterday or day before it may have been, let's go back to . . . you were suggesting we make this habitat a historical landmark."

"It would keep the cops out, yeah. That's all I was thinking. Fire and Rescue wouldn't be allowed all their goddamn poking around, Sanitation trimming our trees."

"It's an interesting thought, a little legislation to preserve our homeland here." We look fondly at the storage cans with the orange metal shavings in them, at the contents of every nearby dumpster which have been placed around us like an expectant feast. Important leaves, old coupons, tobacco butts, coffee cups, plastic shopping bags catch the freeway downdraft, skipping, leaping merrily for us. George's fire smells like a ghost story as it pastes our shadow heads up on the roadway's big concrete underside, snatching them back instantly. A tour of our landmark begins here, where—with unexpected grandeur—a rise of loose earth meets a spacious cement curve. Does life get any better?

I go, "Did my trees need trimming? Tell me that. Of course not. It was happy how it was, my tree was."

"It seems the enforcement of landmark status might require the assistance of a full-time staff person."

"Hunh?" I'm completely proud of myself for not—as before I would have—pretending to understand. I take this as a sign of how far George's and my friendship now has progressed.

"Just a thought."

An ambulance rushes by overhead, slicing an emergency path through the unspooled cassette tapes and shatterproof pebbles that decorate the oil-ruined, rubber-skidded freeway. Its siren provokes a cat fight somewhere out near the grocery carts in the parking lot. We can see none of it but it sounds pretty nasty.

"Some," George goes, "people, you know, get songs stuck in their head. It's just that you got a whole band."

"A whole band and their like goddamn cheerleader mascot, yeah. Who just won't shut up."

"Apparently he can't rest in the afterlife until these few certain things are seen to."

"It's like that."

"I saw this in a movie. Bring him by, I can speak to him."

"He won't come," I whimper, suddenly beyond consolation, tears welling up. "You think I haven't thought of that? Tornado said the same thing, we tried it with him. The mighty Tornado, ha! Guy will do what Guy always does. He'll get back on his motorcycle and ride the fuck off until I'm alone again."

"That is because he appears in your head."

"Fuck you, in my head. That make you smart? Fuck you!"

"I'm just saying."

I leave Old Useless George then and get back to my tree, where I used to sleep, back when I could sleep, a couple hundred yards away, still within landmark reach but enough distance that it usually daunts Rojo and his lazy ass and I am pretty much unmolested except when—as happened a while back—some thief loses control, swerves from the fast lane all the way across, skids around the off-ramp sign, slams hard into my barkwood tree, then flees on foot, his vehicle stopped two feet from the bed where I sleep, used to sleep when I was allowed to, but no longer sleep. Unmolested except when Guy comes by at midnight and keeps me up, declaiming, which is all that really happens anymore.

"J.C.," murmurs Guy, "was the darkest of *les existentialistes*." Time has passed but maybe not, who can tell, here we are at it again. Guy smacks his lips most uncharacteristically, raises a gloved finger, and, as he speaks, weaves it dramatically through the air as if from the ocean floor he were stirring dangling threads of kelp—"Let us take 'Lodi' for example, a song known by *tout le monde*—vainly one inquires as to its meaning. A gent gallops forth to keep his appointed rendezvous with Messrs. Fame et Fortune, and ends up mired in Lodi—by the way, Camden—" he has taken to addressing me as Camden though he knows it is not my name—"one finds Lodi a pleasant enough village, encamped 'twixt Modesto and Sacramento, a stone's throw beyond Stockton, rich in leafy green trees and small-town kindness—*quelle ironie!*"—and here Guy bangs down his cane for emphasis, startling the other patrons (*am I missing something?*)—"ironic that the town will now only be remembered from this song, which implies it is a mucky tar-trap of a place, hell-hole USA—why stuck? What has happened? 'Things got bad and things got worse'—we are in receipt of no clearer explanation than this—'looks like my plans fell through' he observes. 'Somewhere I lost connection'—'looks like they took my friends'—there is the dim awareness of a conspiracy of circumstance."

Guy shuts his eyes. "And let us not dismiss the added suspense of the song running a slight bit longer than one expects, the wishfulness in that extra verse when one surmises the song is concluding and instead it climbs a key: 'If I only had a dollar for every song I sung.' Ah, such obstinate drama! In short, we learn nothing of this singer but for the abstract qualities with which we identify! And the community Lodi—in this song—becomes but a state of mind! And that—" and here Guy's pince-nez glimmers fantastically in the freeway headlights and the salon gas lamps—"*C'est la poésie existentialiste, mon ami.*

"Creedence (which was the name of their friend) Clearwater (a word taken from a beer advertisement) Revival (a statement of their musical aims), or (as they shall be periodically referred to herein) Creedence or CCR were first and foremost a band belonging to Fantasy, as in Saul Zaentz's Fantasy Records, and ironically of all the musical bands of their day probably the sound of CCR least deserved to be on a label called Fantasy—more they should have been signed to Reality Records or Authentic Ditch Recordings and bands like Simon & Garfunkel or Crosby Stills Nash & Young signed to Fantasy—although in the end maybe working for Fantasy was apropos; for Fantasy bilked them out of royalties, led Fogerty and Co. into an involved Bahamian investment plan which lost them all their profits, laying siege to all copyrights, and incessantly repackaging the same Fogerty material under new names (*1968-1969, 1970, Creedence Gold, More Creedence Gold, Chronicle, Chronicle II, Chooglin', The Movie Album, Rollin' on the River,* &c.)—and when Fantasy tiptoed from the bank vaults, arms laden with certificates and private securities and pots of gold which once rightfully belonged to the band—well then, *who* was it who was living in Fantasy? (The band, sad to acknowledge, the band!)

"Let us turn now to address the Climatic Interrogatories (as they have come to be called), a pair of them, the question at first in early 1970 phrased somewhat laconically as 'Who'll stop the rain?' and then later the same year, more desperately (as though having perhaps been asked 'What rain?') rephrased as 'Have you ever *seen* the rain?'"

Jesus I'm thinking how I've gotta get Old Man George to help on this, I've gotta get him to talk to Guy and get him to stop bothering me like he said he would but "Not now!" is how I imagine George will greet me. Except it's not my imagination, that's really George right in front of me there, and I'm somehow back beneath the freeway, and this is what he's yelling at me: "Not now!" How did I get here? I cannot possibly grasp this, but you know, who knows, here I am, indisputably.

Rojo is circling Tornado with another brawl plainly in the offing.

"Go away!" George yells but shitty luck has glued my feet to the earth and I cannot move.

A snapshot taken at this moment would reveal the following: bats and cats and rats and squirrels in eternal interplay, a fleet of state vehicles upstairs, an armada of thieves really, doing their machine-of-the-unconscious stuff, the flecking lightstorm patterns from Old Man Fire going yellow, yellow, then white, words I never had much time to fully digest before looming in giant spraypaint on walls around us — "MUFTAH DESTROYAH!" "I luv you Janine baby" and — of course — "Creedence hopes you are quite prepared to die" — and a few fabulous feelings, not a lot of complaints really, this memory, that memory, the cold dirt which surrounds us, it tickles underneath my toes, and a pretty good life it's been all told, let me add, as these things go, this is what the snapshot would conclude.

Rojo spots me, and Tornado — sensing what's to come — attempts one of those purely spectacular tackling dives, a feat of utter heroism, the quiver and flexing of comic book muscle, though in the end his attempt falls short. There is the glint of something in Rojo's hand, it first blinks at me in the firelight than can no longer be seen, and then Rojo stands over me, pissing, and where he has opened up my chest it stings. Another snapshot taken at this moment would tell us nothing. Tornado's questions sound iced, strange, and I'm unclear on how much time has elapsed.

"Guy," I call, because there he is now, he's finally followed me beneath the freeway. It's an unexpected pleasure, his sudden presence, despite his appearing very upset. He uses the back of a palm to paint his face all around with tears. "Oh hey, I'll be fine."

Guy nods like it's the last thing he'll believe. "Come on, man." It's an invitation.

"Nah." I don't feel like going anywhere.

"Yeah. C'mon." Then we're moving.

"I'm cold, Guy." He leads me by the arm. As we walk, I feel

I'm leaving the greater part of me behind but that's okay.

"Here." He drapes his jacket about my shoulders. I try to shake it off. "Fuck." Not the jacket. "Not your jacket," I mumble. Makes me feel like shit and now I'm also crying. "Oh man. I'm so sorry."

"Nothing to be sorry about."

We walk to his motorcycle. He kicks it to life, sets me snug behind him on the seat. "Now hold onto me," he says. "Friend." And off we go at last, down the road, and up around the bend.